Playing on
Yggdrasil

Alex McGilvery

Yggdrasil: the World Tree of Norse Mythology.
Pronounced yingdrasil or yg/drasil

**Dedicated to Alexandra who told me
the story of her friend who was a tree.**

Cover Illustration by Wil Oberdier

Copyright Alex McGilvery 2013

Second Edition, 2017
ISBN 978-1-7751286-2-5

Prologue

"No Father wants to lose a child," the preacher said. "In First Peter, we hear the faithful told to be patient as God does not want anyone to be lost."

Too late, Patrick thought. He tried to look away from the box that held all that was left of Ingrid. Justine held his hand and leaned her head on his arm. He was all that Justine had now. He needed to be strong for her. He hadn't been strong enough for Ingrid and now she was gone. Lost, in spite of what Pastor Daniel was saying.

There was a rustle as the people in the church all stood and Patrick saw the funeral director waiting for him and his daughter to lead everyone out of the church.

At the cemetery, they put the obscenely small box of his wife's ashes in the hole. He threw a handful of dirt in after it and the tears pricked at his eyes. He forced them back with an iron will. He was not going to cry in front of his daughter.

"Is Mommy in that box?" Justine asked looking at him with her blue eyes.

"No." Patrick had to stop and take a deep breath. "No, Justine, that's just what is left of her. She's out there somewhere."

"Is she lost? Can we help her come home?"

"She isn't lost. Nothing we really love is ever lost." Patrick had to take another breath and push back the tears. He could feel the weakness trying to claw its way out. He wanted to howl and tear his clothes.

"She can't come home," Patrick said, "She's with God."

He felt a bitter acid in his stomach at the G word. It was a cop-out, but Ingrid had given an ironclad faith in the big guy to Justine. He wondered what he really believed. All he knew was the jagged hole in his life no amount of words could ever to fill.

"Say hi to God for me, Mommy." Justine threw some dirt into the hole, then brushed her hands off. "I'm going to talk to Molly, OK Dad?"

1

"OK," Patrick said. He watched her run off. Her blond hair streamed out behind her. He wanted to call her back and hold on to her and make sure that she was safe. Instead he looked back at the hole. "You can fill it in now," he told the funeral director. She just nodded and a man in overalls quietly shovelled the dirt into the grave. It didn't take long. Patrick wanted to let the tears flow, but the traitorous weakness mocked him by keeping his eyes as dry as the dirt covering his wife and lover's grave.

It should be raining. The heavens should have opened and the whole world should be deluged. Let the clouds weep the tears that he couldn't. He heard the squeals of Justine and Molly playing. He envied them at the same time as he felt bereft of company.

"If you need anything, just call." The minister handed him yet another card. Patrick was sure he had twenty of them lying around the house.

"Give one to Justine," he said. Then he thought how ungracious he sounded. "Thanks for all your help."

"I heard what you told Justine," Reverend Daniel said, "about nothing loved ever being lost. Remember that." He patted Patrick's shoulder and ambled off toward Justine. Patrick watched him kneel in the grass to talk to her. She took the card and ran arrow straight back to Patrick.

"Can we go home?" she asked.

"Sure thing, Justine."

They walked back to the limousine he'd rented, not certain of his ability to drive, not wanting to put anyone else at risk. The driver was leaning against the door waiting for them. He didn't say anything, but opened the door for Justine and closed it behind Patrick.

The ride home was lost in the fog of grief that threatened to overwhelm Patrick. Justine sat beside him and chattered about the service and the other people who were there. The fog followed him into the house. He couldn't remember talking to people, though he was sure he must have said something in response to their endless words of sorrow and support.

"Justine wanted spaghetti," Patrick's sister was saying to him. "So I made her some. It's ready if you would like some."

2

Patrick thought of the awful void inside him. No amount of spaghetti would ever fill it.

"Sure, thanks." He was aware that she was shepherding the last of the people out the door before she went out herself. He followed the garlic and tomato smell to the kitchen as if he could get lost in his own house. Yet he felt lost.

"Hi, Daddy," Justine said, "you need to eat something." She was echoing what she had heard every other woman in the house tell him. She pulled him into a chair and climbed into his lap. She whispered in his ear, as if her words were the secret of the universe. "I know Mommy's with God, but I'm still sad. The minister said it was OK to cry. Is it?"

Patrick looked into his daughter's eyes and saw the same dry pain that he knew was in his.

"Yes," he said, "it's OK to cry." The floodgates opened and he saw her tears as he felt his. Then she clung to him with all the strength of her eight-year-old arms. He felt her wet face against his and their tears and their grief and their love mixed.

"I'll always be there for you." Patrick whispered into the blond hair. "Always."

Chapter One

Patrick finished assembling the sauce for their Friday spaghetti night as Justine came in. The smell filled their kitchen as it did every time, it reminded him of Ingrid. She loved this kitchen with the walls painted dark green and white cabinets. The old wooden table that was marked by years of being the centre of his family's home stood in the centre of the room.

"How was your day?" Patrick asked as he set aside his memories to focus on his daughter.

"OK, I guess." She dropped her bag in the corner. "Ms. Palenz had chocolate chip cookies for snack today. Real ones too."

"Did you bring me any?"

"No, silly, we ate them all, then we played Space Invaders," Justine said.

"Space Invaders?"

"Yeah, it's this dinosaur age computer game. It's so old it's kinda cool."

"I used to play that game."

"Well, you see then? Mz Palenz wanted me to ask if you needed anything. I told her your usual answer."

"Thanks." Patrick gave the sauce a stir sending up a waft of garlic and memories. Two years and it still brought him to the edge of tears. "How was school?"

"Oh, school." Patrick heard how his daughter's voice changed. "We did reading and math. We're starting a new book about a swan that has no voice. Ms. Hall was going to do Charlotte's Web, but she was afraid with Charlotte dying at the end that it would bring up 'issues'."

Brother, were they still at that? Justine had no problem reading Charlotte's Web and weeping over the spider's death at the end. She cried every time she read the book. While it didn't bother her; all through the last two grades her tears terrified her teachers. They had called him in a panic when Justine cried through 'Are You My Mother?' She had tried to explain the minister had said it was OK, but that didn't go over well.

"And Kelly?" he asked.

"Kelly is just dealing with her depressed issues."

"I think it's repressed."

"Whatever, she's still a bully."

Patrick sighed and poured the noodles into the strainer and gave it a shake. He heard Justine setting the table behind him.

"How was your day?" Justine asked.

"Well, I got one client's report done and the boss gave me three more to do."

"What about Wanda?"

"Wanda is nice, but, she's just nice."

"Oh Dad, you aren't getting any younger."

"I'm not worried." Patrick wished a curse on the writers of all movies and books in which the grieving father miraculously found a new true love by the end of the story.

"She doesn't like spaghetti," Patrick said as he piled the noodles on their plates.

"So that's that." Justine came over and slopped sauce on the noodles and put 'shaky cheese' on top. Patrick carried the plates over to the table.

"Thanks for the food," Justine prayed, "and say hello to Mom for me."

"Amen."

He twirled the spaghetti on his fork, while Justine tried to do the same. She managed a reasonable amount, but it fell off on the way to her mouth.

"O darn," she said. Then she sighed and picked up her knife to cut the spaghetti into manageable bits. "Do you miss Mom?"

"Every day."

"Me too."

They finished their meal in companionable silence, then Patrick washed dishes while Justine did her homework.

"I could get you a desk for your room," Patrick said.

"I like the kitchen table. It keeps me close to you."

"And the fridge," he said.

"And the fridge."

She got up and helped herself to a glass of milk, then sat down with her book. Patrick smiled as memory and reality meshed. Ingrid had liked to work at the kitchen table as well. She'd have designs, fabric samples and paint chips all over the table. For a moment Justine's blond head looked just like Ingrid's and Patrick felt the pain of her loss like a dagger in his heart.

"It happens to me too," Justine said. "I see her and think that she's come back." She came around the table and hugged him tight. He hugged her back and thought she had her mother's empathy too. There were many times that Ingrid had seemed to know exactly what he was thinking.

***

Saturday morning Patrick got up to the sound of cartoons and the smell of coffee. He put his robe on and went to the kitchen. The coffee was just finishing up and he poured a cup.

"Let me know when your brain starts working."

Patrick buried his nose in the steam from the coffee and let the aroma carry the grief away. Ingrid used to say that; now it was his daughter's way of saying good morning. He smiled and took a long sip. The bitter heat flowed down his throat and he decided that it was a good day.

"So what are we doing today?" he asked.

"My room," Justine said. "I can't stand it anymore."

"We just did it last year."

"But it's pink!"

"You wanted pink."

"That was last year. There's some paint in the basement. I can mix up some new colours."

"Colours?"

"I want to do some colour blocking on the wall by my bed." Justine looked down. "I was looking through some of Mom's stuff for ideas."

Patrick came and sat beside her. He gave her a squeeze.

"That stuff is as much yours as it is mine. She was your Mom."

"She is STILL my Mom," Justine shouted. "It doesn't matter if she's dead. She's still my Mom." She ran out of the room and Patrick listened as she thundered up the stairs. Her door didn't slam, so it was safe for him to follow. He found his daughter lying on the bed looking at some pictures cut out of magazines, a folder with paint chips and fabric swatches sat on the bedside table. The room was very pink.

"So, you want to talk about it?"

"Just because she isn't here doesn't mean she isn't real." Justine said looking up at him.

"She's real," Patrick said, "and she's still your Mom, but other people have trouble understanding that."

"You understand?"

"Yes." Justine heaved a deep sigh then shook it off.

"Then this is what I want to do." Justine sat up and patted the bed beside her. "I want to paint the whole room this dusty blue that I found downstairs. Then we need to tape off the squares and paint them these other colours, there's a green and some yellow, I think some purple, and I thought I'd leave one square pink."

"Your quilt won't match."

"There's another one in the linen closet that will work. Please, Dad?"

"You start moving everything to the middle of the room, and I'll go check to see if the paint is any good."

They spent the day painting the walls blue except for the square that Justine had very carefully taped off. The trim got a new coat of white since they had some white in the basement. Sunday, Justine came home from Sunday School and started taping off the blocks for the different colours. They worked all afternoon. When they were finished, Patrick had to admit that it was a stunning look.

Justine brought out the other quilt that she had found.

"Ah," Patrick said, "I wondered if you were talking about that one. Your Gran made it in case we ever had a boy. It was the last quilt she ever made."

"You were going to have another baby?"

"Well, we had so much fun with you that we wanted another baby. Gran just hoped it would be a boy."

"Then Mom got cancer."

"That's right."

"And she couldn't have more babies."

"No."

7

Justine buried her nose in the quilt. "It doesn't smell like Mom."

"I wouldn't think it would. Probably more like the cedar balls she put in everything to keep things from smelling musty."

"Remember when we hung a bunch of them on the Christmas tree?"

"Definitely. Wait here, I have something for you." Patrick went to his room and pulled a box from the closet shelf. He carried it back to Justine's room. "Look at this." He put the box on the bed beside her. "This was your Mom's stuff."

Justine opened the box and squealed when she saw the tiny bottles of perfume and all the little containers of makeup.

"You're a bit young to wear any of this yet, but Mom would want you to have it."

Justine was carefully opening each bottle and sniffing it.

"This one," she said, "this is the one she was wearing the last time she read me a story. I remember she was reading Pippi Longstocking to me and she smelled like this." She dabbed a little on her finger and rubbed it on her teddy bear. "Mom used to do that so the bear would smell like her and I would sleep better."

"I never knew that," Patrick said.

"Oh, Daddy, I miss her so much!"

"So do I darling, so do I."

"Do you think she'd like my room?"

Patrick stood and turned around slowly. The new paint had somehow not made her old white furniture look shabby, but just comfortable. The colour wall was striking, but not overwhelming. The new quilt fit perfectly to pull the whole thing together. It was like seeing one of Ingrid's projects completed. The smell of her perfume added her blessing to the room.

"She'd love it. Mom would be so proud of you."

"Thanks, Dad." Justine looked up at him. "What did Mom always cook after she finished a job?"

Patrick had to think for a moment. Ingrid did have a special meal that she cooked to celebrate the successful completion of a contract.

"Meatballs," he said, "I remember I used to tease her that meatballs belonged in spaghetti, but she liked them with this special sauce on rice. She said it reminded her of home."

"Can we cook them? Please?"

"Let's go look up the recipe."

They went out to a twenty-four hour grocery store near where Patrick worked to find the ingredients they needed. Then went to work.

"Ewwww," Justine said as she mixed the meat with her hands. "It's just like play dough, but a lot grosser."

"Your Mom would make a whole bunch of them and freeze them so she didn't have to make them that often." Patrick stirred the sauce and put it on a low heat. The rice was already cooking so he and Justine made rows of tiny balls to put in the oven to cook.

They watched decorating shows on TV while dinner gradually filled the house with familiar odours.

"Let's do this again."

"What, paint your room?" Patrick asked.

"No, cook Mom's recipes. It smells like she is watching us. She doesn't feel so far away now."

"OK then," Patrick said, "you choose the recipe when you get home from Sunday School. We'll go shopping to get what we need."

"Cool," Justine said. "Are they really going to paint the room that colour with that couch?"

For a second Patrick was sure that Ingrid was sitting in her chair and had winked at him. Instead of the sharp stab of grief he expected he felt warmth flow from his heart.

***

Monday morning Patrick watched Justine walk to school. When she turned the corner, he poured the last of the coffee into his travel mug and drove off to work. He went the long way around the block to avoid the church where Ingrid's funeral had been and where Justine went to Sunday School. After two years, the thought of God still made his stomach clench and burn. It just wasn't right that Ingrid had to die so young.

As he pulled into the parking lot, Patrick though how fortunate he was to have a job that didn't involve a long commute. He left his now empty travel mug in the car and pushed through the front doors of the five-story office building that held the law firm for which he did research.

Patrick waved at the young woman behind the deck and made sure his badge was on properly. The elevators wouldn't work unless he was wearing his pass. The first desk as he left the elevator was Wanda's. She smiled at him and turned back to her computer. Patrick walked to the back of the open work area and admired his fine view of a sliver of sky and the top branches of a maple tree before he sat down to work.

He didn't have a very big space. A picture of Ingrid from before she was diagnosed and Justine's most recent school picture sat on a shelf over his monitor. Hard to believe Justine was in Grade Four already. The rest of his space was covered with post-it notes and index cards. Patrick picked up a note that had fallen down over the weekend and pinned it into place. He had all that information on his computer, but he liked seeing it arranged visually too. Patrick hung his jacket on the back of the chair and loosened his tie. Time to work.

Patrick enjoyed his job as a researcher for the law firm. He looked for hidden surprises in contracts or properties. Recently he had been researching titles to old properties. There were clients who wanted to develop land next door to churches. Some of those churches had been around for more than a hundred years without doing any work or updating their deed. One company had started building on land they thought they owned, only to learn a nearby church held a deed to the land and wanted a say, and compensation, for the project. Resolving the dispute had taken time and money that should have been spent on the development. Patrick's job was to ensure that didn't happen to any of their clients.

"Excuse me, sir," he said when Mr. Ball lifted his head. "I'm off to the land registry to look at old records, are there any other things on our list that I should look at?"

"Not that I know of." Mr. Ball stretched and pushed his tie further askew. "Bring back a coffee if you feel like it. The stuff in the office just doesn't taste quite right." Neither the wrinkled suits or buzz cut hair hinted at Mr. Ball's management skills. Patrick didn't mind picking up coffee for a boss who knew what he was doing.

"OK."

The land registry was downtown and parking was tricky, but Patrick had a favourite lot where he knew the attendants. There were almost always able to find him a spot. Today it was easy. He waved at the woman and walked across the street to the office.

The receptionist buzzed for an archivist who led Patrick back into a cool dry room where it felt like time stood still. The smell and temperature stayed exactly the same. Sometimes after a long day Patrick half expected to leave the archives to discover the city had vanished while he had worked.

He put on the gloves they used for the old books and began digging back into history. There were bits and clues as he read. Two of the three properties had been owned by a variety of people, but there were no surprises. The trail of purchase and sale was clear back to the original deed to a farmer for clearing the land. Patrick made a few quick notes, and turned to the third parcel.

Patrick wound his way back into history. The school that had occupied the land burned down and was never replaced since there was a more modern school close by. He went further back and found that the land for the school was deeded by a local church. There was a proviso that if the school closed that the land would revert to the church.

The original church had apparently moved several times and changed its name a couple of times. Patrick took as much information as he could and decided that he needed to visit the most recent incarnation of the church to see if they still held a deed for the property. It was the church where Ingrid's had been. He hadn't driven past it since, though it was only a block away from the house.

***

He sat in his car and stared at the doors before he turned off the car and climbed out. It wasn't like he was going to go into the sanctuary. He would just leave a message with the secretary and be gone. He should have just phoned. He had a vision of the stack of cards that Reverend Daniel had left him. The man had tried. God was the problem. They would be talking land not God. It would be OK.

The doors were unlocked and an arrow pointed toward the church office. There was no one at the desk. He was about to leave when he heard footsteps behind him.

"Hello," Reverend Daniel said, "may I help you?" He hadn't changed much in the two years since the funeral. He still wore a black shirt that looked broken in like a favourite t-shirt. A bit of the white plastic tab that he'd worn for the service poked out from his breast pocket. The frames for his glasses were black and the lenses seemed to magnify not only his blue eyes, but the empathy that rested there. If he weren't a minister, Patrick could imagine him being a good friend.

"I'm Patrick Constance, Justine's dad."

"Right, Justine's in our Sunday School."

"I don't come to church." Patrick said and wondered why he had said that. He wasn't here to talk about either church or God.

"Ah," Reverend Daniel said, "we'll be here if you change your mind. I'm not usually in the office on Mondays, but Grace is off sick and I have some reading to do anyway. I have coffee in my office."

"That sounds good." Patrick followed the minister to his office. The only wall that wasn't either books or a window was an abstract painting that was odd lines and colours that looked like they were either fighting or dancing.

"That's not the kind of painting I think of ministers hanging in their office," Patrick said.

"It was a gift from a parishioner. He was dying when he painted it."

Patrick looked at the painting again. It didn't look different knowing a dying man had painted it. He turned away from it and sat down while the minister poured coffee into a couple of mugs.

"Reverend Daniel," Patrick said.

"Just Daniel will do," he said.

"Daniel," Patrick started again, "I was researching a property on King St. that had been a school. The land was deeded to the school from First Reformed, in 1872. When it burned down in 1936, it wasn't rebuilt so the land should have reverted to First Reformed then, but as far as I can find out First Reformed had closed and moved over to Brock St. and become St. Aidan's."

"Then in 1976, St. Aidan's joined us here at Redeemer."

"I was wondering if you still had the deed to the property."

"Let me look." Daniel pulled open the bottom drawer of the filing cabinet that occupied one corner. "We have copies of all the deeds here. The originals are in a safe." He pulled out several large envelopes. "Here we are." He handed a brown envelope to Patrick.

Patrick opened the deed and compared it to his notes.

"This looks like it," he said and handed the deed back.

"Can I ask why the interest?"

"I can't say," Patrick said, "I just do the research, but you may want to make sure that your deeds to all your properties are up to date and registered. A lot of the land registry only goes back forty years. If you haven't done anything with the property in that time it can get lost. That causes problems down the road."

"I will pass the word onto the trustees."

"I'd better get back to work."

"Thanks for stopping in. Say hello to Justine for me."

"I will."

Patrick climbed into the car and took a deep breath. Then he drove back to work, stopping at a drive-thru to pick up a coffee for Mr. Ball.

13

Chapter Two

Justine set the table in stubborn silence. Patrick sighed and served out the spaghetti.

"Going to school is the law," he said as they sat down.

"Is it the law that I have to listen to that big bully every day?" Justine shook the parmesan cheese viciously. "Kelly is mean, but the teachers like her so they don't care what she does. Today, Kelly had her friends pretending I didn't exist. They kept bumping into me and looking all shocked that I was there. I hate school."

"You still need to learn, and sometimes we need to learn to deal with people we don't like."

"Yeah, right. You don't have Kelly at your work," she said.

"True, I'm lucky I work with some pretty nice people."

"I want to be home-schooled. Jeannette at church is home-schooled," Justine said, "and she's smart."

"I can't stay home all day. I have to work."

"It isn't fair!"

"You're right," Patrick said. "It isn't."

"So aren't you going to fix it?"

"I don't know if it's that easy, Justine."

"It should be."

"I wish it was."

Justine tried twirling the spaghetti, but kept catching up too much to put in her mouth. She cut the strands into tiny little pieces. Then ate in silence. She stayed silent through her homework then went to bed early.

Patrick finished cleaning up, then looked at the fridge. Maybe Justine had said something to Ms. Palenz. Justine always enjoyed her time there between school and when Patrick got home. Ms. Palenz answered the phone on the first ring and Patrick could hear people eating in the background.

"I don't want to disturb your dinner," he said, "but this is Justine's dad. She came home in a real state today."

"Oh dear," said the voice on the other end. "She is having some trouble with the girls at school."

"She only mentions one name to me. Someone named Kelly."

"Kelly's the ring leader, but the rest of the class follows her. I have another child from that class so I hear stuff that you mightn't."

"Should I be talking to Justine's teacher?"

"Probably, but I don't know that it would do any good. This type of girl is usually expert at getting the teacher to think that she is a perfect angel."

"Thanks for your input. I should really let you get back to your meal."

"It's OK, I have a couple of kids who stay for supper, then Michael and I eat."

"Right then, say hello to Michael."

The voice on the other end of the line laughed.

"Michael is my dog, named after the archangel of battle. I'll keep my ears open. Goodnight, Mr. Constance."

"Call me Patrick."

"Then you must call me Lee."

"Goodnight."

Patrick hung up the phone and saw Justine watching him from the door.

"I told you that Michael was a dog," she said.

"I forgot."

"Can I have a glass of milk?"

"Sure, help yourself."

"Did talking to Ms. Palenz make you feel better?"

"I'm not sure. Should it?"

"She's nice, but she likes to tell me what to do. Sometimes that's good, like showing me how to bake a pie."

"You know how to bake pies?"

"Don't interrupt, Daddy." Their eyes met over the table and Justine started giggling. "I sounded just like her." Patrick smiled at her.

"You're right though, I shouldn't interrupt."

Justine nodded at him and sat at the table.

"She isn't as helpful with things like Kelly. She means well, but Kelly is, well, Kelly. She has the teacher wrapped around her finger and everyone in the class is either in love with her or scared of her. It's hard to even say what she does. It's like she'll say, "We shouldn't ask Justine to bring cookies because she doesn't have a mom to bake them and everyone will think *How sweet*. When Kelly's looking at me thinking *Your mom is dead, you poor sap*. Justine finished her milk, but made no move to go back to bed. Patrick put some cookies on a plate and slid them in front of her. She looked up at him.

"I didn't send you to bed early," he said. "You just needed some space to be angry."

"But it isn't fair to be angry at you about Kelly."

"No, it isn't," Patrick said, "but I can deal with it a lot better than Kelly."

"Thanks, Dad." She stared into her empty glass a while. "What do you think Mom would do?"

"I don't really know." Patrick picked a cookie up off the plate and nibbled at it. "But she wouldn't have let Kelly get her down. I know there were people who gave her a hard time when she started as a designer, but she would just shrug and say they'd be sorry when she was on the cover of Better Homes and Gardens."

"Was she? On the cover I mean."

"No," Patrick said, "she was just getting well known when she got sick, then it didn't seem important anymore."

"That's not fair."

"A lot of life isn't fair."

"Why not?"

"I wish I knew. The minister would be able to answer better than me."

"It's Pastor Daniel," Justine said.

"I know, it's just…"

"You're still mad at him."

"I'm not mad at him. It's just whenever I go near the church I start thinking about how unfair it all is."

"Like me tonight, being mad at you instead of Kelly, except you're mad at God."

"I think so."

Justine nodded her head again.

"Dad?"

"Yes."

"Thanks for letting me be mad sometimes."

Patrick hugged Justine and they didn't say anything for a while.

When Justine had gone back to bed he sat in the kitchen for a long time thinking. She was right. He was still mad at God. Patrick didn't know what to do with that knowledge, and finally decided there was nothing he could do. He washed the glass and the plate and went to bed.

He woke to the sound of the smoke alarm and was out of bed and down to Justine's room before he was even properly awake. She wasn't there.

"Dad, Dad?" He heard her calling from downstairs. "I'm sorry, I was trying to bake cookies and they got all burnt."

Patrick went down the stairs and looked into the kitchen.

"We'd better open some windows and turn on the fan. Maybe you should ask Ms. Palenz to teach you how to bake cookies."

"Really?" Justine ran to the phone. "I'll call her right now."

"I'd better go upstairs and get dressed then."

By the time he was dressed and downstairs again the smoke had cleared and he could hear voices in the kitchen.

"Some ovens are hotter than others. It can make a big difference with cookies. Also, some kinds burn very easily."

"Good morning," Patrick said. "Thanks for coming over." He poured himself a cup of coffee and waved the pot in her direction.

"Thanks. Justine made me a cup, but I wouldn't mind a refill."

Patrick poured her more coffee then sat and watched them work. Lee was much younger than he'd thought. He had imagined some grandmotherly soul. His sister had recommended her and since she lived just a couple of blocks away it was convenient for Justine to go there after school until he got home. He couldn't believe that he had talked to her on the phone barely a half dozen times in two years and had never met her.

She was good with Justine, showing her how to do each

step of baking cookies. By the time they were done they had what looked like hundreds of cookies.

"I can't believe we had this much baking stuff in our house."

"Oh, I brought stuff from my place. This is my weekly baking for the kids," Lee said.

"I hope you leave a few cookies behind."

Justine and Lee looked at each other and laughed.

"You were right," Lee said.

"I told her you would like the cookies," Justine said. "Mom was a great cook, but she didn't like baking, so Dad was always starved for cookies and pies and stuff."

Lee grinned at him.

"Ah, so I know what to do to get on your good side."

Lee ended up staying for supper and Justine cooked her meatballs and rice.

He and Justine were doing dishes after Lee had gone home to make up with Michael for leaving him all day.

"That was a pretty good day, for a day that started with a fire alarm."

"I'm sorry about that. The recipe looked so simple."

"Not everything that's simple is easy. It turned out well, but maybe next time wake me up before you start experimenting in the kitchen."

"OK, Dad."

***

On Monday Patrick called the school and made an appointment to meet with Justine's teacher. Ms. Hall had some time after school that day, so he left work early to go to the school.

The classroom was bright and cheerful with the same smell of chalk dust that he remembered.

"Thank you, Kelly." The young girl who was cleaning the blackboards smiled and left. Patrick looked at her curiously. She didn't look like a monster.

"Now, Mr. Constance, what can I do for you?" Ms. Hall said.

Now that he was here Patrick was at a loss for words. He took a second to organize his thinking and he was sure that Ms.

Hall's lips were trying to bend into a frown.

"Justine came home very upset on Friday," he said, "something about Kelly saying that she shouldn't bring cookies since she had no mom to bake them."

"We are having a bake sale to raise money for a class project. Some of the kids were adamant that everything should be fresh baked and not store bought. Kelly was just trying to be thoughtful."

"That's not how Justine took it. She heard it as her lack of a mother being rubbed in her face."

"I assure you. I was in the room and that is not how it was said." She dusted her hands together as if that were the final statement on the matter. "I am glad that you came in. I do have some concerns about Justine."

"I see. She seems to be getting her homework done."

"Oh, it's not about her work. She's an exemplary student, but she doesn't seem to be very emotionally stable. We are reading Trumpet of the Swan because Justine can't read Charlotte's Web without crying. It's been two years. I think you might want to consider getting her counselling to help her move on."

Patrick felt a spike of rage rush from his gut into his head.

"Is your mother still alive?" he asked.

"Yes, thank goodness."

"Then you have no idea what Justine is going through. You don't just 'move on' after losing someone as important as a mother."

"Goodness, I'm just trying to do what's best for Justine."

Patrick stood up and tried to slow his breathing. Tried to find the right words to explain but the depth of his emotion was beyond words.

"Stop trying, and just teach," he finally said, and walked out of the room. He passed Kelly and some other girls in the hall. He thought Kelly was whispering to the others, but it was hard to tell through the tears that were clawing their way out of his eyes.

The next day Justine came home and dropped her bag in the corner. She looked at Patrick.

"Were you at school yesterday?" she asked.

"Yes."

"You didn't tell me."

"I didn't know what to say to you." Justine nodded. "Kelly said you were crying when you left Ms. Hall's room." Patrick just nodded. The memory of that conversation was enough to make his eyes sting.

"I know just how you feel." She wrapped her arms around him. "I feel like that every day in that place." Patrick just hugged her.

"What can I do?" he asked finally.

"Nothing, I guess. It's not like you could quit working."

"No, I'm sorry."

"It's OK, Dad. I'm getting used to it."

You shouldn't have to.

***

Patrick watched Justine put her coat on and walk to school the next morning. He wondered at the courage that allowed her to go back every day.

On the drive to work Patrick realized that apart from Wanda, he didn't know anything about any of his co-workers other than their names. He stole glances at the work spaces of the other people on the floor. Some had family pictures up, some had sports stuff. One fellow had pictures from travel brochures plastered all over his walls.

"All the places that I want to take my family to before I retire," he said.

"Where have you been?"

"Nowhere," he said. "Every time I get enough money something breaks." He shrugged. "We go to her parent's cottage. It isn't Disneyland, but the kids like it." He looked back at the wall. "Got to dream though."

"True enough."

Patrick sat down at his computer and put his reports together. He added a summary of the history of the third property and noted that the church had a deed for the land then hit the send button and forgot it. It was Mr. Ball's problem now.

He looked at the next job on the list and dove into the searches.

20

The email notice pinged and he checked it.

Mr. Carson wants to see you in meeting room 412.

It didn't mention a time, so Patrick put his work on standby and headed to the elevator. He didn't spend any time wondering why Mr. Ball's supervisor wanted to talk to him. It wasn't common, but it happened occasionally. Mr. Carson managed the lawyers who weren't partners. Sometimes it was faster for him to ask the questions than to try to schedule a meeting with an already overbooked lawyer.

Room 412 was bare bones with barely enough space for four people. It had a wall monitor, a desk station, and a white board. The white board still had words and lines scribbled on it from an earlier meeting. The only word that stood out was 'pizza'.

"Patrick," Mr. Carson said, "sit down."

He sat in a chair where he could see Mr. Carson and the screen. The other man walked over and closed the door, then leaned against one of the chairs. He was younger than Mr. Ball, but he wore his suit like he'd been born in it.

"You went to this church, Redeemer, and asked about the deed?"

"Yes, sir."

"Why?"

"It seemed like the logical next step. The records weren't completely clear, but if the church had a deed then the situation would be much easier."

"Now they know someone is interested in the property."

"I never mentioned a reason for my visit."

"They will be able to figure it out," Mr. Carson said. "If they starting asking for an exorbitant amount for that parcel it could be trouble."

"Perhaps," Patrick said, "but if a sale was almost completed and they showed up with a deed, it could be more trouble."

"We'll hope so," Mr. Carson waved his hand in dismissal.

Patrick went downstairs to find Mr. Ball waiting at his desk.

"Well, it looks like you still have a job," he said.

Patrick felt a twist in his gut. He hadn't imagined that he could lose his job over something so small.

"You're a good researcher," Mr. Ball said, "but leave the personal contacts to the people paid to do that. As long as the property doesn't suddenly appear on the market you'll be fine. Next time check with me and I'll give you a decision on whether you or someone else should go."

"Thanks, Mr. Ball."

"I'll let you get back to work."

Patrick sat down at his desk and spent a long time looking at Justine's picture before he logged back in and started work.

Chapter Three

"Hi, Dad," Justine walked in and tossed her bag aside. "Spaghetti smells good. There's a bake sale next week. Ms. Palenz said she would help me with some cookies."

"That sounds like fun. So we'd better go shopping first to get everything we need."

"Good idea, Dad." Justine pulled a paper out of her pocket. "Ms. Palenz made me a list."

Patrick laughed.

"We're going to package them at school so we can sell them in trays, but we'll also sell single ones at lunch time."

"That sounds like a good plan."

Early Saturday morning Justine banged on Patrick's door.

"We've got to get going."

"It's too early."

"The store is open twenty-four hours."

Patrick got dressed quickly and opened the door.

"That's not what I meant."

"I know," Justine grinned at him and handed him a travel mug. "Let's go."

It was amazing the variety of things that you could put in cookies. No peanuts though, because one of the kids in kindergarten was allergic, but they had everything else from chocolate chips to coconuts, dried fruit and even maraschino cherries.

They took it all home and Justine called Ms. Palenz. Once again the house filled with the fragrance of baking. Patrick sat and pretended to read while he listened in on their conversation. Ms. Palenz told stories of her trips that had Justine in giggles most of the time. Every once in a while Justine would bring him a cookie to 'test.'

By mid-afternoon they were done and all the cookies were carefully stacked in plastic tubs that Lee had brought with her. She refused the offer of another supper saying that she was heading out with a friend that night. Justine came and sat beside Patrick on the arm of the chair.

"That was a blast."

"Good."

"It's good to do things that Mom did, but sometimes it's nice to do new things too."

"True," Patrick smiled, "so, how about we do another new thing and I'll take you out for dinner."

"For real?" Justine said, "I mean a real restaurant with waiters and everything?"

"There's a place near where I work that you would like."

"Let me go get changed." Justine ran upstairs. Patrick looked at himself and thought that he could probably do with a higher class of clothes himself.

Justine apparently decided that her first time in a "real" restaurant called for a mix of her church clothes and a shirt that Patrick had never seen on her before. It was a bit large, but since she wore it like a jacket, it worked.

"It's a shirt I found in your closet," Justine said. "Do you mind?"

"It looks good on you."

They drove to the restaurant and Patrick walked her to the table. The waiter paid special attention to Justine making her laugh by pretending to pour her wine.

"I'll have a steak, because it's more grown up."

"Since I don't need to prove how old I am, I'll have the salmon."

While they were waiting for their meal, Justine steepled her fingers.

"So how was work this week?"

"I finished up a few projects, but I got in trouble because I did more than I was supposed to do."

"We get extra credit for doing more work."

"Work is more complicated. The bosses were worried that the wrong person doing something might let a secret out and cause problems."

"I thought secrets were bad."

"Some are, like if someone does something wrong and wants to keep it secret. Some are more a matter of timing, like a surprise party."

"Oh, and they think you might have spoiled the surprise?" Justine said.

"Something like that."

"So what did they do to you?"

"They talked to me, then gave me a whole bunch of new work."

"Wow, and I thought Ms. Hall was tough!"

"It's how the world works. If we never made any mistakes nobody would do anything but sit around the pool and drink margaritas."

"What's a margarita?"

"It's an adult drink, with um, adult stuff in it."

"You mean alcohol," Justine made a face. "We learned about that in school. It makes people stupid."

"Fair assessment, but some people enjoy it."

"They enjoy being stupid?"

"Well, some," Patrick said, "but most just like to relax a bit."

Their meals arrived and Justine tucked into her steak. Patrick was astonished that she not only finished the steak but had room for dessert.

She fell asleep on the way home and Patrick had to wake her up to go inside.

"Thanks, Dad," she murmured before sleepwalking into her room.

On Sunday, she looked through the recipe cards for how to cook steak.

"I can't find a recipe for steak," she said as she sat on the arm of Patrick's chair.

"I don't know that they have much in the way of recipes for steak," he said. "Mostly people just cook it, and add spices and stuff to make it taste better. Maybe look on the internet."

"They have recipes on the internet?"

"All kinds." Patrick laughed as she ran to the computer and started typing into it.

"Wow, when you're right, you're right," she said. "We could eat for years and never eat the same thing twice."

"Except spaghetti," Patrick said.

"Well, duh!"

Instead of steak they had satay chicken on skewers.

"Chicken that sticks to the roof of your mouth," Patrick said after they finished dinner. "Tastes good though."

"Not bad," she said, "I can't decide if I want more spice or less."

They had ice cream to finish up. Then Justine organized the cookies to go to school before she went to bed.

"Will you drive me tomorrow? I don't want to take all this stuff on the bus."

"Sure thing."

***

Patrick helped Justine carry the tubs of cookies into the school then headed off to work.

He spent the morning on simple projects. He still felt a little nervous and didn't properly settle into work until after lunch. By then he decided that if they were going to fire him, they would have done it by now. He focused on his research until it was time to go home.

Justine came in the door like a hurricane. Her bag flew across the room and slammed into the wall.

"I could just scream," she said.

"Then why don't you?"

"Really?"

"I won't mind."

She put her head back and let out a shriek. Patrick was sure the neighbours were going to be phoning the police.

"That was a pretty good scream," he said when the echoes had died. "You want to tell me what it's about?"

"Remember how I brought all those cookies to school for the bake sale? Kelly said that they looked store bought. There was no way that I could have made them. Ms. Hall said they did look awfully professional and I just lost it." Justine looked at him. "I yelled at them that I made the cookies, and they should be happy about it. I got sent to the principal's office for yelling at the teacher, but the principal made them sell my cookies anyway. They made all kinds of money off them, so Kelly is saying that it proves I bought them. Every time I tried to say that I baked them, the teacher would ask me if I wanted to go back to the principal's office. I said 'Yes, cause it's better than being called a cheat.'" So I ended up spending the whole day with the principal. He liked my cookies. He bought two dozen, and now everyone hates me."

Patrick felt like doing a little screaming himself, only the phone rang.

"Hello," he said.

"It's Lee. How did the bake sale go?"

Patrick gave her an abbreviated version.

"Oh dear, Tommy is in her class and that's very close to what he said. I'd hoped he was exaggerating."

"The problem seems to be as much this teacher as the girl. She thinks this is all because Justine hasn't moved on from her grief."

"I think she is doing very well, but it might not hurt for her to talk to someone about her feelings. Especially with all this going on at school. I know someone who is very good with children. I can ask her if she'd see Justine."

"I'll talk to Justine and see what she says, but I can call around. I don't want to impose on you."

"It isn't imposing. Justine is a friend, and you'll find that the good counsellors have waiting lists years long."

"Hold on a minute." He put his hand over the phone. "Justine, Ms. Palenz has a friend that you might be able to talk to."

"You mean like a crazy person."

"No, I don't think she's crazy."

"Not her, me. You think I'm crazy."

"No, I don't, but sometimes even sane people need to talk about stuff."

"Let me talk to Ms. Palenz." Patrick handed her the phone. "Alone." He rubbed her hair then left the kitchen, closing the door behind him.

They talked for a long time, and Patrick was sure that he heard Justine crying at one point. She came out of the kitchen and handed the phone to him.

"I'm going to go and see her. I don't feel much like eating right now. I'm going to bed." She walked upstairs and into her room. The door closed firmly behind her.

"Hello?" he said.

"Still here."

"Justine said she was going to go talk to this counsellor."

"You aren't going to ask what we talked about?"

"If she wanted me to know she wouldn't have kicked me out of the room."

"You are wise beyond your years. When she is ready, she'll tell you. In the meantime I'll talk to my friend and set up an appointment."

"OK, just let me know when and where."

Patrick went back to the living room and sat for a long time in the dark. What am I doing wrong? He thought to himself. Being a kid shouldn't be this hard. "Tell me what to do, Ingrid." He whispered, but he didn't hear any answer.

"Dad?"

Justine stood in the dark looking in at him.

"Are you all right, Dad?"

"Yes."

"Then why are you sitting in the dark?"

"I'm thinking."

"Did Ms. Palenz tell you what we talked about?"

"I didn't ask."

"I told her she could tell you if you needed to know, but thanks for trusting me."

"When you're ready, I'll be here to listen."

"I'm hungry."

"I think there's some spaghetti sauce in the fridge."

This time Patrick set the table while Justine boiled water for the noodles and carefully heated up the sauce. She served up the plates and put them on the table.

She tried to twirl the noodles but they still wouldn't cooperate.

"Before you give up, try this," Patrick said. He got a spoon from the drawer and used it to separate a few strands out that he twirled up on his fork. The spoon helped him to get the fork to his mouth without incident.

Justine fetched her own spoon and tried it. She managed

to finish the whole plate with only minor problems.

"Thanks, Dad," she said.

"I just remembered about the spoon trick."

"Not the spoon, or not just the spoon. How many Dads would let their kids eat spaghetti at midnight? Not yell at them for getting into trouble at school? Just, thanks."

"You're very welcome, though I'd prefer that you didn't spend too many days in the principal's office."

"OK." Justine sighed and headed back off to bed.

Patrick cleaned up the kitchen then followed her up the stairs. Justine hadn't closed the door, and Patrick could see her sleeping with her nose in her teddy bear.

"Sleep tight, angel."

"You too, Mom," came the barest whisper.

Patrick went to bed not sure if he should smile or cry.

***

In the morning, Justine packed her bag and headed off to school.

"Try to stay out of trouble," she said.

"You too."

He went and researched old properties while he worried about Justine at school. The day passed and the rest of the week, without much more than the usual grumbling about Kelly and her constant teasing. Friday evening the phone rang. It was Lee letting Patrick know that Justine had an appointment that Monday after school.

Justine watched movies through the weekend. She chose a recipe that didn't involve any shopping and went to bed early.

Patrick dropped her off at the school and went in to talk to the principal.

"I hear you like my daughter's cooking." Patrick said.

"The cookies were delicious," the principal said. "My name's Mr. Houston. I'm very sorry about what happened. While I don't allow yelling at teachers for any reason, Justine did have some cause to be upset."

"I watched her bake the cookies," said Patrick, "all of them. She hasn't had that much fun in a very long time."

"I will speak to Ms. Hall. She means well, but she is

inexperienced."

"I will leave it in your hands then." Patrick stood. "I will be picking Justine up after school. She has an appointment with a counsellor."

"I remember when my father died. It took years for me to work things out. I wish my mother had thought to bring me to a counsellor. Though it probably wouldn't have helped. I wasn't nearly as smart as Justine." He shook hands with Patrick. "My door is always open, Mr. Constance."

Justine was still quiet when he picked her up after school.

"The principal came and talked to Ms. Hall while we were out at recess. She sort of apologized, but I still don't think she likes me."

They arrived at the address to find a pleasant looking red brick house. The sign in front said 'Balanteen Art and Play Therapy'.

"This doesn't look so bad," Justine said, "I like art." The inside matched the exterior, with what Justine called a nicely understated look. She walked around and peered at the paintings while they waited.

"This is cool, Dad."

"I'm glad you like it," Mrs. Balanteen said. "Your mother did most of the design work." The counsellor was an older woman wearing clothes that would be as comfortable on the floor as in a chair.

"You knew my mother?" Justine went from quiet to excited in an instant.

"Let me talk to your Dad for a few minutes, then we'll talk about your mother." She waved to the chairs and Justine plunked herself into one.

"What are you waiting for?" she said. "Go, talk."

Mrs. Balanteen laughed and opened the door to her office. Now that he knew, Patrick could see Ingrid's touches in the decor.

"This was done after she learned about the cancer," he said. "She used much softer colours after."

"It was the last job she had before she had to quit. I was at her funeral."

"I don't remember much about that."

"I understand." She pulled out a pad of paper. "I'm Mrs. Balanteen. When Lee called me, I was very concerned, but seeing Justine for myself, less so. If she is so eager to talk about her mother, she is working through the loss well. Still, talking with her will do no harm, and maybe help her deal with the children at school.

"I have a few simple rules. I will not talk about any of the sessions without Justine's permission and without her in the room. The only exception is if I think she is a danger to herself or to others, or if there are signs of abuse. That's just the law. I will tell you in general terms how she is doing and if there are specific things that you can do to help."

"That all sounds good." Patrick stood.

"You don't want to know how much this will cost."

"If it helps Justine, any cost would be worth it."

"Lee told me, and I didn't believe her. Now I owe her a bottle of wine." She put the pad down beside her. "Ask Justine to come in."

"Justine, it's your turn," he said. He'd barely finished the sentence before she was in the room and the door closed. Patrick picked up an old magazine and started reading.

When she came out she was practically bouncing.

"I'll meet you in the car," he said. "I probably need to pay Mrs. Balanteen."

"I won't charge you for this session, Mr. Constance. Future sessions will be a hundred dollars each."

"All this weekend she has barely moved and now she is practically flying."

"She had a very stressful week, then talked about a great many issues with Lee. That takes a great deal of energy. She will bounce back to her normal self. You did very well to just let her find her own level. Shall I make an appointment for two weeks?"

"Mrs. Balanteen was Mom's last client before she died." Justine said when they got in the car. "She asked Mom to create an atmosphere that was calming, but not deadening. The colours come from a picture of India that she has in her office. It is just this landscape, but the colours are amazing. She was at Mom's funeral. I don't remember her, but she said that was OK. She wants to see pictures of my room too. We can just talk or I can draw pictures. She is so cool."

"I'm glad you like her," Patrick said. "I talked to Mr. Houston today. If you need to talk at school, he said you're welcome to go and talk to him, and you don't need to yell at Ms. Hall first."

"Thanks, Dad."

When they got home, she ran to the phone and called Ms. Palenz.

"I wanted to thank you for getting Mrs. Balanteen to talk to me," Justine said. "She is so cool. She knew my mom."

Justine talked a while longer before she hung up then she hugged Patrick before setting out her books.

Chapter Four

Patrick sat and watched Justine expertly twirl the spaghetti on her fork. It had been a couple of months since she started seeing Mrs. Balanteen and she had a confidence that Patrick hadn't realized she'd lacked. Not so much doing anything different, but she didn't stop and check everything with him anymore.

"So how many reports did the boss give you today?" Justine asked.

"Just two, but they are really big ones," Patrick said. "Sometimes I wish I was back in school and could do something different every day."

"Nice one," Justine said. "OK, I'll work on the science project, but bugs are gross."

"Gross, but important."

"Yeah, I guess." She finished her plate and looked at him. "What's a drasil?"

"I don't know. A kind of bug?"

"No, it's not a bug, and it's not a riddle."

"Well, why don't you look on the web?"

"I already did, and I didn't find anything."

"Strange, I'll keep my ears open."

"OK." Justine gathered up the dishes and put them in the sink. "I have some bug research to do on the computer."

"Sure," Patrick didn't mind washing the dishes. He'd always washed them for Ingrid and it seemed a logical thing to wash them for Justine too.

When he'd finished, he went into the living room and Justine hit a couple of keys to switch the screen to a web site that had assorted pictures of large insects.

"What were you looking at?"

"Noth..." Justine looked at him. "Dad, can I ask you to just trust me?"

"You can, but I have a job as your Dad. I need to make sure you're safe."

"It's for a surprise, but I can't tell you yet. Please?

"OK," Patrick said. "I'll trust you."

"Thanks." Justine heaved a big sigh. "You won't be sorry."

Saturday morning, Ms Palenz came and collected Justine for a quick shopping trip. They came home laughing and joking. Justine took a bag up to her room. While Lee carried some other bags into the kitchen.

"I told Justine it was time she made a pie for you."

"Ah, pie..."

"Apple or peach?" Justine came back in.

"I have to choose?"

"What did I tell you?" Justine said. "It's a good thing we bought enough for both."

Lee brought out bowls from the cupboards and lifted a rolling pin from her bag. Soon they were mixing pastry and Justine was rolling it out carefully. She lifted the pastry and dropped it in a tin pie plate. She rolled out a second crust and put it in another plate. They peeled and chopped the apples and peaches and filled the pie shells heaping full. A mysterious mix of spices, flour and sugar went on next and was covered up with more pastry. Justine trimmed the edges and poked holes it the pie crust. As she slipped them into the oven she asked Ms. Palenz to watch them while she did something upstairs.

Lee put on coffee and sat down.

"She is an extraordinary girl."

"She is indeed," Patrick said, "but I still feel like I'm being softened up for something."

"You are, but you can trust her."

"I know, but it still scares me sometimes. Whenever I think I know what I'm doing she changes and I have to learn the rules all over again."

"I think it's supposed to work like that."

"You know a lot about children. Do you have any of your own?"

Lee sighed and got up to pour coffee.

"That's a story meant to be told over wine, not coffee."

"I'm sorry I intruded."

"It's not an intrusion, but it's also not a story you need to hear right now."

34

They sat in silence for a while drinking their coffee. Patrick could smell the pies.

"How long do they need to cook?" he asked.

"Until they're done," Lee said.

Patrick laughed.

"That sounds like something I would say."

"Usually half an hour or so."

They were on their second cup of coffee when Lee peered into the oven and pronounced the pies done. She pulled them out and put them on racks to cool.

"That's my cue," Justine said from the door. "Come with me." She led Patrick to the computer and had him sit in front of it. "This is your room," she said. "It's nice, because Mom did it, but I think you could use a change. So here are some ideas." With a click of a button she started a slide show. With each slide the furniture was arranged slightly differently and the colours of the wall and the curtains changed.

"We can't afford to do the floor and it's pretty neutral. Which one do you like?" Justine said.

"We?" asked Patrick.

"I've been saving my allowance and helping Ms. Palenz with some stuff."

"I've got no sense of colour at all," Lee said "Justine has been a great help with some decorating at my place."

"You're ten years old and you're a professional decorator?" He tried to return his eyebrows to their proper level.

Justine turned deep red. "I'm almost eleven."

"You're even more amazing than I thought." Patrick looked at his daughter and shook his head. "Well, let's see this again." He finally chose a green wall colour with curtains that were almost bronze. The furniture was turned around so it looked completely different.

After Lee left and Justine had gone to bed, he went back to the computer and went through the slide show again.

"Ingrid, you would be so proud of her."

***

Sunday, Justine came home and told Patrick that Pastor Daniel wanted to talk to him. He was at the office. Patrick decided it was a little silly to phone when he could walk there in a few minutes. There were still people standing around talking, but Daniel was waiting for him in the office.

"I just wanted to let you know where we are with that property you mentioned." Daniel leaned back in his chair. "The trustees had just got the registration sorted out when we received an offer from a company that wants to develop that property for apartments. Since we had been talking about the property, the Board had done some thinking about what if anything they wanted to do with it."

Patrick's stomach started to burn.

"How much more did you ask for?"

"That's the funny part. Their lawyer had this nervous look like we were going to get crazy and ask for a ridiculous price. We have some solid business people on the board and they said the offer was reasonable. No, what we decided was that we wanted the rent on a portion of the units, roughly equivalent to the value of the land, to be geared to low-income housing. We offered to manage the extra work it would create through the church. I think we shocked them. They are considering the proposal and will get back to us next week." The minister grinned. "We've wanted to get some low-income housing in the area for quite some time. This will allow us to do it faster and neater than we could have on our own."

Monday morning there was a note on Patrick's desk. 412 Now was all it said. Patrick took the elevator up trying to calm his stomach. Mr. Carson and one of the middle range lawyers were there. Mr. Carson closed the door.

"We have a development on the church property," he said. "Essentially they want to use the purchase price to permanently subsidize the rent in five units," the lawyer said. "Church people, go figure. You talked to them. Are they serious about this?"

"I would say so, sir," Patrick said and swallowed. "The church is where my daughter goes to Sunday School. The minister seemed very excited about the proposal." He could feel Mr. Carson's eyes on him.

"You didn't tell me you were a member of the church."

"I'm not. I don't go to church, not since my wife died."

"Can't blame you," the lawyer said. "Doesn't seem entirely rational. Anyway, they were very grateful for the offer for the land. I think the clients are going to go for it. This housing stuff is all the rage these days. It will look good on them and they get the land at a very reasonable price." He looked over at Mr. Carson. "No harm, no foul." He left the tiny room. Mr. Carson closed the door after him.

"How long ago did your wife die?" he said.

"A little more than two years," Patrick said.

"Mine died last year. Worst thing that ever happened to me. Try to be more careful Patrick. You're a good researcher, I'd hate to lose you over some silly damn thing." He left the office too. Patrick took the elevator back down to his desk. For some reason it had never occurred to him that other people at the firm might have lost people too.

The next weekend Justine and Lee took over his bedroom. He helped them move furniture, then sat and watched TV as he listened to the bumps and bangs upstairs. He made a snack halfway through the afternoon and called them down.

"How's it going?"

"This is a lot of work," Lee said. "I'm having trouble keeping up with the whirlwind here."

"That's because you have the little brush and I'm using a roller," Justine said.

"Well, the painting is just about done. We've got some stuff at my place to pick up and bring here.

"No peeking!" Justine ordered.

"Trust me," Patrick said. Justine just rolled her eyes, but when they left, he stayed in his chair. Even though he'd seen the pictures, he didn't want to spoil the surprise.

They returned carrying rolls and bags. Justine saw him in the living room and waved as she went upstairs. Just before supper she came and got him.

"It's ready." She led him upstairs then made him close his eyes before she opened the door and pulled him in by the hand. He opened his eyes and looked around.

"Oh wow, this is even better than the pictures."

"I was so scared it wouldn't work," Justine said. "I had this picture in my head and I couldn't get the real room to look just like the picture."

"Your mom used to say that," Patrick said, "whenever she had an especially challenging project."

"Really?" she said. "I thought she always knew what she was doing."

"She always knew what she was doing, but she didn't always know if it would work."

"Right," Justine said, and Patrick and Lee laughed.

"Whatever gave you the idea to redo my room?" Patrick asked when Lee had gone home.

"It was something Drasil said."

"Drasil?"

"Drasil's a new friend of mine."

"Did you meet him at school?"

"Kind of, though I'm not sure Drasil's a he."

"Sounds interesting."

"Yeah, Drasil's....different."

"Well, thank Drasil for me anyway. This was a brilliant idea."

"Oh sure."

Justine went off to bed and left Patrick in a room which strangely made him feel both closer and further from Ingrid. He slept well.

Chapter Five

Justine came through the door and put her bag on its hook before coming into the kitchen.

"Hi Dad," she said. "Sorry I'm late, but I got talking to Drasil and forgot about the time."

"Well," Patrick said, "you aren't very late. I just have the noodles on."

"OK." Justine set the table. "He was telling me about some people he knew. They never fight at all, and they always let people come in the door. It was something about hospitals ... hospi something."

"Hospitality."

"That's it. Anyway, they want people to feel at home so they're safe."

"They sound like interesting people," Patrick said.

"Drasil thought so. He thinks they are very special."

"So this Drasil is a person after all? You keep saying he."

"Well, 'he' sounds much nicer than 'it'."

"True. Can you tell me more about this Drasil?"

"Not really. I'd have to ask him first."

"That's fair enough." Patrick set the plates on the table.

"Thanks for the food." Justine prayed as she always did, "and say hello to Mom."

"How was school?"

"Same old, same old." Justine shrugged.

"Where did you learn that?"

"The other kids say it. It is exactly what school is like."

"It describes work too some days."

"See?" Justine said.

"Kelly isn't bothering you?"

"I don't pay any attention to her, so she doesn't bother with me anymore. I'm no fun. It's something Mz. Balanteen said that when I get angry at Kelly it's like giving her a reward. She taught me some breathing stuff to help stay calm. I had to do lots of breathing at first."

"That's something I guess. So, it's just learning now."

"You won't believe what I learned about frogs today."

"What?"

"Some of them freeze solid in the winter, then thaw out in the spring; and their eyeballs freeze first."

"Frog-sicles?"

"Ewwww, you're not supposed to eat them."

The weekend passed and Justine spent her time drawing room designs and baking.

Patrick realized he never heard his daughter talk about any friends before this mysterious Drasil. He decided that he ought to talk to Lee about it after Justine had gone to bed. He looked around the house and saw that she had been gradually changing it to match her own style. The hooks in the hall for their coats and her bags, different pictures hanging in the kitchen, even cushions she had sewn for the living room. Yet for all the changes there was still a sense that Ingrid was just around the corner.

He called Lee.

"I've never heard Justine talking about any friends, Lee, have you?"

"She plays with some of the children here," she said, "but I wouldn't say they were friends. Some kids don't have many friends; some have dozens. I wouldn't worry about it for now, or you could ask Grace, that's Mrs. Balanteen."

"Thanks, I might do that."

On Monday Justine came home and wandered into the kitchen.

"Drasil took me to see his friends today."

"I would prefer you asked me first."

"Sorry, Dad." Justine hung her head. "I won't go if you don't want me to."

"As long as you're safe and you let Ms. Palenz know if you're going to be late, it's OK."

"Thanks, Dad."

"So tell me about Drasil's friends."

"They live in these neat little houses made of logs. They're so cool, but hard to decorate with all that wood. They pack the cracks between the logs with moss. It keeps the wind and the bugs out. Marisha made tea from some moss too, but it was a different kind of moss. It was kind of funky. I like hot chocolate better. She made biscuits too, I want to try them; they were sooo good."

"I'm glad you made some new friends. Are there any children there?"

"Loads. Marisha and Davvad have three kids, and there's lots more. They're teaching me some of their games."

"What kind of games?"

"Some of them are like ours, you know, tag, hide and seek, but others are really different. There's one called guest or wolf. We keep asking are you guest or wolf. If they say guest that we say, 'Welcome and be at peace in our home and hearth.' If they say wolf, then you run away and they try to catch you."

They ate supper while Justine talked about her new friends. He wondered at all the stuff she talked about doing in the short time between school and going to Ms. Palenz, but decided that he didn't want to spoil the mood.

The next day he got a call from the school.

"Hello, Mr. Constance, it's Mr. Houston from school."

"How can I help you?"

"I wanted to check on Justine after what happened on Monday."

Patrick felt his stomach sink.

"You'd better tell me what happened."

"Mrs. Hall's class has been working on some art projects. Justine handed in a project where she showed how she redecorated a room. It was a very good looking project. Ms. Hall decided that Justine's project deserved to be put up on display in the hallways for other students to see. Unfortunately, on Monday someone tore her project down and ripped it to pieces. They taped up a note with a very crude message printed on it. I was shocked that any student in the school would use such language.

"Justine saw the note and ran out of the school. One of the teachers saw her sitting under a tree sobbing, but when she went to investigate, Justine told her to go away. Since she was safely on school property, we let her stay there as long as she needed to.

"I told her personally that we would try to find out who did it, but she said it didn't matter. I told her it mattered to me and we left it at that."

"Thanks for your call, Mr. Houston. I'll talk to Justine about it."

"She didn't tell you?"

"No. She made some new friends on Monday and that must have pushed it out of her mind."

"Well, if there is anything I can do, please call."

"Thanks, Mr. Houston. I will do that."

When Justine came home she was humming a tune. She spread out her homework and was soon lost in her math. Patrick noticed that her hair was different. She had a braid on one side of her face and it was tied with a scrap of green wool.

"I like the braid," he said.

"Oh, thanks Dad, Marisha helped me with it."

"How's Marisha?"

"Let me finish my homework and I'll tell you all about it."

Well, that's a first. Justine was usually responsible about doing her work, but she was also glad of an excuse to do something else. He busied himself getting dinner and found himself listening for the scratch of the pencil. When did his world suddenly revolve around Justine? Before Ingrid died, they had hired baby sitters and gone out to do adult things. Now he worked all day so that he could come home and talk with his daughter. He realized that he didn't have any friends either.

He decided that was OK as long as Justine was happy.

"OK, all done," Justine said and put her books away in the bag and hung it up. "Drasil says that I must keep up with my responsibilities if I'm going to keep visiting Marisha. Marisha is big on responsibility too. She says that each person has a reason to be, and it is our work to figure out what that reason is and live for it."

"I'm not sure I understand that," Patrick said.

"I don't either, but Drasil says it means that we're not just random."

"I'll have to think about that." Patrick slid plates of stir-fry onto the table and sat down. "So what else do you talk about other than not being random?"

"That was Drasil, but Marisha showed me how to make biscuits. They're really easy once you know the trick. I wanted to

42

show her how to make spaghetti, but they don't have noodles like we do. Can you make spaghetti from scratch?"

"I'm sure you can. We'll look on the web after supper."

"Also Stone showed me how to juggle. Do you want to see?"

"Sure."

Justine stood up and pulled three pieces of cloth from her pocket.

"They have little stones in them so they fall, but slowly." She tossed one in the air, then another and all at once was tossing them in a complex loop. She caught them one after the other and put them back in her pocket. "As I get better, I'm supposed to make the rocks bigger so they move faster."

"I like the way they float." Patrick poured himself another glass of milk.

"How are things at school?"

"Mr. Houston phoned you?" Justine said.

"Yes, I was worried because you didn't say anything about either the project or it being wrecked."

"The project was no big thing. It was like one of Mom's client boards. It had a few pictures and some paint chips and a bit of the cloth from the curtains. I wasn't going to keep it anyway." Justine looked down. "No, that's not true. Sorry, Dad. It was a big deal that it was up on the wall, not because of the project, but because it was me. That's why I lost it so bad when it was destroyed and they put that note up."

"Was the note really that bad?"

"It was all the words that you would kill me for if I said them."

"I don't know that I would kill you, but I know which words you mean."

"So I went outside and sat with Drasil for a while. I'm afraid I yelled at a teacher, but I just needed to be left alone."

"Alone with Drasil."

"Yes, he's my friend. That's when I figured out that I could visit his friends."

"Tell me more about Drasil."

"I'm not supposed to talk about him. It isn't that he'll get in trouble, but he's afraid that I will."

"Because Drasil is a tree."

"That's right." Justine looked Patrick in the eyes. "How did you know?"

"Mr. Houston told me you spend the afternoon under the tree in the schoolyard. You told me you spent the afternoon with Drasil. I just figured that Drasil was the tree."

"Do you think I'm crazy?"

"The girl who walked in and did her homework right away?" Patrick shook his head, "I'm not sure that's normal, but I don't think you're crazy. Crazy means you can't function in the world, but you're functioning better."

"So, do you think I'm crazy or not?"

"Not, but I will be keeping an eye on you in case I'm wrong."

Justine sighed. "That's more than Drasil expected."

"Do I get to meet Drasil?"

"Really?" Justine looked at him wide eyed. "You want to meet him?"

"If he's a friend of yours, for sure."

"Let's go!" Justine jumped up and pulled Patrick with her. They walked along to the school with Justine chattering the whole way.

"This will be so cool. He's a lot like you," she said.

"I'm like a tree?"

"No, I mean he talks like you," Justine said, "like I'm a real person and not some stupid kid who can't understand big words."

"Ah, I see, I think."

Justine pulled him across the school yard.

"Hi, Drasil. My Dad wanted to meet you."

"I know you said that was a risk, but I can't lie to my Dad."

"OK, only Dad." Justine turned and looked at Patrick. "Didn't you hear that?"

"Sorry, Justine, I only heard you."

"Put your hand on him and talk to him."

Patrick put his hand on the rough bark of the tree. Most of the leaves had turned colour, but he could imagine the vital force flowing through the massive trunk.

44

"Greetings, Drasil." he said, somehow not feeling awkward about talking to a tree. "My name is Patrick and I am Justine's father. If you are her friend you will take care of her. Keep her safe." He felt a swell of protectiveness overwhelm him. "She is all I have left. So you be careful. If she gets hurt, I'm coming out here with an axe."

"Wow, Dad, that's intense." Justine cocked her head a moment. "He says you still can't hear him, though he heard you. He promises root and branch that he will look after me. He said you can't hear him because either you're not ready or he's not. It's hard to tell from what he said. Actually, he says he can't tell, but he looks forward to the day when you and he can speak."

"It's time to go home, Justine." Patrick patted the tree. "It's good to know my daughter has a friend."

Justine waved goodbye and they walked home in silence.

Chapter Six

Justine looked at the mound of flour and egg and sighed.

"Who'd have thought spaghetti would be so hard to make?"

"They have pasta machines that are supposed to make it easier."

"I can hardly carry a machine to Marisha's," Justine said as she scraped the mess into the garbage. "Besides I think you still need to get the dough right. I'm trying everything they say on the internet, but it just isn't working."

"Well, there is only one thing left to do."

"I'm not giving up!"

"I was thinking of asking an expert," Patrick said. "There is a little Italian restaurant that's been advertising that they only serve fresh pasta. They might be willing to help."

"Really?" Justine wiped the counter off. "Let's go."

"Let me call and see if they have space." He pulled a sticky note out of his pocket and dialled the number. "Hi, I was wondering if you had a table for two for this evening? Sure, great, thanks." Patrick looked up at Justine and saw she already had her coat on. He laughed and followed her out the door.

The restaurant was busy with waiters almost running to keep up with the orders. Even calling ahead they had to wait for ten minutes until a table came clear. Once they sat down, they were given garlic bread right away with a promise their order would be taken soon.

"Hi," their server said a little while later, "I'm Phillip and I'm your server tonight. What can I get you?"

"I'd like spaghetti, please." Justine said and Phillip laughed.

"What kind of spaghetti?" he said, "If it is made with pasta, we have it. All kinds of sauces too."

"I just want spaghetti and tomato sauce. I'm trying to learn how to make my own spaghetti and I want to taste what good homemade spaghetti tastes like."

"Ah," Phillip said, "very good then. I know exactly what to bring you."

"I'll just have the special," Patrick said. Phillip grinned and took their menus.

A few minutes later a big man in a white coat and a chef's hat came out of the kitchen.

"Phillip tells me you want to learn to make spaghetti," he said to Justine. "He said you wanted to taste good spaghetti. Here, try this." He put a bowl of spaghetti noodles in front of Justine. They glistened a little with oil and there were flecks of what Patrick thought must be herbs.

Justine picked up her forks and twisted a few strands onto it. She put it in her mouth and chewed thoughtfully, then smiled.

"That's amazing!" She pushed the bowl over to Patrick, "Dad, you have to try this."

Patrick took a mouthful and had to agree with his daughter. There was no comparison with the dry spaghetti they usually ate.

"So, this is what you want to learn?" The chef scowled at her. "You will open your own restaurant and put Georgio out of business."

"I just want to cook for my friends."

"Hah," Georgio said, "we make the pasta early, before it gets busy. Right now is busy, too many knives chopping. Come tomorrow, eight am. I will teach you how to make spaghetti for your friends."

Justine finished the small bowl of spaghetti, then the much larger bowl that came with tomato sauce.

In the morning, he brought her to the restaurant where Georgio handed him a cup of wickedly strong coffee and whisked Justine to the kitchen. Patrick sipped his coffee and listened to the conversation. He brought her home with a small bag of fresh spaghetti in her hands and a determined look in her eyes.

"Georgio said I'm using the wrong kind of flour and we need to watch the humidity when I'm making it up. I have to bring him a sample from my first batch."

They went out and bought the right flour, then Justine went to work. Patrick could hear her muttering Georgio's advice to herself as she mixed the dough then rolled it out as thin as she could get it.

The next Friday evening she boiled water and added a

pinch of salt. The noodles were cooked and drained then served out on the plate. She sprinkled a little olive oil and pesto on them.

"Thanks for the food, and say hello to Mom, and please let this work."

"Amen."

"You don't need to say that with such enthusiasm."

"It looks good." He twirled some up on his fork and the strands held together. "Tastes good too," he said past the mouthful of spaghetti. "Dad, that's gross." Justine twirled her own, smaller, mouthful and chewed with a thoughtful expression. "It isn't as good as Chef Georgio's, but it will do."

"So what do you need to bring with you to make the noodles?" Patrick said thinking of sifter, roller, cutter and the rest of the tools.

"I think Marisha has everything I need. The problem was I needed to learn how to use the stuff."

"Right, that makes sense. So are you going tomorrow?"

"Can I?"

"Sure, as long as you're home for dark."

"Drasil always gets me home at the right time."

"See that he does."

"How are things at Marisha's?

"Well," Justine sat back in her chair. "You remember how I told you that everyone welcomes guests with "Welcome and be at peace in our home and hearth."

"Right, I like it but it seemed a little long to say every time."

"It's only the first time that someone comes as a guest. After that it's just 'Welcome.'"

"OK then."

"Well, they take it very seriously. You don't fight inside the house. If you must argue you go outside and argue. People don't argue very long if it's cold and rainy, so they've learned to work things out without arguing."

"Sounds interesting."

"When Marisha and Davvad are discussing something they start making suggestions to the house. Like 'Wouldn't the house be nice with red gingham curtains?' or 'The house would be so happy with an extra shed to store tools.' They can go on for days like that."

"Mmmhmmm."

"The kids do the same thing outside. We'll be talking about playing a game and instead of saying 'I want to play tag.' they'll say 'Doesn't it look like the field wants to play tag?' I found it tricky to catch on to at first. It's considered rude to just say what you want straight out unless you're asked."

"So if all this is about guests, why do families not argue?"

"I think they are supposed to be guests in each other's homes. Marisha's daughter is getting married soon and I'm sure that there is something about that in the wedding vows. Risha is really nice. She's helping me with figuring out how to fit in there. Everything is so different, I'm afraid sometimes that I'll say something that will make everyone hate me."

"If they are the kind of people you say they are, they will forgive you if you make an honest mistake."

"It's funny you said that. We were playing guest or wolf, and I was asked. I started to say guest and changed my mind to wolf. Everyone shrieked as loud as they could and chased me all over the place. When they caught me, they tickled me until I begged for mercy. Then it was like nothing happened and they went back to the game. I asked Stone and he said you had to be guest or wolf, you couldn't be both even for a second. He also told me that the tickling was his favourite part of the game."

"Speaking of Stone, how's the juggling coming along?"

"I can do spoons now!" Justine picked up spoons from the table and started tossing them in the air. Patrick clapped.

"That's great! I love watching you juggle."

"I think I'm going to bed now." Justine put the spoons down. "I'll leave after breakfast."

In the morning, Justine looked at her recipe and notes very carefully. Then hugged Patrick.

"Thanks for letting me go."

"You'll be home by dark?" Patrick said.

"Yes, Dad, home by dark."

"Say hello to Drasil for me."

Justine waved and left, he saw her running down the street a moment later and smiled. It was good to see her so happy. He sat with his coffee and wondered what he was going to do with his day. He picked up the phone and dialled.

"Hi Lee, it's Patrick," he said. "Justine ran off to friends for the day and I wondered if you were up for lunch? Sure, brunch would be good too. Come over whenever you're ready and I'll start throwing things around the kitchen."

He hung up and started pulling out pans and looking in the fridge. Where were Justine's breakfast recipes?

Lee arrived a few minutes later and he waved at the coffee pot.

"Help yourself. I'll be with you in a minute."

She poured a cup and sat at the table looking at him. "So tell me about Justine's friends. They can't be school kids or I would likely know about them."

"Just let me serve this up." He slid the omelettes onto plates and placed the grilled tomatoes beside them.

"Here you go." He handed her a plate and put his on the table. "I'm so used to Justine setting the table that I forgot." He set the table with cutlery and sat down across from her. "Dig in."

There was silence for a short time as they ate their food.

"Friends, Patrick, give."

"I was going to talk to you anyway, because Justine already trusts you." He heaved a big sigh and shook his head. "I'm not sure that the friends that she's visiting are real."

"What?" Lee raised her eyebrows. "You'd better explain that."

"Well, she took me to the school ground and introduced me to a tree she called Drasil. She acted like she could hear him talk, but I of course couldn't hear anything. The friends that she's off to visit today are friends of Drasil's."

"How has her behaviour been? Any inconsistencies or breaks in functioning?"

"Actually, she has been very responsible. The homework gets done, the dinners get cooked. She is being Justine, only more so."

"Hmmm, I'm no expert, but I recall reading that exceptional children will sometimes build elaborate worlds to inhabit to challenge them beyond what the normal world will."

"You're saying Justine is exceptional?"

"Don't you think she is?" Lee said.

"I'm her father, I'm supposed to."

"Let's look at it objectively then." Lee counted points off on her fingers. "She is able to pull together from looking at her mother's notes a sufficient understanding of the principles of colour and balance to be a professional designer. You've seen her work. She has learned the basics of cooking and how to read a recipe and is confident enough to try making pasta from scratch."

"She's headed off to cook a spaghetti dinner for her friends from scratch today."

"Well, there you go."

"She's learned how to juggle."

"Juggle? You mean as in tossing multiple balls about and keeping them in the air?"

"Yes, only she using spoons now."

"I would bet if you checked her homework, you would find that she hasn't made a single mistake. That's probably why most of her class hate her. She makes them look bad."

"She's ten, I mean eleven years old."

"Exactly. Most eleven year olds are playing computer games and trading knock, knock jokes."

"So what do I do?"

"What did you do when she introduced you to Drasil?"

"I told him to make sure he took care of Justine."

Lee looked at him for a long time.

"What, did I do something wrong?" Patrick asked finally." There are so few things that make her happy these days. I don't want to take this little bit of happiness in her life."

"I think you're fairly exceptional yourself. I can't think of too many parents who would have a conversation with a tree instead of telling their kid to come back to earth."

"Well, I did threaten to chop him down if Justine got hurt."

Lee laughed, "How did Justine take that?"

"She said that Drasil understood and swore to keep her safe."

"You two are an amazing pair. I'll bet that you weren't even thinking you had to play along to humour your poor crazy daughter."

"No, you're right. Justine and I already decided that she wasn't crazy."

"You had a conversation with your eleven-year daughter about her level of sanity?"

Patrick stared down into his cup.

"She brought it up."

Lee coughed on her coffee and turned red. She waved off Patrick's concern and regained control.

"I knew there was a reason I liked this family." She looked at her coffee cup. "I better leave this alone. This stuff is dangerous." She looked at him and Patrick thought there was a subtle shift in her eyes.

"You have all day, right? Let's go to the zoo."

"I haven't been to the zoo since Justine and I went with Wanda and the twerp."

"The twerp?"

"That's what Justine called Wanda's son when she wasn't trying to match us up."

"I'm glad to hear that she's normal in some respects."

"She was ten."

"Never mind. It's off to the zoo; lions and tigers and bears."

"Oh my."

The two of them giggled all the way to the car. Occasionally Patrick would hum a song from the Wizard of Oz while driving and they would start over.

***

It was a beautiful sunny day but cool enough for the animals to be moving around in their enclosures.

"Look," Lee said, "they've named the lion Maximus."

"He doesn't look much like a Maximus, more like a Minimus, or maybe a Medius."

"Give him time."

"They didn't give the rhinoceros a name."

"How about Arnold?"

Lee laughed, and Patrick felt something in him shift ever so slightly.

The zoo was a delight, or rather being at the zoo with Lee

was a delight, but the afternoon went far too quickly. They finished the day off at a gift shop with entire walls of stuffed animals.

"So, what are you going to buy for Justine?" Lee was petting the fur on a huge plush lion.

"I don't know," Patrick lifted a much smaller lion from the shelf. "Maybe I should get a couple of things." He picked up a tiger too. "Do they have any bears?" Lee laughed again and Patrick laughed with her as she tossed him a small plush bear.

They got home mid-afternoon, and Patrick put together some chilli and left it to simmer in the slow cooker. Just as the afternoon light began to dim, Justine waltzed in through the door.

"Drasil didn't know what you meant by dark so he sent me home before there was a significant loss of light." Justine saw Lee and stopped dead. She looked at Patrick and sighed.

"So does she think I'm crazy?"

"It isn't polite to talk about people in the third person."

"So, Ms. Palenz, am I crazy?"

"Far from it. I've convinced your father that you are a certified genius and need to be challenged."

"Oh," Justine hung up her coat. "So what's a certified genius supposed to be like?"

"Different."

"Well, that fits." She saw the three animals sitting on the table. "What, the zoo didn't have any flying monkeys?"

Lee and Patrick looked at each other and went off in howls of laughter. Justine just shook her head and went to check on the chilli.

"When you're ready," she said, "we can eat."

It was a little while longer before they sat down to eat. Lee and Patrick took turns telling Justine about the zoo and soon had her in fits of giggles. After Lee left, Justine insisted on doing the dishes.

"Dad, you told her about Drasil."

"I did," he said. "I didn't know if I was doing the right thing. Lee helped me figure it out."

"By saying I was a genius. Did she say that I was making it all up because I was bored?"

"That was one theory, yes."

"And what is your theory?" Justine turned away from him to scrub at the slow cooker.

Patrick went and knelt beside her and turned her so he could look in her eyes. They were wet with tears.

"I am so glad to see you happy, that's more important than understanding where you're going. I think I will just trust my daughter."

Justine flung her arms around him and squeezed him hard.

"The spaghetti was a huge hit." She paced back and forth in the kitchen as she talked. "I couldn't believe that I got the noodles right on the first try. I tried to teach them how to twirl the noodles, but they couldn't do it. Well, Stone figured it out, But the rest wouldn't cut up the spaghetti. What's the use of making long noodles if you cut them to pieces? they said.

So, Marisha got out these things like chopsticks and they ate them like Chinese noodles. What a mess! There was sauce everywhere. But they liked it and Marisha asked me to show her again how to make it. Then we played tag, and Stone and I juggled together, and he kissed me goodbye."

She put her hand up to her mouth.

"Oops, I wasn't going to tell you that part."

"Why not?

"I didn't think you would like if I had a boyfriend."

"I'm not sure what I think about it, but what you think about it is more important."

"I don't know. He's twelve or something. He's fun and he listens when I talk and answers my questions sensibly most of the time."

"He sounds like a good friend."

"They all are, but Stone especially. I think he understands me."

"That's always good."

"I think I will just stick with being friends."

"May I ask why?"

"Because I like the juggling more than the kiss, and if I'm his girlfriend he'll want me to kiss more than juggle."

"Makes sense."

54

"Thanks, Dad." Justine blew him a kiss and went upstairs.

Patrick sat down at the table and stared at the lion and tiger and bear.

"My daughter was kissed by a boy," he said to them, "oh my."

Chapter Seven

"So Thamos just disappeared," Justine said as she shovelled fresh tortellini into her mouth. "He had wanted to marry Risha, but she chose Hisen because he was gentler. The night before the wedding Hisen went to see Thamos, and Thamos actually hit him. Hisen was in shock because of course no one had ever hit him before so he just sat there while Thamos ran away. Risha was in tears, because, while she wanted to marry Hisen, Thamos was still her friend. She asked me what to do, and I told her that she needed to forgive him if he was sorry. Hisen said Thamos had whispered he was sorry before he ran away, so Risha and I looked everywhere trying to find him, but he was gone. It was like something had just snatched him away."

"He broke the rules, didn't he?" said Patrick as he served himself more of the pasta. Fridays were much different since Justine had started experimenting with all kinds of pasta. He wondered about putting cooking gadgets on his Christmas list for her. The season was getting close quickly.

"Well, Hisen would have welcomed him, so Thamos broke the Peace by hitting him, but why would he have run away?"

"In the game, when you changed your mind everyone chased you down."

"Yeah, but nobody wanted to chase Thamos. We looked for him because we were worried about him."

"So is the wedding still happening?"

"Yes, Risha said that she's been waiting too long for this to stop now. She really loves Hisen."

"So when is the wedding?"

"Next week I think. Drasil will make sure I make it to the wedding."

"How are you and Stone doing?"

"Well, he's decided he'll just wait for me to change my mind. He'd rather be my friend than not. So, he's back to teaching me juggling tricks."

"I'm relieved. I'm not ready for my daughter to have boyfriends."

"Well, duh, I'm only eleven, but Stone is my friend and I needed to honour him by thinking about it."

"Honour, huh?"

"The Pax are big on honour. Not like their own honour, but protecting the honour of others. Marisha said that they used to be this really violent people and they were always killing each other over stupid things, and when they weren't killing each other, they were fighting wars against their neighbours."

"What happened?"

"A guy named Darsh decided that he didn't feel like killing his neighbour because one took his cow. So, he didn't, then a different neighbour took his horse. People started coming and just helping themselves to everything that Darsh had. Soon he had nothing but his wife and children and the rock he happened to be sitting on.

"One of his neighbours came by and saw his wife and decided he liked Darsh's wife, so he went to take her away. Darsh's wife asked him if he was going to do anything to stop this neighbour, and Darsh asked her if shedding this man's blood would make her happy. She looked at her children and realized if Darsh killed the man, then his kids would kill Darsh and then her kids would kill them.

"I get the idea."

"So Darsh's wife went with the neighbour and served him as his maid, but she kept reminding him she only did so to preserve her children's lives. The man wasn't happy because she was making him look bad, but if he let her go he would look weak. So, he went to Darsh and asked him if, now that he had nothing but his children and the rock he sat on, if he would come and be the neighbour's servant too.

"Darsh replied that he would rather starve swiftly than slowly, but would the neighbour take in his children to preserve their lives? So, the neighbour ended up with a whole lot of extra children who he couldn't honourably get rid of and a servant who was making him look bad.

"He decided that he would give the whole bunch back to Darsh, only Darsh by this time was down to skin and bones, so the neighbour had to give back some of the other stuff he'd taken so Darsh could feed himself and his family. The other neighbours came to take the stuff away again, only Darsh would ask them to take care of his family. They knew what had happened with the first guy so they left him his family and even brought back more stuff.

"While all this was going on the King noticed everyone was a lot better off now that they weren't spending all their energy trying to kill each other. The neighbours who brought Darsh's stuff back were the richest of all.

"The King asked the priests to go figure out what was going on. So, they went and talked to Darsh and then his neighbours. They went back to the King and said the Goddess of the land was blessing Darsh and his neighbour because they stopped shedding the blood of her children. Then King asked all his people, rich and poor, strong and weak to come to the City and have a meeting. The meeting went on for three years, but in the end, they decided that they would rather be rich and peaceful than strong and warlike. That's when they created the guest code, and they've been living that way pretty much ever since."

"That's quite a story."

"Marisha says that it isn't told often enough. People are forgetting why they are who they are."

"I'm with Marisha. It's important for people to remember their stories."

"So what's your story?"

"Ouch, that's a good question, and I'm afraid that I don't have a good answer for you. I'll think about it though."

"I think I like Darsh. He's a bit like Jesus because he refuses to do bad things, but his story has a happier ending."

"I don't know, the minister might disagree with you on that. As I remember Easter is a pretty good happy ending," Patrick said.

"But he had to die first. That had to suck."

"True, but some things can only be accomplished if we do the stuff that sucks."

"I guess. I still like Darsh's story."

"Me too."

They washed up the dishes while Justine talked about what

she was going to wear at Risha's wedding. None of the clothes sounded familiar.

"Where do you have all these clothes?" Patrick asked.

"I borrow clothes from Tami and Cinda; they're Stone's friends; and Marisha has some put in a trunk for me when I visit. My own clothes look really strange with everyone else dressed different, so I like to change while I'm there."

"All right. I was wondering if we needed to get you a bigger closet."

"Nah, I have enough stuff."

"I'm glad to hear that. So, you won't mind if I give all your Christmas presents to the poor."

"That's a great idea!" Justine said.

"I was joking."

"No really, I don't need anything and there are all kinds of people who don't have anything. We should help them out."

"OK then, you make a shopping list of what you want to give away for Christmas and I'll do the same thing."

Justine had her list done on Saturday and they went shopping. Patrick invited Lee to come along on the spur of the moment. They had a great time buying clothes and toys and dropping them in the collection bins. Justine insisted this was just between them and no one else was to know.

Patrick hadn't done his list yet, but he'd been giving it careful thought. Then he saw a poster and he knew exactly what he wanted. While Lee and Justine were sipping hot chocolate he slipped away to make a phone call.

"What was that about?" Justine asked. "You never use your cell phone on weekends."

"I was checking to see if my Christmas present is available."

"Well?" Justine said.

"It is."

"So are you going to tell us what it is?"

"I'll tell you on the way."

They finished up their hot chocolate and Patrick led them out to the car.

"Buckle up," he said.

He drove through the City to a nondescript building

situated by a strip mall.

"Isn't this the Women's Shelter?" asked Lee.

"Yes, Ingrid did some work for them, so I was able to ask a favour."

"And ..." said Justine.

"For Christmas I would like you to design me a new living room. Theirs. They're advertising for paint and such to redecorate so I asked them if they wanted Ingrid's daughter to design their new living space. They were delighted. So here we are. Are you up for it?"

"Are you kidding? Let's go see."

They got out of the car and walked up to the door. Patrick buzzed and a woman's voice squawked at them from a speaker beside the door.

"May I help you?"

"My name is Patrick Constance. I talked to your director about my daughter helping to do the design for the living room decor."

"Please wait."

A couple of minutes later a woman came out through the door. She had blond hair tied back in a ponytail and wore a comfortable suit, but her face looked tired and sad.

"I'm Natalie Jones, the director of the Shelter. I didn't realize that Justine was so young."

"I'll vouch for her skills. I'm Lee Palenz and Justine did my home."

"It's not her skills that I'm worried about, but this isn't always a very pleasant place. We try, but it is hard on children."

"Then you need me more than ever," Justine said, "I can help design a room that will help everyone feel more at home and relaxed. They might be hurt and scared, but they still deserve a nice place to live."

"I wish more people felt like you do," Natalie said.

"I just need to see the room and I can do most of the work at home. It's my Dad's Christmas present."

Natalie looked at Patrick. "You asked for a decorating job in a Woman's Shelter for Christmas?"

"My wife believed very strongly in what you do here. She

did the original design for the shelter when it was built."

"You won't be able to come in today, but Justine and Lee can come in and look at the room."

"Thanks, I really appreciate it."

"Now Justine, I have to ask you to keep anything you see in the Shelter absolutely in confidence. You can't talk about anything you see here. If you recognize someone, you can't talk to them about being in the shelter outside of these walls. This is really important."

"I understand," Justine said, "this is their home."

"It's more than just their home. The families are here because they don't feel safe anywhere else. There are some dangerous people who would hurt these women if they could."

"Then we'd better work hard at keeping them safe and helping them to feel safe too."

"That's some girl you have here," Natalie said to Patrick. She put her hand on Justine's shoulder. "Let's go look at that room."

The three women went through the door and Patrick got in his car and went for coffee. When his phone buzzed, Natalie said that Justine and Lee were ready to be picked up. He went and collected them. Justine was silent all the way home.

"Are you all right?" Patrick asked as they pulled into the drive.

"Oh, yeah Dad, I'm just thinking about the design. Natalie gave me pictures of the room to work with and we took all kinds of measurements. She said I could talk to you about the design if I needed to."

Lee said goodnight and walked off into the dusk. Patrick followed Justine into the house. She went straight to the computer and loaded the pictures into the computer. She got out a sheet of paper and began carefully measuring and drawing lines. A room quickly took shape. She cut out rectangles to represent furniture.

"I'd show you pictures of the room, but there is someone there that you aren't allowed to see."

"Someone you know?"

"I'm not allowed to talk about it."

"You can talk about how you feel without talking about the person."

"Let's just say I'm really glad you're my Dad."

Chapter Eight

"The wedding was amazing, Dad." Justine was setting the table while Patrick served up the spaghetti.

"Risha was beautiful. She wore a green dress and flowers in her hair. Hisen never stopped grinning the whole time. The priest read a poem about love being a guest in our homes and they kissed. Then they said the welcome thing to each other, only they added a bit about being cast out into the darkness if they ever broke their vows. Then they kissed each other again."

"That's a lot of kissing."

"Well, they were getting married. After they finished with the kissing then we ate. They loved the cannelloni, you were right about them being easier to eat. Stone keeps bugging me to make spaghetti again so he can show off his twirling skills. We all sang songs and danced. If you stepped on your partner's toes, you had to give them a kiss."

"I'm guessing that Stone was a clumsy dancer."

"Oh Dad! I only let him step on my toes once."

"I'm glad that your friends are so happy."

"They are mostly."

"Mostly?"

"There are rumours that the country next door has a new Emperor and he wants to have a bigger country."

"And the people are afraid they will be asked to play Darsh?"

"I think so. They don't talk about it much when the children are around."

"We'll hope that it just stays rumours."

"I've got to work on the room for the shelter. Do you mind cleaning up tonight?"

"Not a problem if I get a peek at the design before you go to bed."

"Did Mom let you look at her designs?"

"Sometimes."

"I still miss her, but it doesn't hurt as much. Is that bad?"

"No, it means that you're healing. Mom wouldn't want you

to be miserable your whole life. She wanted you to have a full and happy life."

"That makes sense, I wouldn't want you to be miserable either. Mrs. Balanteen says stuff like that too.

She switched on the computer and was immediately lost in her work. She had the furniture arranged the way she wanted, but she kept changing the colours. She had been researching colour and mood for days. Patrick watched her for a while then picked up a book.

On Monday, Justine came straight in and went to the computer.

"Hi, Dad, I was talking to Mrs. Balanteen and realized that she was brilliant."

"Mrs. Balanteen?"

"No, Mom. She used a picture to pull all the colours together. I just need to find a picture that will create the mood I want."

"Maybe a visit to an art gallery is in order."

"After school tomorrow?"

"Sure, I'll get off a bit early and pick you up," Patrick said.

"You won't get in trouble, will you?"

"Don't worry, I'll get permission."

The next day after school Patrick took Justine to a gallery downtown.

"Not only did Mr. Ball say I could leave early, he recommended this gallery."

"Cool."

The paintings in the gallery ranged from landscapes to abstracts. Justine stood in front of one painting after another with her head tilted to the side. The woman behind the desk came over to Patrick.

"May I help you?" she said.

"My daughter is looking for a colour scheme for a room she is designing." The woman peered at Justine who had come back to stand beside a portrait of a woman that was almost abstract. She wandered over to Justine.

"What mood are you looking for?"

"I want a room that will help people to feel safe and

comfortable, like they are at home."

"I see, so how is the painting going to help?"

"My mother used pictures to choose her palette sometimes," Justine said. "I thought looking at pictures would help."

"You see anything you like?"

"Oh, I love the paintings, especially this one, but she looks too angry."

"The artist called her 'Justice'."

"I didn't know that justice was angry."

"If there is injustice around."

"I guess so."

"I have a painting upstairs that you might want to look at."

"Really? Let's go."

Patrick followed them up to a tiny office. There was a painting on the wall that depicted a desert oasis. It was a splash of green and blue in the midst of a vast expanse of sand.

"This is my haven. The picture was painted by a school teacher who lived in the desert teaching the people and their children."

Justine peered at it and looked at it from different angles.

"The greens are too strong to be the main colour, but they could be picked up as accents. That sandy colour is warm and almost sleepy. The furniture would be the darker brown. This would work really well." She reached into her backpack and pulled out a stack of colour cards. "Would you help me find the right colours?" She was soon deep in conversation about shades and tones. Patrick wandered back downstairs and looked at the paintings. He looked at the painting of Justice that his daughter had thought too angry. He thought she looked sad.

They came downstairs with Justine waving her colour cards.

"I've got it and it is going to be just perfect! Thanks so much, Ms. Rowland."

"You are very welcome, Justine. Come in any time." She came over to Patrick as Justine took a last long look at Justice. "You have an extraordinary daughter," she said. "I have a friend who teaches art who would pay to have her in her class."

"Thank you," Patrick said, "I'll remember that."

Justine waved and they drove home. She was almost bouncing on the seat she was so eager to add her colour scheme to her design. She spent some time finding fabrics and printing out samples.

"Can we go tomorrow so I can show Natalie?"

"Sure thing."

He called the Shelter and arranged for Justine to visit. She brought her proposal in while Patrick went for coffee. When Natalie phoned, he went and collected Justine. Justine was looking stubborn while Natalie talked and patted her shoulder.

"It's too much money." Justine said as Patrick opened the car door.

"How much?"

"Hundreds," she said, "thousands, I don't know exactly. I'll have to go through and figure it out, but I'm going to do this room and I'm going to do it right!" She glared at Natalie. "I'll raise the extra money myself if I have to."

"OK," Natalie said, "I'll talk to the Board and let them know. I can give you another week before we should start on the room. They want it done by Christmas."

"You got it." Justine put the design board in the car. "Let's go, Dad, I have work to do."

The next day she came home from school and announced the class was holding another bake sale.

"I told them that it didn't matter who made the cookies as long as people would eat them."

"So we're up for another weekend of mad baking?"

"Yup, but I have something to ask you."

"What is it?" Patrick said.

"I really want to change up one of the couches. It's all torn and ugly, but the couch I want to put there is way too expensive for a school bake sale. Do you think you could ask at work and raise money for a couch?"

"How much do you need?"

"A thousand dollars," Justine said, "but it's a beautiful couch and it will last a really long time. It's just so perfect for the room I want to do for them."

"I'll try," he said.

***

Patrick went into work the morning following the trip to the museum and looked at his co-workers. He didn't know them well. Researching precedents and old titles didn't lead to much interaction. Most of his time was spent on the computer or looking through dusty archives. How would they react if he started asking for money? The only way he would find out was to begin. He decided that he had better talk to the boss first and get permission.

"Excuse me, Sir," he said tapping on the door. "Can I bother you for a moment?"

"Sure Patrick, what's up?"

"My daughter's class is raising money for the Women's Shelter. They're redecorating the main living room."

"Mmm hmmm."

"She asked me to raise money for a new couch for the room. She promised me that it was an extraordinary couch."

"How much was she asking?"

"The couch is worth a thousand dollars."

"Doesn't think small, does she?"

"No sir, she never has."

"I like that. Bring her in some time so I can meet her." He pulled out his wallet and took two fifties from it. "Here's your first donation. I'll mention it at the management meeting this morning. You can ask people in this department, but no harassing folks. If they say no, that's it. No arguing."

"Thank you, sir." Patrick went back to his desk and put the money in an envelope and marked it "Couch Fund for Shelter."

He started with Wanda, and got a donation for twenty. Jim with his vacation pictures still covering his walls emptied his wallet and pockets into Patrick's envelope.

"Don't ask," he said. "It's too long a story and I don't like crying at work."

Patrick wandered down to the reception area and got ten dollars from the receptionist and fifty from the security guards.

The rest of the morning was hit and miss. Some people put in five or ten, some put in nothing. One woman wrote him a check for a hundred dollars.

Mr. Ball called him in just before five.

"How'd it go?"

"We have four hundred and thirty-seven dollars and thirty cents."

"Who put in thirty cents?" He waved his hand, and said, "Never mind, I don't want to know. The management team kicked in another five hundred. They didn't want to be out done by me. Mr. Carson was there to get a report from me and he said he'd top it up to the even thousand."

"That's wonderful, Justine will be so pleased."

"Hold your horses, I'm not done yet. It seems that one of the partners has a sister who used the shelter in the past. She put in another thousand, and the other partners put in five hundred each. So, by my count, your little girl has got her couch and another two thousand to buy some extraordinary chairs to go with that couch."

"She is going to be beside herself."

"Just ask her to save some cookies for me."

Patrick sat at home waiting impatiently for Justine to get home. The phone rang and he picked it up.

"Mr. Constance, Mr. Houston here, I just missed you at your office. There has been an incident at the school and Justine has been taken to the hospital." Patrick dropped the phone and ran to the car.

At the hospital, the emergency nurse directed him to a room in the back. Ms. Hall was sitting in the room while Justine lay curled up on the bed.

"Someone came onto school property and tried to abduct another student. Justine intervened and was struck several times. The other students said she just stood between the man and his intended victim. I'm told she said she wasn't going to let him hurt anybody. While she distracted him, the other student was able to escape."

"How is she?" Patrick could feel a void opening beneath him. He was failing Ingrid. Their little girl was hurt.

"I'm OK, Dad, but my face hurts." Justine's voice was blurred, like she couldn't talk properly.

She rolled over to look at him. Justine's face was bruised and swollen and she had a cut over her eye.

"We'd like to keep her here overnight, just in case." A doctor had come in behind them. "Besides it isn't often that we get a genuine hero in this place."

"I'm no hero," Justine said. "I just couldn't stand there and let him take Kelly."

"I think you're a hero," Ms. Hall said. "I couldn't do what you did. My stomach aches just thinking about it."

"You'd do it if you had to, Ms. Hall."

"I hope so." Ms. Hall turned to Patrick. "You have an amazing daughter. If you don't mind I'm going to go home and hug my kids and have a good cry."

"We'll move you into a nicer room in a bit," the doctor said. "Rest, but try not to go to sleep just yet."

"OK."

"So, can you tell me what happened?" Patrick asked.

"Ms. Hall told you most of it."

"What made you think that you could stand up to this man?"

"I couldn't just stand and watch him drag Kelly off. She'd turned all white and was crying. I thought about her and her mom in that place and it just sort of happened."

"The man was Kelly's father?"

"I guess so. He wasn't anything like you."

"So you stood in his way and told him he couldn't take Kelly."

"Yeah, and he hit me, and I got up and told him he was still wrong, and he hit me again. Things got a little weird then. I heard Drasil telling me something, but I couldn't understand it. Then I thought I heard Mom's voice. She told me she loved me, then I woke up here with Ms. Hall. I miss Mom, Daddy, I wish she was here."

"From what you said, I think she is."

"Daddy, do you mind if I call the Pastor?"

"I'll go look up the number."

"It's in my bag over there."

Patrick picked up the bag and looked in the little pocket.

The card was there, complete with a smudge of dirt.

"I'll call him and see if he can come."

"Thanks, Dad."

Patrick found a pay-phone and put some change in. He dialled the number, feeling the anger he always did when he thought about the church or God. *Justine wants this.* He forced the anger away.

"Pastor Daniel," a voice said.

"This is Patrick Constance." He tried to say more but the words stuck in his throat.

"What can I do for you?"

"It isn't me, it's Justine, she wants to talk to you."

"Can she come by my office?" Patrick heard the flipping of pages. "I have some time tomorrow afternoon."

"Sorry, I didn't make myself clear." Patrick felt the anger in his voice again and tried to fight it down. "She's in the hospital. She got hurt and wants to talk to you."

"I'll be right there." Patrick heard Pastor Daniel excusing himself to some other people. "Are you still in emergency or have they moved her upstairs?"

"We're still downstairs, but they're talking about moving her upstairs."

"I'll look downstairs first then."

Patrick walked back to the room and carefully put the card back in its pocket.

"You're mad at me."

"Not at you, never at you," Patrick said, "I am angry that grown men hit little girls."

"I'm not that little."

"You're smaller than him."

Pastor Daniel arrived much faster than Patrick expected. He walked into the room.

"Hello Justine. That looks scary."

"I thought he was going to kill me."

"Maybe you'd better tell me all about it." He pulled a chair over and sat down beside her.

Justine told her story all over again, interrupted a couple times by doctors looking into her eyes or checking her blood pressure.

"Ah, that is scary."

"Why are there people like that?" Justine asked, "Why does God let people hurt each other?"

"Good questions, and I don't have any easy answers." He picked up her hand from the bed and looked at it like it was the most marvellous thing in the world. "Why does God make people like you who help others despite the risk?"

"It's just who I am."

"Partly, but it is also who you chose to be. You have chosen to help so often that when you see someone who needs you, you don't think about it."

"You're right, I didn't really think about it. I just needed to stop him."

"I believe that is how God wants us to be, but some people get stuck in other places so they hurt people."

"So we just unstick the people and everything will be perfect?" Patrick found himself asking.

"No, sadly there are far too many people who are content to be stuck. Remember it comes down to what you choose."

"What about cancer? What choice did Ingrid make that she needed to die of cancer?"

"Dad!"

"No, Justine, it's OK," Pastor Daniel said, "It's a question I ask a lot. I've never found an answer that works."

Patrick found himself weeping with rage. There was so much he needed to say to God. He tried to force it out with words, but they wouldn't come. Patrick thought of how close he had come to losing Justine to the same abyss that had stolen Ingrid. His hands wouldn't stop shaking. Pastor Daniel slid a chair over to him. Patrick sat down and let the tears burn down his face.

He felt Justine's small hand grip his and Pastor Daniel's hand on his shoulder. He didn't know how long he cried, but somehow when he was ready, Pastor Daniel handed him a tissue.

"Sometimes there just are no words, and our souls cry out with tears and anger. God hears, and weeps for your sorrows." Pastor Daniel looked at Justine. "Your Dad is a special person.

He called me for you even when he knew the pain he would feel."

"Do you mind if I say a prayer with Justine?

Patrick just shook his head.

"God, I give thanks for giving your daughter Justine courage and strength. Heal her quickly."

"And my Dad, too."

"Yes, and her Dad, too. Help him to find peace."

"And say hello to Mom for me."

"Amen.

Pastor Daniel smiled at them both and left. Patrick looked at Justine with her eye turning black, and felt something surprising. He didn't know what to call it but it wasn't the anger he had just minutes ago.

The doctor came in and arranged for Justine to be transferred upstairs for the night.

"If you have someone who can bring you pyjamas and other necessities, direct them to paediatrics on the third floor."

"I'll call Lee."

"Ask her to bring my teddy bear."

"All right." The nurses let him use the phone at the desk and he dialled Lee.

She answered on the first ring.

"Yes."

"Lee, it's Patrick..."

"What happened?" she said, "I was walking Michael and the door was open. Your phone was lying on the floor with the battery half way across the room."

"Justine's OK, but she's at the hospital."

"I heard on the news that there was an attack at the school. Was that her?"

"She has some bruises, and the doctors are worried about concussion so they're keeping her here."

"What can I do?"

"I'd like you to pick up some stuff for us at the house. Justine would like her teddy bear from her room and bring whatever pj's are under her pillow. We'll need toothbrushes and stuff from the bathroom too."

"I closed the door and locked it."

"If you look under the green rock beside the door there's a key. That will open the shed, and there's a house key hanging just inside the door of the shed."

"I'll be there as soon as I can."

"Come to the third-floor paediatrics; they're moving us up now."

"See you soon."

Patrick went back to the room, but the nurse sent him upstairs to meet Justine. They just sat in silence with Justine holding his hand until Lee came rushing in the door with a bright pink bag. She hugged Justine like she was made of glass, then hugged Patrick too.

"I heard on the news and thought you'd be so upset when you got back from your friends. I never imagined that it was you that got hurt. What happened? The news was all confused. A girl had been assaulted, the man had been shot dead by police, another girl is still missing."

"Kelly's missing?" Justine tried to sit up in bed. "She must be so scared, and she won't know about her Dad either." She looked at Patrick. "We have to do something."

"You are staying right here until the doctors say you can go home," Patrick said.

"You could go," Justine said.

"Go where?"

"Go see Drasil, whenever we play hide and seek that's a favourite spot. He's easy to climb. If she ran away at school she might be there, too scared to come out."

Patrick looked at Lee.

"Go," she said, "it will help Justine rest. I'll stay with her."

Patrick went to the school yard. He passed the corner a block away where a half dozen police cruisers parked with their lights flashing. Yellow tape blocked off a large part of one side. The school yard itself was dark. His eyes slowly adjusted to the light and he could see Drasil as a darker blob.

He got to the tree and walked all the way around it. No girl. Justine had said it was easy to climb, but he wasn't going to try it in the dark. He put his hand on the rough bark.

"Justine is going to be OK, but she's awfully scared."

73

"You're Justine's, dad?" a young voice floated down from above him.

"You'd be Kelly," Patrick said. "Justine's worried about you."

"Why would she care? I was mean to her. I bet she hates me."

"She stood up for you."

"I've never seen anyone get up after my dad hit them." Kelly's voice shook. "Everyone was so afraid of him. I never want to see him again. Isn't that bad?"

"I don't think it's bad." Patrick said slowly, "I think it's sad that your dad hurt you and your mom."

"Mostly my mom," Kelly said. "Sometimes when I was younger he would carry me on his shoulders and I would be taller than anyone. I want to go home, but I'm too scared to move."

"Help isn't far away." Patrick pulled out his phone and called the police. A car was there within minutes and a young police officer climbed into the tree while Patrick held the flood light for him.

Kelly was white as a ghost, but she clung to the officer until he gently peeled her off.

"We need to get you to the hospital, and let your mom know you're OK." The police officer looked at Patrick. "You going back to the hospital?"

"Yes."

"I'll stop in and get some information from you there."

"We're on the paediatrics floor."

The officer bundled Kelly into the car and drove off leaving Patrick again blind in the dark. He put his hand on the tree.

"Justine would want me to thank you for looking after Kelly."

Back at the hospital, Patrick filled Justine and Lee in on Kelly's rescue. Soon after he finished the young officer knocked on the door.

"May I come in?" he asked. Justine waved him in and hugged her teddy bear tighter. "I need to get your story of what happened so we've got it straight."

Justine went through her story again in a small, thin voice.

"I realize that you're tired, so I won't keep you long, but I wanted to let you know that your friend is OK. She's just tired and scared. Her mom's here with her now, and they'll be going home in a little while." Justine nodded.

"Sir, can I talk to you for a minute outside?"

Patrick stepped out in the hall with the police officer.

"I just need to know how you came to be under that tree."

"Justine sent me. She said a lot of the kids liked climbing that tree. She thought her friend might have hidden there."

"That's some smart girl you've got there, brave too from what I heard."

"She is both of those things and more."

"I'll let you get back to your family." He started to leave. "Oh, the other girl wanted to come up for a minute."

"It will have to be quick."

"Right then. Thank you, sir. You and your daughter may have saved that girl's life. It's supposed to get really cold tonight."

He walked off down the hall. Patrick went back in the room to find Justine almost in tears.

"My head hurts."

"I'll go talk to the nurses," Lee said. Patrick sat down beside his daughter and held her hand. The doctor came in with Lee.

"I'm really sorry Justine, but we can't give you anything for the headache. Not until we're sure that there's no concussion." Justine nodded, but Patrick could see the tears leaking out her eyes.

"Mom might be able to help." Kelly stood in the door with a tall woman behind her.

"I'm Kelly's mom," the woman said. "I'm a reflexologist. I may be able to reduce the pain."

The doctor smiled, "It's certainly worth a try, but it's up to Justine."

"Please." Justine said.

Kelly's mom took her hand and began massaging it between the thumb and fingers. Justine sighed and relaxed.

"The headache's getting better."

"I'm sorry I almost got you killed." Kelly said.

"I'm glad I helped. I would be really sad if you were hurt."

"Even if I was mean to you?"

"Forget that," Justine said.

"You mean it?"

"Sure."

"I'm going to make sure that we have the best bake sale ever." Kelly said.

"I made all kinds of cookies," Justine said.

"I'll bet. Did you do the ones with the cherries in the middle?"

"Yup."

"I wish I cook bake like that."

"Why don't you come over some time and I'll show you how."

"For real?" Kelly looked at her mom, "Please, can I?"

She looked at Patrick and he nodded.

"Why not? It would be good for you." Kelly's mom said.

"So what are all these cookies for?" asked the doctor.

"We're raising money to paint the Shelter," Kelly said. "It was Justine's idea."

"Bring some by here and I'll buy a dozen, those cherry ones sound good. For now, it's time to let Justine rest."

"If your head starts hurting again, just call," Kelly's mom said.

"Thanks," Patrick said.

Justine, Lee and Patrick were left in the dim room. Lee sat on the chair and closed her eyes.

"Thanks for watching over Justine and Kelly," Patrick whispered, "And say hello to Ingrid for me."

"Amen" came a whisper from the bed.

Chapter Nine

Patrick heard the car door slam and a few minutes later Justine walked in. She looked like a child who'd been in a prize fight.

"How'd it go?"

"The doctor said everything was healing up the way it should. He liked the cookies, though he only got to eat one. He said the nursing staff was voracious." Justine laughed, then winced slightly. "The bruises have gone down a lot but he said I could keep taking the pills for the pain since I was fine neurologically."

"I love listening to those big words sliding off your tongue," Patrick said. "It's surreal."

"Ms. Hall has started a word of the day club. She puts the word up on the board and we write down what we think it means. Anyone who gets it right gets a star. The person with the most stars will win a prize."

"So what are you winning?"

"I'm working at coming in second." Justine said, "You should have seen the class the week after I didn't win the first one. They were all sounding it out and scratching their heads."

"You'd make a good teacher someday."

"Really? Ms. Hall said that too."

"Supper's ready. Didn't Lee want to come in?"

"She said it was spaghetti night and she didn't want to intrude on our sacred ritual."

"I think spending the night in your hospital room gave her a ticket."

"She's trying to decide something."

"OK." He slid the plates on to the table.

"Thanks for the food," they said together.

"And say hello to Mom, Amen," Justine added.

"How was your talk with Mrs. Balanteen?"

"She is concerned I might get post-traumatic stress disorder. That just means that I might get all jiggly and have nightmares and stuff."

"So do you feel jiggly?"

"Not really, but it's something to watch for she said, not to worry about. I don't want to have nightmares again."

"You remember those?" Patrick asked.

"I remember I would wake up and scream until you came into the room and rocked me back to sleep."

"On a happier note, are you ready for tomorrow?"

"I'm not sure. I don't know what all the fuss is about. Well, I do, but I don't think it should be about me."

"What do you think it should be about?"

"Well, they should be doing something about the people like Kelly and her mom who have to run away and hide. They should be doing something about people like her dad who don't think about what they are doing to other people. I keep telling Kelly that it isn't her fault that her dad got shot, but she hates herself right now."

"Maybe she needs someone to talk to."

"Like Mrs. Balanteen?" Justine said, "She's great, and Kelly needs her a lot more than I do, really."

"Let me give her a call."

Justine jumped up and fetched the phone. She handed him the card off the fridge.

"OK, but I can't promise that she will be able to do anything."

He dialled the emergency number and got an answering service.

"Yes, it is an emergency, at least my daughter thinks it is and I trust her judgement. Thank you."

"They said they would give her the message and she will call back."

"How did your boss like his cookies?"

"He loved them. He was very touched that you sent enough for all the staff too."

"They all helped."

"They did," he agreed. "They have that picture of you from the paper up in the lunch room."

"Oh no, that's a horrible picture." Justine said, "I look so young."

"It's last year's school picture."

78

"I'll send them a nice one when we get our pictures taken this year."

"That's not too soon, is it?" Patrick said, visions of sending evidence of Justine's bruises to all their family running through his mind.

"A couple of weeks. The bruises should have gone down by then."

"Well, that's good then."

He started on the dishes while Justine did her homework.

"I miss hearing about Marisha and her family." Patrick said, "You aren't visiting them anymore?"

"Drasil won't let me. He says I need to heal first and get stronger."

"Well, I think he's right. You don't want to be at Marisha's and have one of your headaches come on."

"No, I keep trying to do that thing that Kelly's mom did in the hospital and I just can't get it to work."

"It must be like juggling, some people can do it and others can't."

"You just don't practice enough, Dad," she said. "You'll get it yet."

The phone rang and Justine answered it. She took the phone into the living room and talked for what seemed like a very long time.

"She said she would try calling the shelter and offering to talk to Kelly," Justine said, "but it's up to Kelly's mom and Kelly herself."

"If it's a financial thing," Patrick said, "I guess I could help out a little."

"I told her Kelly could have my time if she needed it."

"That's my girl."

Saturday morning, Justine spent extra time getting dressed.

"I'm just not sure what to wear, there's nothing I really want to meet the mayor in."

"There was one sure-fire thing that your mom used to do when she had that problem."

"What was that?"

"Go shopping," Patrick said.

"Great, let's go."

"I haven't finished my coffee yet."

"You can buy one at the mall."

Patrick was putting on his coat when there was a knock at the door.

He opened it to find Kelly on the other side.

"Hello, Mr. Constance," she said, "I talked to Mrs. Balanteen last night. It helped."

"It was Justine's idea."

"I know, that's what Mrs. Balanteen said."

"We're going shopping for some new clothes. Do you want to come along?"

"Let me ask my mom." Kelly ran back to the car that was parked in the drive then back to Patrick.

"Mom says, yes as long as I'm back in time to go to City Hall with her."

"We'll be heading there ourselves. She could always meet us there."

Kelly ran back to the car and had a longer conversation.

"She said OK."

Justine came out of the kitchen.

"Hi, Kelly."

Kelly flew at her and hugged her. Patrick could hear whispering and Justine patted the other girl's back a few times.

"Kelly's coming with us," she said. "I'd like her advice on clothes."

"That's good, because I already invited her."

"That's my Dad," Justine said. She took Kelly's hand, "We'll sit in the back seat."

Patrick could hear them conspiring in the back. Kelly already looked better.

At the mall, the girls abandoned Patrick at the coffee shop.

"We'll come and get you when it's time to pay," said Justine, laughing.

Patrick sat and sipped his coffee, and watched the people go by. There were some who looked like they needed pack mules to carry the piles of bags and boxes while others were empty handed. Christmas music played and the Salvation Army kettle was off near the door. He could just hear the bell from where he sat.

"People watching, huh?" Patrick's boss sat down in the seat across from him. "You don't mind?"

"No, no, not at all sir."

"We're not at work, just call me Bob."

"OK, Bob. Thanks."

"How's the little girl?"

"She's out spending my money."

Bob laughed. "Mine too, though she's twenty-four and has plenty of money of her own. Wanted to tell you I think you're doing incredibly well raising that kid of yours on your own. You ever need anything, my door is open." Justine and Kelly found them then.

"Come on, Dad," Justine said, "time to go to work, we have some outfits to show you."

Bob laughed, "Be sure you don't wear him out too much. He's one of my best researchers"

"What does he research?"

"I send him into the dungeons to look at old papers and find out whatever I need to know about buildings, laws, even people sometimes."

"You told me you just wrote reports."

"He does that, and very good ones. You'd better go, Patrick, before I tell all your secrets."

The girls dragged him to half a dozen different stores showing him a shirt here and pants there, but at the end of the afternoon both girls had satisfied looks and Patrick was lugging a fair collection of bags. They piled back into the car and drove home. Since they had a while yet before heading over to City Hall, Justine took Kelly up to her room, while Patrick put the kettle on for hot chocolate.

"Hot chocolate's ready," he yelled up the stairs and heard some incoherent response. He went back into the kitchen and dropped another marshmallow in his cup and blew across it.

Justine walked in and spun on her toes.

"What do you think?"

"Turn a little slower," Patrick said.

She pirouetted in slow motion.

"It looks very good on you."

"Kelly is a genius when it comes to clothes."

"Thanks, Justine," Kelly said coming in behind her. She handed Justine a shirt. "So you don't get hot chocolate on your clothes."

"Good idea." Justine put the shirt on and buttoned it up.

"I still think we should do your hair to cover those bruises." Kelly said, "You'd look so much better for the Mayor."

"I want the bruises to show," Justine said.

Kelly shrugged and picked up her cup. "We don't get this at the Shelter."

They finished up their drinks and put on coats and hats. Kelly laughed because Justine almost left the shirt on over her new clothes.

There was a large crowd at the City Hall, but Kelly's mom found them and reclaimed Kelly. Patrick and Justine were shown into the Mayor's office.

"Well, young lady," the Mayor said, "it's good to meet you. I've been hearing so many good things about you. One of our councillors is on the Board of the Woman's Shelter and she told me that you're raising money and redecorating the living room.

"Yes, sir," Justine said. "Dad's work gave us a whole lot of money to buy furniture and we had a bake sale to help pay for the paint and curtains. Other people have been donating too."

"But you're doing the design and choosing the colours."

"Yes, I am." Justine said.

"So, what do you think of my office?"

Justine turned around in a slow circle.

"I think it suits you. People will come in here and know they're meeting a real person, not some phoney."

"I like it too, but if I ever decide to change it, I'll give you a call."

"Thank you, sir."

"Now, what's going to happen is that we'll go out and I'll explain what's going on. There's a couple of other people who will say things and that will be it."

"Will I be able to say something?"

"Sure, if you want to. Do you have something written out, or are you just going to talk. I like to have stuff written out ahead. It keeps me on time."

"I've written something out." Justine pulled a sheet out of her pocket and handed it to the Mayor. "Will this be OK?"

He put some reading glasses on and read through the page.

"Do you mind some advice from an old hand?" he asked.

"Sure."

"You have a great little speech here, and I like what you're saying, but you're jumping right in. You need to add something at the beginning so people get a sense of who you are."

They put their heads together and worked over the speech for a few minutes.

"Five minutes, Mr. Mayor."

"Thanks, Denise, we'll be right out." He handed the paper to Justine. "You sure you're comfortable with this now?"

"Thanks for your help, Mr. Mayor."

"Let's go. We'll let your dad go first, then you come with me." Patrick led them out of the room and Denise showed him where to stand. The Mayor stopped to whisper to Denise for a second then walked outside with Justine beside him. The air was cold, but there was very little wind. Flashes went off as the photographers began their work and Patrick could see the TV vans in the back. He was standing over at the far end of the line of dignitaries.

"Good afternoon, friends," the Mayor said. "I'm glad you came to help thank a true hero of our City. I've rarely had so many different groups wanting us to recognize one individual. What makes it even more special is that she is only eleven years old.

"Last week as you heard on the news, there was an unfortunate incident at one of our schools. A very unhappy man tried to abduct his young daughter. I shudder to think of what would have happened had he succeeded. Justine Constance quite literally put herself in harm's way to protect her friend. Her classmates say that she stood between the man and his daughter and asked him not to hurt her. Even when she was struck to the ground she stood up and again put herself between her friend and this man a second time. The other girl fled the scene and found safety, but Justine spent the night in hospital being treated for her injuries.

"Had the story stopped there that would have been heroics enough, but she heard in the hospital her friend was missing. Though her head must have been pounding and she must have wanted her father with her - if I was in her situation I would have wanted my Daddy." The crowd laughed.

"She thought about where her friend may have hidden in her panic and sent her dad to go look. He found the girl cold and scared, hiding in a tree where her father wouldn't be able to find her. It is quite possible that, owing to the bitter cold, Justine saved her friend's life, not once but twice that night.

"I have a letter from Justine's friend, her mother has asked that she not be identified." The Mayor looked over at the reporters and they gave him a thumbs-up. "I knew I could count on you. Anyway, this young girl writes.

"My dad came and tried to take me away. He was screaming and I was screaming too. Justine told him to stop, and he hit her, then hit her again. I ran away and hid until her dad found me. I used to be mean to Justine, but she saved me anyway, and now we are best friends. She is my hero."

The crowd cheered and clapped for a while. Patrick saw Kelly turning red and her mom kiss her head.

The Chief of Police spoke next and presented her with a medal and then the School Board superintendent spoke and presented her with a plaque. Denise came out and put a chair behind the podium and the Mayor helped Justine up on the chair.

"Hi," she said, "my name is Justine. I'm just a kid like any other, I like to paint and bake cookies."

"Yeah, cookies!" yelled someone in the crowd. Justine waved at him.

"What I did shouldn't be special." She pulled the hair back from her face. "I have bruises, but they'll fade. There are people who are bruised all the time on the inside. They live their lives afraid of being hurt or killed. Nobody should have to live like that. I stepped in to help my friend because I don't want her to be hurt, or anybody else." She paused and looked out at the crowd.

"If every one of us is ready to stop violence when we see it happening, then there will be no violence. We might get hurt, but bruises fade. Failing to help my friend; I would have had to live with that forever."

"I also wanted to thank the police and my dad and the hospital for being there with me and my friend when we needed you." She jumped down from the chair and the crowd cheered and clapped while she waved.

"Now folks," the Mayor said after a while. "There is one other thing I wanted to mention that I know is near and dear to my friend Justine's heart. She's been working on a little project. When she said, she liked to paint, she meant she likes to paint rooms. She's been working on making the living room at the Woman's Shelter feel a lot more homey and safe. She and her classmates have raised most of the money themselves. In recognition of her work, I am honoured to present her with the Junior Citizen of the Year Award and a check from City Council for ten thousand dollars so she can continue her good work at the Woman's Shelter.

Justine screamed and threw her arms around the Mayor. That was the picture that made it into the paper the next day.

"You look so good, even with that bruise," Lee said that night after they had watched the news, "and you've made a good friend in the Mayor."

"I like him," Justine said.

"He's a good Mayor."

"It's too bad Kelly's mom didn't want Kelly's picture in the paper."

"Well," said Patrick, "when you've lived in fear for that long, it becomes a habit."

"It's still sad." Justine said.

Chapter Ten

"Should I wear the red or the green?" Justine asked from the door.

"I like the green myself, but either one will look good."

"Great help you are, maybe I should call Kelly."

"Good idea, the noodles are just about ready. You'll have a few minutes to change after supper, then we'll have to be off."

"I'm so nervous," she said. "What if they don't like it?"

"Your mom was usually nervous before a big reveal too." Patrick said, "I'll tell you the same thing I told her. Take a deep breath, have fun, and tonight, just listen to the positive comments."

"Thanks, Dad." Justine took a deep breath, then came in and started setting the table. "I think I'll wear the green dress. It doesn't make me look like I'm trying to be twenty-nine or something."

The spaghetti was served and they ate quickly.

"Drasil said that I should be able to visit Marisha tomorrow. I can't wait to hear all the stuff that has been going on. It's been ages since I've been there."

"That will be good. How are you going to explain the bruises?"

"I'll just tell them what happened, what else?"

"Well," Patrick said, "if they are as peaceful as you have said, the idea of someone hitting a young girl could be really upsetting for them."

"I hadn't thought of that. What would you suggest?"

"You might want to talk about the difference between where you live and where they live. That way they can see this whole thing, while not normal for here, isn't as scary as it would be in their homes."

"Stone is going to be really angry."

"Good, he should be, but then he needs to let it go again or it will be a problem for him."

"What do you mean?"

"Well, I was really angry at God for a long time, but I held on to my anger instead of just letting it out and being done with it. It made things harder for me."

"I think I know what you're talking about," Justine said. "You don't go around the long way to avoid the church anymore."

"No, I don't still need to avoid the church." Patrick stood up and started clearing the plates. "We'd better get a move on. You don't want to be late. I'll leave the dishes until we get home."

The parking lot at the shelter was already full so Patrick parked at the strip mall next door. When the clerk who came out to ask them to move saw Justine, he asked for her autograph, then promised to watch out for the car.

"I've never signed an autograph before," Justine said. "It was a little weird."

"You're famous now, that means you can do things that other people can't, but it also means that you have more responsibility. People will watch how you act"

"I'm really glad I wore the green dress then. Maybe it'll remind people that I'm only eleven."

Natalie met them at the door. She smiled at Patrick, but gave Justine a hug.

"I heard what you said on the news," Natalie said. "I'm so proud of you, and I'm sure your mom is too."

"Thanks," Justine said, "for not putting Mom in the past tense."

"My mom just died last year," Natalie said. "I still talk about her like she's right here. It helps."

"It does," Justine said. "If you want to talk about your mom, I would be glad to listen." She laughed. "That didn't sound much like a kid did it?" She shook her head, then she saw Kelly.

"Kelly!" She hugged the other girl. "I was trying to decide what dress to wear, and my dad was like "They both look nice, dear, which was soooo helpful." Kelly laughed and the girls ran into the building.

"You have an amazing daughter, Mr. Constance," Natalie said.

"Call me Patrick, it looks like I'm going to be around a lot."

"Patrick then." Natalie looked at where the girls had been. "I wish I had a friend like Justine when I was that age. She has been so good for Kelly, and Mrs. Balanteen has been a godsend. She has a student she is going to send once a week to be here for the children. I can't believe all this is happening just like this."

"It seems all of a sudden, but we've been building up to this for a while." Patrick said, "I think is part of Justine's reason for being."

"Are you always this philosophical?"

"It's something that a friend of Justine's said."

"Ah, that explains everything."

Lee came up at that moment.

"Hi, Patrick. Am I too late?"

"No, Lee, we're just getting organized," Natalie said. "It's been a challenge since we gave all the women a choice of staying here and having the public through or going to a motel for the night. Most have decided to stay, but it does mean that I have to keep an eye on who's coming in."

"We won't distract you anymore," Patrick said. He took Lee's hand and led her into the building. "I haven't been in here before, so you will have to show me around." He looked at her and she was a little pinker than usual, than he realized that he was still holding her hand.

"No, please," she said when he went to let go. "I don't mind." She gave his hand a squeeze. "I could use the support today."

"Rough day?" he asked.

"Today always is," she said, "but I won't go into it now. This is Justine's day." She smiled a little. "Thanks for being here."

They walked down the hall to the living room and joined the crowd already there. Patrick took a long look around this room that had been the centre of Justine's life for weeks. It did indeed feel like an oasis. The walls were the colour of the desert sand and trim the green of living things ran around the room was. The curtains were an abstract pattern that made Patrick think of palm trees. There was a large plaque on the wall that was covered with a curtain. He went to have a closer look at the couches. The leather felt extraordinarily soft. They all had people in them, so he'd have to wait to try them out. They looked very comfortable.

Justine looked at her dad, then nudged Kelly and pointed

to them. They whispered something to each other and Kelly went toward the table of food while Justine came over to them.

"You look so cute," she said. "Kelly is helping with the food, so you're stuck with me." She took them around the room and introduced them to the women who were standing around, some looking defiant and some nervous, but they all smiled at Justine.

"We had a woman who was a professional painter come in and paint, and another woman who did the trim," Justine said when they completed the circuit. "This is the first time in ages that there've been men in past the front door." She saw the Mayor come in. "Excuse me, I need to say hello to the Mayor." She went over and the Mayor knelt to hug her. He introduced her to the others with him, who Patrick guessed were some of the City council.

"If I could have your attention for a moment," Natalie said, "I just have a couple of things to say, then we can go back to the party. Our Board approved a fundraising campaign to get supplies to spruce up our living room a bit. Mr. Constance, Justine's dad, asked us if Justine could do the design for the room as an early Christmas present. After meeting Justine and seeing her ideas the Board unanimously approved. Justine raised money with her classmates, while Mr. Constance received a very generous gift from Taylor and Taylor and their staff. All of you know about the press conference and the City's pledge, so you know this room is just the beginning. Justine already has plans on how to spend the City's grant. In the meantime, we are gathered tonight to celebrate the completion of this room. From its warm paint tones to the wonderful curtains, to the addition of new furniture, which I might add are all fold out beds for emergency use, we have been given a room to enjoy and feel safe.

"I wanted to name the room after Justine, but she had other ideas."

Justine stepped forward from Patrick and Lee.

"Not all of you would know that my Mom did the original design for this room. She was a firm believer everyone should have a home that was not only safe, but felt like a home. All the work I did here, was what I learned from her notes." Her voice broke and she took a deep breath. "So I would like to name this room after her. Let's call this Ingrid's Room." Natalie pulled a cloth from a plaque to one side that Patrick hadn't noticed. On it was a picture of Ingrid with a wide smile, and the words Ingrid's Room.

Justine had stepped back and Patrick hugged her with his free arm. He felt the tears running down his cheeks, but he didn't care. Lee's hand squeezed his. Justine looked up at him and he saw the same smile on her face that was on Ingrid's picture along with his tears. People clapped and cheered, then by tacit consent turned away to give them space.

"I am so proud of you," Patrick said. "This is the best Christmas present I ever got."

"So you don't mind that we named it after Mom?"

"She would love it. It looks wonderful." Patrick hugged her.

"I'm going to go help Kelly with the food."

"It's no wonder everyone loves that girl," Lee said. "Every time I think I know what she is going to do, she goes and surprises me again."

"Try living with her," Patrick said. "My head is whirling half the time." The Mayor came over to talk to them, then Bob introduced him to the partners.

"You and your girl are special people," Ms. Taylor said. "My son and I are very glad you're a part of our firm." They wandered off to talk to the council members who had come in with the Mayor.

"Hey," Justine said, "would it be all right if I stay with Kelly for the night?"

"Sure, if it's OK with Natalie and Kelly's mom."

"Great, 'cause Natalie already said it was fine and so did Kelly's mom."

"Well, that's settled then." Patrick said, "Have fun and stay out of trouble."

"Sure thing, Dad."

"Are you sure she's not a twenty-year-old in an eleven year old's body?"

"Sometimes I wonder what she'll be like as a teenager,"

Patrick said, "then I decide it's just as well I don't know."

Lee laughed. "It looks like things are winding down. Do you think Justine would mind if we made an exit?"

They said goodbye to Justine. Kelly's mom said she would drop Justine off in the morning.

Outside, the wind had picked up and Lee shivered. Patrick wrapped his arm around her to keep her warm. He walked her to the car, then got in to drive home.

"I'm glad I took a taxi here," Lee said. "I really didn't feel like driving tonight. Thanks." They sat in silence for a while.

"It's hard to believe," Lee said, "all that's come out of your asking Justine to do a little design work for the Shelter. She almost gets killed, but ends up as a hero and bringing all kinds of attention and money for the shelter."

"Terrifying is what it is," Patrick said. "All I want to do is give Justine a good life, but there is so much I can't control."

"Maybe the best thing you are giving her is your trust. She's an amazing kid."

Patrick dropped Lee off at her house and went home. It felt empty without Justine so he decided to go to bed. He had just finished brushing his teeth when he heard a knock on the door. He put his shirt back on and went downstairs. Lee was standing at the door, her teeth chattering and holding a bottle of wine.

"Come in before you freeze," he said. "Why aren't you wearing a coat?"

"I went home," Lee said, "but I just couldn't face sitting there by myself, so I grabbed a bottle of wine and ran over here. I guess I forgot to put on my coat."

Patrick led her into the living room and wrapped a blanket around her.

"Could you open the wine?" Lee pleaded. Patrick opened the wine and poured out two glasses. Lee took a huge gulp from hers and started shaking more. Patrick sat beside her and rubbed her hands to warm them up. Lee put her head on his shoulder.

"That's feeling better," she said. "I have to talk to you, and the only way I can talk to you is if I drink wine."

"You do what you need to do," Patrick said. "I have all night."

"You are so sweet," Lee kissed him on the cheek. Then she finished her glass and held it out for more. He refilled it and took a sip of his.

"I was a rebellious kid," Lee said. "I horrified my parents all the time. They finally had to send me away because they couldn't do anything with me. I went into foster care at fourteen. I hated my parents for giving up on me, but I hated myself more for forcing them to. When I was fifteen I met a boy that everyone told me was bad news. I didn't care, I was bad news myself. We got into some bad stuff and we were sleeping together every chance we got.

"When I got pregnant he ran off and never looked back. My parents didn't want me back. My foster mom was kind enough, but she was religious. By the time I worked up the courage to tell her I was pregnant it was too late to do anything but go through with it. She lectured me all the time about what a terrible thing I had done and what a bad person I was. I had the baby and he went straight to adoption, lucky kid. I called him Michael, but I don't know what name they put on the birth certificate. That was sixteen years ago. Today is his birthday. I always have a hard time on his birthday." She held her glass out and Patrick filled it again.

"I was twenty when I met a great guy at college. We got married and he wanted to have children. We tried and tried. I finally went to the doctor and after all kinds of tests, learned that somehow that first pregnancy had messed up my insides. I was never going to have children again. I was only going to have one child and I had given him away." She started crying and Patrick wrapped his arms around her.

"Tom, that was my husband, was furious. He called me all kinds of names and told me that God was punishing me for my sin. He beat me up and left me broken and bleeding on the floor. If a friend hadn't happened to come over I would have died. I never heard from Tom again. I just got papers from his lawyer to sign to annul the marriage. He said it was a lie because I couldn't have children." She started rocking and crying harder. Patrick picked her up and rocked her like he had with Justine when she wakened in the night missing her mom. He found tears in his own eyes and let them come. Lee was whispering that she was sorry. He didn't know if she was talking to him, or Tom, or Michael or even God. It didn't matter.

She was as lost as he was. How long had he let his anger at Ingrid's death poison his life? Too long. Faith was part of Ingrid's life. To be honest, it was the core of her life. She had never blamed God for the cancer. Only Patrick had raged at God. Ingrid said something good came out of every circumstance. Patrick hadn't seen it then, but maybe he was beginning to. Kelly was now Justine's best friend. The Women's Shelter had a much needed boost. What did he know?

Patrick whispered to Lee that she was forgiven. He didn't think God would mind. After a long time, fell asleep. Patrick tucked the blanket tighter around her.

"You take care of Lee, God," he said. "Maybe you could help me out too. I'm sorry I was angry for so long." He took a long deep breath. "Say hello to Ingrid for me."

He didn't remember falling asleep, but he was still cradling Lee in his arms when Justine came in.

"Well, I got out for one night and look what you get up to," she said.

Lee woke with a start and saw Justine.

"Oh God, Justine," she said as she struggled to untangle herself. "It isn't, I mean we didn't..." Tears started down her face. "I'm not like that anymore."

Justine threw her arms around Lee and held her tight.

"I'm sorry," she said, "I was just joking. There's nobody in the world I'd rather have with my Dad than you. Please don't go."

"I have to," Lee said. "I have to go take care of Michael, he'll be frantic."

"Promise you'll come back," Justine said.

"Not today, but I will come back. I will."

"It's all right, Justine," Patrick said. "It was a very hard day for Lee. Someday she will tell you about it."

Justine reluctantly let go of Lee and let her go to the door.

Patrick stood at the door with her.

"I would like you to come back too," he said.

"You're sweet," Lee said, and kissed him briefly on the lips.

"Thank you." Then she was gone.

"I'm guessing you need some coffee," Justine said.

Chapter Eleven

Patrick gave the sauce another stir and looked at the window. It was almost fully dark and Justine wasn't home yet.

He had just decided that he was officially worried when she came in the door.

"I'm really sorry I'm late," she said. "Drasil had me back in time, but I wanted to think. I walked the long way around the block. Pastor Daniel was at the church and he let me sit in the church and think. He told me to say hello for him.

"So what's happening that's causing all this thinking?"

"Well, you know that woman thing that we have to learn about in school? That all started while I was visiting Marisha. It was like eewwww, but she helped me out and it's all cool. She said I'm not really a child anymore and I have to start taking up adult responsibilities."

Patrick looked at her and realized that despite all the things that had happened she was still a child growing up, though faster than he was ready for.

"You look weird, Dad. Do you need to scream or something?"

"I need to sit down." He pulled out a chair and sat in it. "So you're OK with all this?"

"It's still kind of icky, but it isn't like I have any choice. Kelly's had hers since last year. I'll get some stuff from her tomorrow. What I needed to think about was not having Mom around to give me the talk and tell me that everything is fine, then I started thinking about how she wouldn't be here for when I get married or have kids or anything. I started bawling then, so I needed to sit and think."

The phone rang.

"That will be Pastor Daniel making sure I got home OK."

It was and Patrick thanked him for being there for Justine.

"I'm always glad to help out."

"You must live at that church."

"Not quite, but I think I have help being there at the right times."

"Well, if you do, then that help is appreciated too."

Daniel laughed. "I'll pass that on to the Boss. Goodnight and remember, either one of you can call whenever you need to."

"So, how was the rest of your visit?" Patrick asked after hanging up the phone.

"Risha is really scared. There are all kinds of rumours going around about an invasion. They haven't traded much with the other countries in the last few years. They don't need much. Davvad doesn't know what they will do if an army comes. Some of the younger men want to form an army and fight back. Marisha gets mad at them and tells them that they have no idea how to fight and why would they break the Peace. Stone says the army will have broken the Peace first and so it would be all right."

"Forming an army is a pretty drastic step. I remember stories my Granddad told about being in the army and it didn't sound like much fun. He never talked about the fighting, but he cried every Remembrance Day.

"What should they do?" asked Justine. "They keep asking me, and I don't know what to say."

"I think the most important thing is to be true to themselves." Patrick had said. "I know it sounds trite, but it's like you standing up to Kelly's dad. That wasn't something that you thought and decided about, but just something you did because that's who you are."

"So you think they shouldn't fight?"

"Wouldn't fighting be a betrayal of what they believe?"

"Stone says it's like when someone says Wolf in the game."

"But you don't fight the wolf in the game, you just run away, don't you?"

"He'd say it is like when I changed my mind and everyone chased me."

"Fighting isn't as easy as it sounds, and it changes you. I don't think they could fight and then go back to the Peace."

"That's what I keep saying to them." Justine sighed. "I'm tired and stuff. Goodnight, Dad." She went upstairs and Patrick heard the shower running.

"Ingrid, I'm sorry," he said to the silent kitchen, "I never thought to say anything to her. Thank God that she was with someone who understood. I know there are some other conversations that I'm going to have to have with her. I wish you were here to tell me what to say. I don't want to mess it up."

"I made a pillow and drew a face on it," Justine said a few days later as she put her homework in her bag, "and told Stone to hit it, but he couldn't. Davvad said that they aren't a fighting people anymore, but it isn't fair that these soldiers can just come in and push them around. There was a man from another village and he said that men in white came to their village. They welcomed them and made them a meal, but then the soldiers drove them out of their homes and burnt the houses down. It isn't right."

"No, it isn't."

"There must be something they can do."

"I wish I knew."

Justine started decorating the house for Christmas. She set out candles and figurines. Every year was different, but each one was the same too. Patrick felt like the house was being filled with light. Kelly came over and helped with the decorating. The last weekend before Christmas she spent the weekend helping bake huge batches of cookies. She took a lot back to the shelter.

Yet while their house grew full of light, the stories from the Pax grew darker. There were more people who had met the soldiers in white. Stone and the other young men still wanted to fight, and Justine was losing patience with them.

"I keep telling them, but they won't listen. These men in white are real soldiers, they aren't going to be stopped by a bunch of boys with sticks."

"I bet you Stone wasn't happy to hear that."

"No, he hardly talks to me anymore." Justine wiped her eyes and sniffled. "I want to help and I can't."

"Maybe you need to talk about what they can do instead of what they can't."

"I can't think of anything they can do except leave before the soldiers come to their village."

"Ask them what they did last time this happened."

The next night Justine came home and sat at the table.

"I asked them what happened last time this happened and

they just looked at me. As far back as they can remember this has never happened. Davvad said that years ago they had people who used to trade in the neighbouring countries and who talked about the Peace to people, but they weren't protected by the Peace and so some never came home. No one has gone out since before he was born, and he's older than you.

"Marisha said it was a good question though, that maybe they would have the answer in the Library at the City. It is days and days away. I think she wants them to leave before the soldiers come, and if they are going to somewhere instead of running from something it would be better."

"Smart woman, how do the others feel about it?"

"Risha and Hisen like the idea. Risha is expecting and doesn't want to have the baby if her house is going to be invaded. Stone and his friends hate it and they're saying they will stay and fight even if the others leave.

What am I supposed to do? Patrick wondered. This world of Justine's was making her as miserable as the bullying at school had before she made friends with Kelly. He felt even worse than when Ingrid had cancer. At least then there were doctors and tests. This invasion of the Pax was beyond him. He needed help. Patrick went to the phone to call Lee, but stopped. She had put him off when he had tried to call before, saying she needed time to sort herself out. He didn't want her worrying about Justine too.

He found himself dialling Daniel's number at the church. It rang through to a message machine. He didn't want to disturb the man at home so he just left a brief message that he would like to talk. Patrick immediately regretted it, but it was done. He was sitting staring at the TV when the phone rang.

"I checked the messages at the church," Daniel said. "One of my young mothers is expecting any day and I wanted to make sure I didn't miss any calls. How can I help you?"

"I'm worried about Justine," Patrick said.

"She's recovered from her injuries, hasn't she? She looked all right the other night."

"It isn't her physical injuries that I'm worried about."

"How about I come over for a bit?" Daniel said.

"OK," Patrick looked around the room. The last time

Pastor Daniel was in the house was the day after Ingrid died. Patrick remembered sitting on this couch and thinking a part of him had died. He didn't want to see Daniel here. He went into the kitchen and got out some of Justine's cookies and set up the coffee. It would only take a minute to run through if Daniel wanted any.

There was a knock on the door and he opened it to let Daniel in.

"We'll sit in the kitchen," he said and mentally kicked himself for sounding angry. Daniel just smiled and followed him into the kitchen.

"Kitchens are the heart of a home," Daniel said, "or at least that is what my wife tells me."

Patrick thought about everything that happened around the table in this room.

"I think she's right." He pushed the plate of cookies over. "Coffee?"

"Water is fine, thanks." Daniel accepted the glass with a smile and bit into a chocolate chip cookie.

"Wonderful." He munched on the cookie, apparently willing to wait all night for whatever Patrick needed to say. Patrick sat down and helped himself to a cookie. They munched in silence for a while.

"Let me tell you a story," Patrick said. "Then you tell me what you think."

"Sounds good."

Patrick told the minister about the Pax as Justine called her friends. He talked about their customs and then the recent trouble with the invasion.

"What do you think they should do?" he asked at the end.

"Well, that is quite a tale," Daniel said, and helped himself to another cookie. "You have a people who live by rules of peace, but that is different from living in peace. It is a custom for them, but I wonder if they've forgotten the meaning behind the custom. So when there is a challenge to their habits, they don't know how to react. There's no depth to them."

"They're good people."

"Yes, but even good people can forget why they are good.

The strongest test of good isn't in joy, but in sorrow. If I were writing the story, they would hold to their peace, but learn the depths of it and make it a conscious choice again. Is this something Justine is working on?"

"In a way," Patrick said. He didn't want to reveal all her secrets to Daniel.

"It must be a way for her to work out what happened at school. That would be very hard for a young woman like her. She blazes with so much goodness that it's hard to remember there is a great deal of evil in the world too."

"Why?"

"When we are surrounded by good things, we are most comfortable forgetting the bad."

"No, why is there evil?"

"Now that's a question for the ages. There are more answers than I can count, and likely many I don't know. Evil is necessary for us to have free choice. It is the result of the Fall in the Garden. It is the handiwork of the devil. It exists because we don't trust God enough. I don't know what answer I like best. Sometimes it's one and sometimes another."

"So you don't think God created evil?"

"That's a tough question too. Let's say that I don't think that God plans evil for us, but God is certainly able to turn what evil happens to good, and I think he's there whether we are in the midst of good or evil."

"That doesn't really answer my question."

"No, I'm afraid it doesn't. I sometimes think that answers are overrated. It is the questions that count. I will say that Christmas is a big part of God's response to evil. It is all about shining as bright a light as we can in the darkness instead of trying to pretend the darkness doesn't exist."

"I haven't thought about Christmas that way in a long time."

"Merry Christmas," Daniel said as he left. Patrick ate another cookie and sat in the kitchen to think.

"Daddy," Justine wandered into the kitchen looking more asleep than awake. "Was someone here?"

"Pastor Daniel came over for a chat."

"Right," Justine sat down and helped herself to a cookie. "I really must be dreaming. You asked Pastor Daniel over to talk about God?"

"Almost."

"How can you almost talk about God?"

"We talked about evil."

"Yech," Justine made a face. "I'd rather talk about God, but I guess you're still angry with him."

"Maybe," Patrick thought for a moment. "I don't think so, but I'm trying to figure out what it feels like to not be angry at God. I needed someone to talk to and I couldn't call Lee."

"I'm sorry, Dad, I really messed that up."

"Not your fault, Justine. Give her time."

"Not too much. So what did Pastor Daniel say about evil?"

"Not much I understood, to tell the truth. Just that, for whatever reason, it's here and, God is with us."

"Uh huh," she nodded. "I could have told you that."

"He also said that if he were writing the end to the story, that the people would learn the reason for the Peace and live the Peace by choice instead of custom."

"Story?"

"He thinks it's a story you are writing."

"What do you think?" Justine looked at him and Patrick saw a deeper question hidden in her blue eyes.

"I don't know what I think. If there is a God who cares for us, why not another world? What I do know is that you are my daughter and so I'm going to love you as much as I can regardless of whether I understand you or not.

"OK." Justine made the last cookie vanish. "I love you too." Then she stumbled back upstairs to her room.

Chapter Twelve

"I still think spaghetti is a strange thing to eat on Christmas Eve," Kelly said.

"It's Friday," Justine said.

"Good spaghetti." Kelly put another forkful in her mouth. "I'd eat this any time."

"Eat all you want," Patrick said.

"Service starts in an hour," Justine said.

Kelly just nodded and took another huge bite of pasta.

"Excuse me for a moment, ladies." Patrick pushed back from the table. He went upstairs and changed into a suit and tie. He thought about his conversation with Pastor Daniel a few days before. In a moment, there would be no turning back. He went back downstairs and sat in the living room and listened to the girls talking.

"I can't believe I was so mean to you," Kelly said, "and now you're like my best friend."

"Mrs. Balanteen says it's easy to be mean when you're hurting."

"I didn't think I was hurting that much. It's still hard sometimes. I don't want to miss my dad, but I do anyway. Then I feel guilty because I miss him and he was so mean to my mom."

"What do you miss?"

"Things like Christmas when he would buy us all kinds of presents," Kelly said. "Christmas morning there would be wrapping paper all over the place. It's strange that you guys don't have anything under your tree at all."

"We already gave each other our presents."

"I know, that's so weird. Cool, but weird. We didn't do much for Christmas. Mom's trying to move on from Dad, and since he made such a big deal about it...We haven't got much under the tree either, but everyone should have at least one present under the tree. You can open this now or tomorrow."

Patrick heard paper tearing, then Justine's gasp.

"Kelly, that's beautiful!"

"I made it myself. There are all kinds of these neat beads in

102

the craft room. I made my Mom one too."

Justine ran into the living room.

"Dad! Look what Kelly made... Why are you wearing a suit?"

"I thought I would join you at the service this evening."

"Really!" Justine said, "But you haven't gone since Mom died."

"I think it's time."

"Could you help me with this bracelet? Kelly made it for me."

"It's gorgeous," Patrick said. "Kelly, you have a talent for colour."

"You think so?"

"Definitely."

Justine put her hand to her mouth.

"I didn't get you anything."

"If it weren't for you, I wouldn't be here. I wouldn't have a best friend who is the smartest girl in the world." Kelly gave Justine a hug. "I just wanted to give you something for a change."

"Speaking of change," Patrick said. "You two had better change quickly, or we'll have to sit in the choir loft."

The girls ran upstairs and were down again almost immediately.

"Let's go," Justine said. They put on their coats and walked to church. The girls went ahead and whispered to each other while Patrick walked behind.

The church was crowded and they needed to sit near the front. Patrick was sure that Justine had introduced him to everybody there by the time they found a seat. She gave his hand a squeeze as they stood for the first carol.

Patrick could smell the Christmas tree that stood up front and the familiar words of the carol rolled through him. He had expected to feel sad or angry, but what filled him was a sense of rightness. He was supposed to be here.

They listened to readings from the Scriptures talking about Jesus and his birth, then sang more carols. Then Pastor Daniel stepped into the pulpit.

"The last few weeks I have been thinking more than usual

about the question of evil. Now I know that some of you are wondering about what evil has to do with Christmas. This is, after all, a celebration of light and joy. No evil to be found here. Except that the world that Jesus was born into was filled with evil. His country was occupied by an empire that was cruel and heartless. The reason he was born in a stable was the Emperor wanted to know how many people he ruled over, so he would know if he was collecting enough taxes.

"There was a King over Judea, but only because he cooperated with the Romans. His only concern was himself. Very soon after Jesus was born, Joseph would flee with Jesus and Mary to live in Egypt as refugees until Herod had died.

"They were harsh times and dark. Yet we celebrate Christmas not because the birth of Jesus was all peace and joy, but because Jesus is God's answer to evil. God doesn't try to explain evil to us, instead we are given God's Son to free us from evil. The angels sang 'Peace on Earth and goodwill to all' not because the world was a pleasant place, but to show God's promise to the world that peace will win. Christmas isn't about us, but about God, just as our hope isn't in us but in God."

He continued in the same vein for a bit longer, but Patrick was lost in his own thoughts. Maybe he'd been so fixed on why, he'd forgotten about the who. At the end of the service they sang Silent Night and filed out wishing each other a Merry Christmas until Patrick was hoarse. Since they were sitting almost at the front, they were the last people out of the church.

"Glad you could make it," Pastor Daniel said.

"Thank you," Patrick shook his hand. "Merry Christmas."

Justine hugged the Pastor and introduced him to Kelly. They walked home quietly and found Kelly's mom waiting patiently in the driveway.

"Merry Christmas," she said to Patrick and Justine before pulling out of the drive.

Patrick followed Justine into the kitchen. She put the kettle on for hot chocolate and sat at the table with him.

"Merry Christmas, Dad," she said.

"Merry Christmas, Justine."

"Do you think the Pastor was right about evil and stuff?"

"It is certainly a different way of looking at it. I like it though. It means we don't have to wait until we understand to start doing good in the world."

"But what if we don't know what is good?"

"Thinking about your friends, the Pax?"

"Yeah, I don't know what the good thing to do is. What if I do the wrong thing?"

"I think that's part of what the Pastor was trying to say. We don't always need to know. God knows, so we trust God."

They finished their drinks and put the cups in the sink.

"It does look strange," Justine said looking at the tree as they walked through the living room, "but I feel good anyway."

"Me too."

Christmas morning Patrick woke to Justine knocking on his door and the smell of coffee.

"Wake up, sleepy head."

"I thought since we didn't have any presents we could sleep in," Patrick said, but he was putting his robe on as he spoke.

"Dream on." Justine handed him a coffee and they walked downstairs.

"You know how we said we weren't giving each other presents?" she said. "I sort of lied." She led him around the corner into the living room and he saw a painting leaning against the wall. It was an abstract that immediately reminded him of the painting of Justice they had seen at the gallery.

"The artist who painted Justice lives at the shelter. I think that's why she made Justice so angry looking. This one is called Peace. She insisted on giving it to me after the Shelter and all that stuff. It reminded me of Mom. I recall her having a light to her."

"It is amazing." Patrick walked around to look at it from different angles. "Where should we hang it?"

"We could hang it right here. The colours will work. It will fit where the seashore picture is now."

"Your mom bought that picture on our honeymoon." He carefully lifted it down and leaned it against the wall and hung Peace in its place. "It does look good." He looked over to the seashore picture. "Wouldn't that look good in your room?" Justine picked it up and disappeared upstairs. He went to find his hammer and nails and walked up to join her.

Justine was holding the picture up against the wall opposite the colour blocks.

"Here looks good," she said.

"Your mom always said that pictures should be hung at eye height."

"Mine or yours?"

"It's your room."

They got the picture hung and sat on Justine's bed to admire it.

"It's almost like I designed the room around the picture," she said.

"It does look good."

"Merry Christmas, Dad. Thanks for the painting."

"You're welcome. Thanks for the painting of Peace. It reminds me of your Mom, too. Speaking of which. I sort of lied about the presents too." He pulled a small book out of his robe pocket and handed it to her. "Your mom always kept a journal. She wrote about everything from design ideas to lists of books she wanted to read. She never got to start this one. She wanted me to give it to you when I thought you were ready for it."

Justine opened it and ran her fingers across the elegant script 'Ingrid Constance'.

"Wow," she said and hugged the journal. "Thanks." She leaned against him and they sat like that until his stomach rumbled. Justine laughed and they went downstairs to cook breakfast.

Chapter Thirteen

Patrick stirred the spaghetti sauce and watched for his daughter to come home. It was almost dark and Justine had been coming in later and later. Worse, she hadn't mentioned the Pax at all since Christmas even though she had been spending almost as much time with the Pax as with Kelly. It worried him more than when she did talk about them. Oddly, he also worried for her friends. She had talked about them so much he almost felt he knew them. Regardless of what Justine needed, he needed help.

As much as he was learning to appreciate Pastor Daniel, what Patrick wanted was Lee's down to earth advice. He also missed her. He hadn't got to speak more than a couple of words to her since she had run out of his house in tears. He missed their conversations not just because she helped him with understanding Justine. There was something about being with her that made him feel good. He didn't think her having given up her son for adoption made her bad, but obviously she did.

It was time they talked, if not about Lee, then about Justine. He picked up the phone to call Lee. Patrick had just dialled her number when Justine ran into the house crying. Then he noticed she was wearing a brown dress that came down to her knees. Her hair was done in dozens of braids with feathers and stones woven into the braids.

"Dad, you have to come. Please, Dad, now, I need you." She grabbed his arm and pulled at him. Patrick looked at her face and let the fear and anger he felt drift away. There was something more important happening. He put the phone on the counter and ran out the door with his daughter.

They ran through the night to the schoolyard. He remembered that night feeling his way along to the tree Justine called Drasil; but she ran sure footed across the grass.

"Drasil, we're here." She put her hands on the tree. "Please, Drasil, you have to let him through." He could hear her hitting the tree. "Dad, just close your eyes and hold on to my hand." He felt her small hand grip his tightly then she pulled him forward and he fell off the edge of the world.

Patrick opened his eyes and tried to scream, but there was no air in his lungs. He wasn't sure he even had lungs. Objects that were either galaxies or atoms flew past him. He knew he was falling but there was no ground below, no sky above. The only fixed thing in this madness was Justine's hand holding his. He focused on slowing his heart. He trusted Justine, trusted her with his life. Then he felt a presence beyond him. It receded to infinite distances and yet was close beside him. Was this God? He wondered and felt a great amusement, but also a negative. Not God then, but something immense beyond his imagining. Drasil.

::Yggdrasil:: the presence said. ::The World Tree. I connect what needs to be connected.::

"How does Justine come into this?" Patrick asked, "She's just a little girl."

The amusement changed and he felt something else, as if the universe had decided to give him a hug. He was filled with the hugeness of the compassion of this being. There was something beyond words that Drasil was trying to tell him, but Patrick couldn't make it out. There was a cosmic sigh and they stopped.

"You can open your eyes now," Justine said.

They stood beside a tree in a field. The sun shone warm on his face and the sky bright blue. In the distance stood a collection of tiny cottages, but something was wrong with them. He couldn't get his thoughts straight to figure out what it was. Patrick slipped to his knees and waited for his head to stop spinning. The scent of strange flowers tickled his nose. It was real. All those stories were real. Davvad, Marisha, Stone, the soldiers in white. Patrick was ready to drag Justin back to the tree and force it somehow to take them home.

"Welcome to Pax, Dad," Justine said. "Let's go find my friends."

Justine pulled him to his feet. "See you later, Drasil."

"I thought that Drasil was the tree in the schoolyard?" Patrick looked at the tree. It didn't look anything like the tree at home. He didn't understand. He felt a comforting nudge and the world's spinning slowed. Somehow Drasil, Yggdrasil was helping him bridge the gap.

"He is," Justine said, "but this is Drasil too. He is here and there and in between."

Patrick felt another nudge in the affirmative.

"I think I met him," Patrick said. "He gave me a hug."

"Isn't that awesome?" Justine said as she pulled him down the hill toward those odd-looking cottages.

"But what is he?" Patrick asked.

"He's Drasil. He connects places that need to be connected."

"Right." Patrick stumbled over a hole in the field. "This is going to take a bit to get my head around." He stopped, "I left the stove on."

"It's OK, Dad."

"But our house, it could burn down, and I left the door open again."

"Drasil says it will be OK."

"You're talking to him now?"

"When we were travelling. He told me that it would be all right, that whatever happened it would be all right."

"That doesn't sound good."

"That's just Drasil, he always talks like that."

Patrick found his feet again and looked down at the village.

"Something isn't right down there." He pulled Justine down to the ground.

A man in a white uniform walked out of one of the houses and yelled. Patrick could hear the sound if not the words. Others in white appeared and formed up in front of the first one. He waved his hands at the village, then toward the forest on the other side of the houses from Patrick and Justine.

Two of the men went into houses and came out with lit torches. Patrick could see flames leaping out the windows. They went into each of the houses, then joined the rest of the group and marched off.

"Oh no, we're too late!" Justine said, "We have to put the fires out."

"How?" Patrick said. "If we're seen those men will come back. I just hope your friends got away."

Justine buried her face in Patrick's shoulder and cried.

"We're too late. I can't believe we're too late.

"We can go back to Drasil and go home," he said.

"I can't leave my friends."

"You have that option now, but you may not later."

"Dad," Justine looked at him, "I have to help my friends. It's like with Kelly. I have to."

"These men have swords."

"I am scared, but I still have to."

Patrick kissed her on the forehead.

"That's my girl. We'll wait here for a while and see what happens. Then go down in a while to look for your friends."

The sun got hotter and Patrick was too warm. He pulled off his sweater and tied it around his waist.

"I think we can go now." He stood up and helped Justine up. They walked in silence down to the burning village. Patrick saw nothing moving until a boy ran up and clung to Justine.

"They burned everything," he said. "Everything,"

"What are you doing here?" Justine asked.

"Mom and Dad finally agreed that we needed to go to the City where it would be safe. I stayed behind to watch for the men in white. I was going to drive them away." He hung his head. "There were too many of them and I just hid and watched them burn my home to the ground." He looked at Justine. "It's too late; you have to go home and stay safe."

"No, Stone," Justine said, "I am here to help, and so's my Dad."

"Are you a great warrior?" Stone looked at Patrick. "Can you defeat these evil men?"

Patrick looked at Stone. He saw a boy only slightly taller than Justine with curly hair and skin that looked like fine bronze. He wore loose pants and a vest tied closed with a string. There were tears pouring out of his brown eyes, but he held Patrick's gaze.

"I'm no warrior, Stone, but I will do what I can."

"Oh great!" He threw his hands in the air. "Who's going to teach me to fight?"

"Stone," Justine said, "you are forgetting something."

It was as if she had slapped him. He became absolutely still,

110

then he took in a deep breath.

"Welcome and be at peace in our home and hearth," he said in a formal voice. "You are our guest as long as you are at peace in this land."

"Thank you, Stone."

"You won't tell Mom that I forgot, will you?"

"Not if you promise to stop talking about fighting back," Justine said. "You'll just get yourself killed."

"I could handle them. I just need someone to show me how."

"I've been in a fight," Justine said grabbing his shoulders and spinning him to face her. "You can't handle them, I can't handle them."

"Sorry." Stone hung his head. "But I need to do something."

"We will, Stone," Patrick said, "but it needs to be the right thing."

Patrick heard some shouting in the distance. He turned to see some of the soldiers in white pointing at them. One of them was waving a sword.

"I think the thing now is to get away from here and these soldiers." He half expected Stone to argue, but the boy led them at a run to the forest away from the village. The shouts behind them continued. When they'd started running he'd worried about Justine keeping up, but the children were pulling him along.

"Just up here," Stone said, "there's a ravine that no one who doesn't live here would notice." He dropped into the undergrowth and vanished. Justine followed him. Patrick went to his hands and knees to crawl under the bushes. The ground vanished under him and only Stone and Justine grabbing him stopped a face first tumble onto the rocks.

"Where are they?" Patrick heard a voice, accompanied by the swish of a sword through the brush.

"What does it matter?" another voice said, "We'll just tell them to go to the City anyway."

"Maybe I'll have a little fun first."

"Orders are to warn only," a different voice came from further back. "Do I need to describe to you what happens to those who don't follow orders?"

"Look, I'm just kidding, OK?" the first voice sounded nervous now and the swishing stopped. "It's just there is no honour to be gained in sending villagers away."

"We're not here for honour, soldier," the third voice had taken on a hard edge. "We are here to serve the Prince. We return. We'll report that we saw the villagers, but they escaped. There will be no punishment for that."

"So there is nothing left in the village," Stone said, "I guess we need to find my parents and go to the City. The road is this way."

He took Justine's hand and started off down the ravine. It was difficult walking in his suit pants and dress shirt. The sweater kept catching on branched, but Patrick didn't want to leave it behind. The ravine let out on another stretch of open ground.

Stone led them along the edge of the fields for quite a way before they got to anything resembling a track. He seemed to know exactly what he was doing and Justine trusted him, so Patrick contented himself with watching for more of the soldiers in white.

Patrick watched the children walk hand in hand, and found he missed Lee. He shrugged it off. Nothing he could do about it now, and he had a suspicion it would be a long time before he saw her again.

They followed the track and it began looking more like a road as the forest disappeared behind them. Patrick relaxed, a little.

"What happened while I was gone?" Justine asked.

"More and more people were disappearing and we figured they were either hiding from the invaders or were driven out. There haven't been many people killed, mostly the soldiers are content to scare the people away, then burn the villages."

Has anyone tried to talk to them?" asked Patrick.

"Hisen said a cousin of his had given them formal welcome. Most of the time, the welcome is the first thing we say to a stranger. I was...upset." Stone hunched his shoulders. "We need to do something, and welcoming people who are burning us out doesn't seem to be very helpful."

"Yet refusing to welcome them is the first step in changing yourself into something different from what you are. You don't welcome soldiers, then you don't welcome any stranger. After a while you can justify buying a sword to hang from a nail beside the door to make sure that the strangers know they aren't welcome."

"You sound just like my Dad," Stone said. "Dad wanted to stay and welcome the soldiers. He didn't believe there was anybody he couldn't reason with. Mom wanted to go the City and see what the Council was doing. Justine told my Dad she was going to fetch you to help. She didn't say how, but if you came through the Goddess Tree that would have to mean something." He tried to pick up his pace but Justine wouldn't walk any faster, so if he wanted to hold her hand he needed to stay at their pace.

"It was really scary the way Mom and Dad were arguing. Almost like the Peace had already been broken. They stood out in the rain and talked and talked. All we could do was watch." Stone's voice broke on the last sentence and Patrick was reminded this boy was only a year or so older than Justine. "We waited for ages for you to come, but once they agreed it was like they were driven. Mom had everything packed and the rest of the village followed. They left a note for you on the table. I ran away and came back with some of the others who wanted to fight. We had sticks, but we saw the swords and the way the men in white moved. One of them must have made a mistake because the lead one knocked him down. He didn't even look back when he walked away. The others ran away, but I had to stay and watch." His voice lifted into a wail. "Why did you take so long?"

"Drasil says he can control when I get home, cause I belong there. When I'm coming here, all he can do is get me here when I'm supposed to be here. I'm sorry I was too late."

"So," Patrick said, "you're here in time for something, just not what you expected."

They walked in silence after that. It had been a long time since Patrick had done any distance walking. He'd forgotten how tired he could get just walking. His shoes weren't the best either and his feet ached. Justine must be tired too, but she didn't say anything.

They came on another circle of cottages. These hadn't been burned yet, but they were abandoned. The walls weren't straight. They bowed outward which made them look like they'd been carved from some immense pumpkin.

"I need to take a break and get a drink of water," Patrick said.

"Sit in the shade, and I'll find some water." Stone went into one of the houses and came out with a pitcher and three cups. "They would make us welcome if they were here. It's sort of a basic assumption. We can take what we need and only what we need. When we meet the owner, we'll make it good or pass it on to the next person."

"I like your country, Stone." Patrick sipped on the cool water. "Justine told me about how hospitality is so important here; that feels right to me."

"I used to like it too," Stone said. Justine stood up and poured her water over his head.

"Hey!" Stone shouted. "What's that about?"

"You were getting hot headed again, and I thought you needed cooling off," Justine said. "You're carrying on like this invasion is some personal insult. I don't want to listen to you grumping all the way to the City."

"It isn't your country being destroyed!" Stone shouted. "It isn't you being driven out of your home and not knowing why. You're not the one feeling completely helpless and wondering what you did to deserve this."

"No," Justine said, "you're right, but I'm here, and I plan to help, and complaining about things isn't going to help."

"You sound just like my Mom."

"Good, at least one of us is making sense."

There was a long pause, then Stone started giggling and soon Justine joined him. They laughed until the tears ran down their faces. Then Stone sighed.

"Thank you, friend, I needed that." He stood and collected the pitcher and glasses. "I'll be right back."

"I wouldn't mind some more sensible clothes," Patrick said, "if that's allowed. Mine are just too warm for this climate.

"Let me look." Stone took the dishes back into the cottage

and came out with some clothes. The loose pants and shirt were much more comfortable than the warm clothes that Patrick had been wearing. Stone also had a bag with some bread and cheese in it.

"Let's go."

They stopped a couple more times to drink water. When it was getting dark Stone wanted to rest in one of the villages.

"I don't think that's a good idea," Patrick said. "Those soldiers seem to be concentrating on villages, and we don't want to get caught in one." Stone shrugged and led them off the road a little way into a copse of trees.

Patrick sat down with his back against a tree with smooth bark. Justine sat beside him and put her head on his shoulder. Stone leaned against another tree. Within minutes both children were sleeping. Patrick tried to stay awake to watch, but he couldn't see anything. He finally decided he needed the sleep enough to risk not keeping watch.

He brushed his hand over Justine's hair. He should insist on them going home in the morning. He didn't know that he could do anything. Justine trusted him, but he didn't trust himself. He was afraid they couldn't go home, that they would go to Drasil and it would be just another tree. He was afraid he would let Justine down like he had let Ingrid down.

"God, I don't know if you can hear me from this place," he prayed, "but watch over Justine. I don't care about myself, but I can't lose her." He let his head fall back against the rough bark. "Oh yes, and say hello to Ingrid for me."

The last thing he felt before he slept was the movement of the tree in the wind.

Justine's Journal

Dear Mom, It's so cool, Dad giving me your journal. It's like I'm talking to you. I miss you and I love you. I'm scared too. I don't know what to do about the Pax and Drasil. It's even worse than Kelly's dad. That just sort of happened. This time I have to think about it. They're my friends, but I don't know what to do. I'm just a kid. Maybe Dad can help.

Love you,

Justine.

Chapter Fourteen

The birds woke him before the dawn and he saw the glint of Stone's eyes across the way.

"Some men went by, just a little while ago," the boy said, "I don't know if they were soldiers or villagers."

"We'll wait until it's light before we move on. We want to be able to see who's on the road." Justine had slid down in the night and her head was pillowed on Patrick's leg. He felt every bump under him, and yet his legs were numb. He moved his limbs cautiously and hissed at the pain of returning circulation.

Soon the light was bright enough to see by, and he shook Justine.

"Time to get up, Justine."

"Hmm, what?" She mumbled and stared blearily at Patrick, then Stone. "Oh, right," she said. "I was hoping it was a dream."

"You and me both, kiddo," Patrick pushed himself to his feet and tried to stretch out the worst of the kinks. Justine and Stone both simply stood up and appeared ready for another day of walking. They ate the last of the bread and cheese. Patrick and Stone used one side of the clearing while Justine used the other to attend to nature's call.

"That's just gross," she said. "Remind me never to go camping." She led the way back to the road and started walking. Stone followed and Patrick took up the rear. He tried to keep an ear tuned to noises behind him, but he couldn't hear anything but the crunch of their feet on the sand and gravel of the road.

This land they were walking through looked subtly different from what Patrick was used to. Some of the trees looked familiar, but others had oddities that made them stand out to remind him that he was no longer in the same universe. The rules here might not what he assumed them to be.

Birds called from the forest, but nothing that sounded familiar. The dust from the road lifted from their feet and clogged their noses, but it carried the scent of cloves. Why would a road smell of cloves? The flowers along the side of the road wafted perfumes that didn't quite fit what he expected. He couldn't have said what was different, but he knew they were.

Whatever the odours of the road said, they still had to put one foot in front of the other to walk. Neither he nor Justine were used to walking long distances. Justine started out fine, but she was fading quickly by midmorning. Stone walked with a steady pace just a little bit faster than Patrick or Justine could manage. He kept getting ahead, then would wait impatiently when Justine called for him to slow. Finally, she took his hand to force him to her pace. Patrick saw the look that Stone gave her when she wasn't watching. He sighed and let the two lead down the road and tried not to listen in on their conversation.

At noon, they met the first of the refugees. They were a family walking along with just one bag to hold whatever was left of their lives.

"The men in white came," the man said, "and we welcomed them and gave them water and food. Then they drove us out of our homes and set fire to them. They told us to run to the City and that our land had been claimed by the Kingdom of Graffire. I've never heard of Graffire. I don't know what they want with our land."

"Graffire is to the East," Stone said, "and it doesn't matter what they want with our land, only that they are taking it from us."

The man shrugged. "They'll know what to do in the City."

They walked with the family for a while, but Stone grew impatient with the slow pace and pulled ahead.

"Did you hear that man? He didn't even know our neighbours."

"You do?" asked Justine.

"I know that Graffire is to the East. Rakkikt is to the North. The mountains are to the West and the ocean to the South."

"What direction are we walking then?" asked Justine.

"We're walking west and a little north," Patrick said. "If I'm reading our shadows right."

Stone nodded. "The City is set in the centre of Pax."

They passed more clumps of refugees. None were carrying much, and all told similar stories. The soldiers in white had driven them out of their homes and sent them to the City. They all walked slowly almost shuffling as if they were carrying burdens much greater that the few bags and bundles they had. Stone was impatient with the refugees and finally refused to talk with them. Justine spoke to each new group. She listened as if this was the first time she had heard the tale of sorrow and offered sympathy. All the refugees put their hope in the City.

"Soldiers!" The cry was passed up the road and people scrambled for the bush on the sides of the road. Patrick followed Stone and Justine. He made them hide behind trees. An old tree had fallen and its roots had pulled a huge wall of dirt and stone out of the forest floor. Patrick lay on the trunk and peered through a small gap. He wanted to see what was going on.

A squad of six men in white rode horses. They didn't look threatening; they looked tired and bored. Patrick was sure they were still dangerous. The swords hanging from their belts would be deadly against unarmed villagers.

"People," one of the soldiers called out in a voice so bored Patrick was sure he'd been saying the same thing all day. "You will not be harmed. Go to the City. If you try to return to your homes they will be burned and you will be punished." They walked along a little way and a different soldier called out exactly the same message. Eventually it faded away into the distance.

"At least they aren't killing people," Justine said as they climbed back on the road, but Patrick wasn't too sure. He wondered what this influx of refugees would do to the City, and what the invaders would do when they got there.

They spent another night in the woods, sharing a clearing with a half dozen dispirited families. When Patrick had suggested taking turns to keep watch, he was met with blank stares.

"I'm a light sleeper," Stone said. "I'll sleep between the road and here."

Again, Patrick was stiff when he woke up, but it wasn't as bad. Stone and Justine were already up and talking with the other families. The birds sang in the trees, ignoring the people on the ground. Nobody had lit a fire, so breakfast was cold water and a hunk of bread more stale than fresh.

Patrick was desperate for a cup of coffee.

"We're about a day out from the City," Stone said. "We'll need to watch for my family and the rest of the village."

They set out, passing others on the road. Stone and Justine walked together again while Patrick limped behind. He couldn't remember his feet ever being this sore. Still he saw some people walking in bare feet or in sandals. He was hungry too. Because they shared food with everyone on the road, it meant no one had quite enough. Today Stone was as silent as his namesake, while Justine spoke to everyone, especially the children.

At one of the breaks Patrick took off his shoes and was trying to rub the soreness out of his feet.

"I forgot that you come from a different place," Stone squatted beside him. "Justine tells me she lives in a City with people crowded together like trees in a forest."

"That's as good a way of thinking about it as any other," Patrick said. "I'm not used to walking so much. We have other ways of getting around."

"Yes, the cars that Justine speaks about. Wagons that don't need horses to pull."

"They aren't magic," Patrick said. "They just use different principles."

"Justine called them machines. Like the pump for our well, just more complicated. Do you miss your world?"

"I haven't been gone long enough to miss my world much. I miss coffee in the morning and perhaps a better pair of shoes for walking, but I am more concerned about what is happening here."

"Ah," Stone nodded, "that is good. Justine said we needed your help. She said you were good at finding answers." He looked around him at the clusters of dispirited refugees. "We really need answers." He wandered away again and Patrick decided he'd better have a talk with Justine about why she'd brought him here. The events of the last few days had driven the subject from his mind.

Stone came back with a long stick. He had peeled the bark from one end.

"It won't make your feet hurt less, but it may help keep you moving," he said. Patrick took the stick and levered himself to his feet.

120

"Thanks," he said. After he found a rhythm, the stick did help. He noticed others walking with sticks as well. He also noticed that they all looked a good bit older than him. Patrick shrugged his shoulders. He wasn't going to give up his stick out of pride.

As he listened to Justine talk to the other people on the road, Patrick noticed most of the people on the road knew as little or even less about their world than the first man they had talked to. The invasion from the East was as strange to them as if the rocks had begun walking about. They were a peaceful people, but they were also insular. Only a handful had ever been to the City. The people headed to a new and strange place expecting welcome and aid, because that was simply the way things were. Patrick wondered if the people in the City would have the same ideas.

He was beginning to think that Pax, as pleasant as it was, was ripe for an invasion. They had their Peace, but there was something missing. It reminded him of the conversation he had with Daniel what felt like a lifetime ago. The Peace was there, but it was habit. They didn't know the reason behind their custom. Before he judged them too harshly Patrick wondered what habits he took for granted.

He was so deep in thought he didn't see Stone and Justine run ahead until he heard the commotion. A man who was much taller than Patrick was holding on to Stone, while Justine was hugging a woman who was short and powerfully built. When he caught up to them Justine made introductions.

"Dad, this is Davvad and Marisha," she said.

"Please call me Patrick," he said and took Davvad's hand.

"We have heard much about you," Davvad said in a deep voice. "Welcome, and be at peace in our home and hearth. Though the welcome is little enough in these times."

"I am glad to meet Justine's friends," Patrick said. "I feel I know you. I have heard so many stories about you. I am also glad to be made welcome in trying times or not. It is easy to welcome people when times are good. In these difficult days, you do me honour to make me welcome."

"You see?" Davvad said. "You see? This is how it is done. This is a man who thinks." He waved at the crowd around him.

"My family. I try to teach them the way, but it is so easy to fall into easy habits."

The big man turned and headed up the road, "Walk with me, friend Patrick, and we will talk of these difficult days."

Patrick walked ahead with Davvad who stayed quiet for a long time. Patrick just let the silence settle into him. He found he no longer strained to hear the sounds of approaching marauders; now he listened to the songs of birds in the trees beside the road and the murmur of countless conversations going on around him.

"The Goddess must be displeased with us to allow us to be thrown off our land."

"We must learn to fight and defend ourselves like other people."

"If we are patient the Goddess will come and save us."

"I'm hungry."

"I'm tired."

"How far to the City?"

"What will we find there?"

The words swirled around him and painted a picture of a dispirited and defeated people.

"You hear it," Davvad said, "the pain of my people."

"Yes," Patrick said.

"We have been lost for a while." Davvad paused for a long while. "It isn't that the Goddess didn't promise we would prosper because of my ancestor's desire for peace, but she also didn't say that it would be easy. When we first changed the name of our land to Pax, there were people who went out to the nations around us to explain who we had become. Trade was constant and many people made their fortunes through the peace, and not just in Pax.

"Yet as the Peace settled into our bones we travelled less. If you are willing to share whatever you have with your neighbour and them with you; there is little need for luxury. Someone always has something that will do. We stopped travelling to other lands, and in time we discouraged it for fear that our children would bring back foreign ideas."

"Peace and hospitality stopped being a choice and became a custom," Patrick said.

"Yes, that is it exactly!" Davvad said. "but while a custom will carry us in good times, choosing peace every day creates a depth that a habit will not. I fear that most of our people do not have the courage to live in peace if it means to die for peace."

"We have some of the same problems where I'm from," Patrick said. "We are a much more violent people, but we desire peace. Yet most of us are unwilling to take the risks that lead to peace."

"So, friend Patrick, tell me about your land."

"It is too complicated to fit into an easy discussion. I think you may get more from Justine. She sees deeper than I do."

"Some of our young people want to learn to fight these men in white." Davvad looked at Patrick from the corner of his eyes.

"Learning to fight effectively takes a lot of training. More, it takes a willingness to let a little bit of your humanity go. It is very hard to fight evil without becoming evil in turn."

"Ah, you are wise indeed. I will think on this."

Late in the day they saw the buildings of the City in the distance. Even from this distance Patrick could see the vast camp surrounding the City. At first he thought it was the invaders, but then he realized it was a different kind of invasion. It was the refugees.

They slept the night huddled under the shelter of the trees. Justine curled up with her head on Patrick's leg, while Stone slept nearby. The boy seemed to be both more relaxed and yet more tightly wound now that they had joined up with his family. Patrick hadn't sorted out all the kids yet. Risha and Hisen were the couple that got married; Risha was just beginning to show her pregnancy. The two girls, Tammi and Cinda he thought belonged to other families. They were about Justine's age. The girls were a mix of shy and extroverted. They ran and chattered to all the children in the group. Justine and Stone talked and played with them, but they wouldn't say a word to Patrick or any other adult. Patrick couldn't remember which girl was which, and he didn't want to upset them by asking. Stone's little brother, Boddi, was a boy who couldn't be more than four. He spent his time in the company of his mother mostly because he was attached by a leash to his mother's waist. He hid behind her anytime that Patrick looked at him.

Marisha was the essence of practicality. She had a bag full of the small useful items that others forgot or had misplaced. One of those things was a flint and steel to light a fire. They didn't need it for heat, but the cheeriness of its flames was very welcome.

Patrick listened to the conversations around him. Now that they had stopped for the night, the talk had become more philosophical in tone. Some wanted to change and others were hoping to return to the comfortable old ways. Yet the tone of both groups was one of fear. This was not a situation they had ever imagined and they were struggling to maintain any kind of equilibrium. They all were putting their hopes in the City. A few talked about the Goddess, but more of her expectations of them than in any hope she would intervene in the crisis. Patrick couldn't get any more understanding of her role than the sense that somehow she had established the Peace. He wondered where Darsh fit into the scheme of things. It was probably a good question to ask Davvad.

The big man was the quietest person Patrick had ever met. They had walked for miles without saying anything, but somehow in Davvad's presence the silence was full of things almost heard. Patrick, who was used to talking or listening to other people talk constantly, found the silence a powerful experience.

Even with the warmth of fire and conversation Patrick was feeling out of sorts. He still hadn't had time to pry Justine away from Stone long enough to ask her what she had hoped he could do for her friends. For all his listening in on the discussion around him and his talk with Davvad, he didn't think he understood what was going on any better. Most of the people were simply following the people in front of them. They were too much in shock to do anything else. It worried him that the soldiers in white were sending the people to the City. They were all doing what the invading force wanted them to and not thinking about why. He felt out of his depth in this situation. He wanted to be home eating spaghetti and talking with Lee and Justine.

Patrick wished the tree he was leaning against was Drasil and that he and Justine could be whirled away home, but the tree stayed silent and he fell asleep with a root in his back and the weight of Justine's head on his knee.

Justine's Journal

I wasn't sure what Dad would think of Marisha and Davvad and their family, but I didn't think he would fit in quite so quickly. Even Stone is listening to him! I'm still scared, but I think I'm supposed to be here. It's like there's something pushing me along. I wish you were here, Mom.

Love you,

Justine

Chapter Fifteen

Morning came too soon. More of the birds started singing before the sun was up, but the people didn't want to stir until the light of the sun shone into their camp. Patrick went to talk to Davvad.

"Get everyone to gather as much loose wood as they can carry," he said.

Davvad just looked at him.

"The people of the City will offer hospitality," Patrick said, "because that is the way you folks do things, but it doesn't mean you don't take basic action to care for yourselves. From the size of that camp outside the City, there won't be much in the way of water, food, or fuel available. We can't do anything about the water or food, but we can carry wood."

"You are right," Davvad said "we need to be as self-sufficient as we can, and not impose on others." He went over to Marisha.

"The loose wood might be happier as firewood to heat food for the people of the City. Marisha looked thoughtful, then nodded. The two of them wandered through the camp talking to others. Stone and Justine were already gathering sticks and bundling them for the smaller children.

"Spread out," Stone said. "The sticks further away will want to come to the City. It won't matter if we take some time to pick up the wood. We'll be at the City soon enough anyway." The youngsters automatically followed his suggestions. Marisha had a large ball of twine in her bag. Justine showed others how to tie the bundles. She left the other children and came over to Patrick.

"I never thought that all that gardening we did would come in handy, but at least I can tie a bundle of sticks." She held his hand for a bit while they watched the other refugees slowly move to gather wood.

"What did you and Stone's dad talk about yesterday?" she asked. "Am I allowed to know?"

"Davvad is afraid that his people have lost their centre. They are good at being peaceful, but they have forgotten the reason for the Peace."

"So what do we do?"

"I don't know," Patrick said. "We go along for now. If we are supposed to be here there will be something for us to do only we can accomplish. At least that's how it works in the books." He shrugged, "In reality, I don't think it will be that simple." He looked down at Justine and felt a rush of fierce pride and protectiveness. "What were you hoping I could do here?"

"Marisha and Davvad were arguing about whether to go to the City. Davvad had been there before and he didn't want to go back. Marisha was worried about what would happen when the soldiers came. Davvad said the only good thing about the City was the Library, and I thought about what your boss said you did. If anyone could help in the Library, it would be you. Then Stone wanted to start an army and Davvad and Marisha were almost fighting. You always knew what to say to me to make me feel better. I thought maybe you could fix things." Justine took a deep breath and looked at Patrick. "You will help, won't you?"

"I don't know if I can read in this world," Patrick said.

"Oh no!" Justine looked at him in horror. "What do we do now?"

"I guess we'd better find out if I can read."

"Wait here, I'll ask Marisha." She left Patrick wondering how Marisha would know if he could read, but she came back a moment later with a little book.

"Look at this." She handed him the book.

He opened it to the first page. "When the world was ripe" he read out loud, "the Mother plucked it from the Tree and gave it to her children to rule. Lyylen was as fair at the sunrise and she chose to bring peace to the world they had been given and the people who lived on it, but her brother Naxic said 'Peace is false, the world is won through struggle and pain.' He was silver and black like the full moon." Patrick closed the book and looked at Justine. "I guess I can read OK." He handed the book to Justine stared at it for a while.

"It's all old mythy language like the Bible," she said. "I can't make out what's real and what's just people hoping is real." She gave it back to him. "Marisha said you can hang on to it, but be careful, it's been in Davvad's family for donkey's ages."

"Well, I'll look at it some more later, and I'll do what I can at the Library."

"I'd better go help some more." Justine hugged him. "Thanks, Dad."

Patrick watched Justine go take charge of the bundle tying again and wondered what he had done to deserve all the thanks Justine gave him. People were getting ready to set out now. Some were carrying huge bundles of sticks while others carried nothing. These folks were not that much different that the people he was used to at home. He went and picked up the bundle Justine had made for him.

"Thanks, Justine."

"For what?" she asked.

"Just for being you." She rewarded him with a brilliant smile.

If he had thought walking was tiring, walking with the huge bundle of sticks was a hundred times worse. He kept shifting the bundle from one shoulder to another. He saw the truly mammoth bundle Davvad carried with apparently no effort at all and determined that he wasn't going to complain. *There's a use for macho competition after all.*

At about midday they met a City official who directed them off to one section of the camp.

"Welcome and be at peace in our home and hearth. Tents will be made available to you and there is a well. Trenches have been dug for toilets, use them. We don't need to have disease making the rounds along with everything else." He didn't say anything about the bundles of sticks, but Patrick thought he gave an approving nod.

The tent City was even more depressing than the road. People sat listlessly in front of their tents. Some eyed the bundles of sticks, but most just stared at the ground. They looked like a people already defeated.

What was worse was the group of young men only a few years older than Stone who stopped them to stare at Patrick and Justine. These boys wore ragged clothes and frowns. They didn't look friendly.

"They look like the invaders," one said.

"What are they doing here?" another asked.

"They are my guests," Davvad said.

"Is that wise?" the first one said. "They may be spies."

"Whether it is wise or not, they are my guests."

"They should be kept separate, maybe questioned."

"Are you suggesting that I should break the Peace?"

There was a long uncomfortable silence, then the youths stood aside one by one. They still stared at Patrick with suspicion.

"That's going to be trouble," he said to Justine. "Try not to wander alone."

"They wouldn't break the Peace," Justine said firmly.

"It isn't that they will decide to," Patrick said, "but one thing will lead to another and the Peace may very well get broken. I don't want you getting broken with it."

Justine looked like she was going to argue with him, but they arrived at the tents designated for their use. They were really just canvass draped over poles. There had no floor and the door was just a flap without even ties. Davvad and his family had been given two.

"I think the tents would be happiest if you stayed in one and my family in the other," he said.

"No, Davvad," Patrick said, "let Risha and Hishen stay in the second one. We'll make do in one or the other." Davvad nodded and began prowling around the tents. He adjusted some ropes here and moved a few sticks and soon the tents were looking a good deal straighter. He discovered that one tent had an extra flap that divided off a tiny room to one side.

"This tent insists that you and Justine make use of this room."

"Thank you, friend Davvad," Patrick said, "we will be most comfortable."

"Dad," said Justine, "you're even beginning to talk like him. It's kind of scary."

"I'm trying to learn how this system works," Patrick said. "Davvad seems to have as good a grip on that as anybody. Like any community, the idea is to keep as many people content while still leaving space for individuals. I think they have the comfortable part down, but a lot of them have stopped trying to grow."

"The ideal is for everyone to be self-sufficient." Davvad turned around taking in the camp. "But the community is responsible for making up any lack. In our own villages, this works very well, but I fear the strain the invaders are putting us under."

"I saw many people who looked like they'd just given up."

"I was more worried about those who looked like they had given up on the Peace." Davvad put a hand on Justine's shoulder. "Please don't walk about by yourself, or you either," he said to Patrick. "While it wouldn't be your fault, I would hate for you to be at the centre of the Peace being broken."

"Justine and I have already talked about this," Patrick said. "We will be careful."

Their little corner of the tent was stifling, but there was room for both Patrick and Justine to stretch out. The ground was uneven enough to make Patrick wish for a tree to lean against.

"Dad," Justine said in the dimness of the tent, "are we going to get home again?"

"You always got home before."

"I was never this far from Drasil before."

"Well, we're here now, and I'm sure there are things we can do to be useful." He sighed and wondered why he'd let them leave Yggdrasil behind. Justine and Stone had swept him along while he was still trying to adjust to the reality of this world.

"I can't think of anything. Maybe it's time to focus on whatever I can do, but I don't even know how to find the Library."

"Neither do I, but Davvad does." Justine said.

"I'll talk with him about it in the morning," Patrick said. "Just be yourself and what will be will be."

"OK, Dad." She reached out and gripped his hand. "I'm glad you're here with me."

"So am I."

In the morning, Patrick was awakened by the shouting of children at play. He could hear Stone and Justine's voices mixed in. He crawled out of the little room and stretched until he heard his joints pop.

Outside a mob of children ran about. Every once in a while two would stop and talk, then either part quietly or one would chase the other madly. Stone's little brother must have changed his mind, because suddenly the whole group shouted in glee and chased him down.

A few minutes later a wagon came through the street serving up a thick gruel for breakfast. Patrick heard grumbling from some of the people in the other tents. Obviously, they were tired of gruel. He had to admit it didn't look terribly appetizing.

"Thank you for your kindness," Patrick said as he took his bowl.

"New here, right?" the man who was serving it said. "You won't be so thankful in a week."

"If there is anything I can do to help," Patrick replied. "You can find me here. My daughter is also good with food."

"Grain is all we have in quantity enough to feed everyone," the man said, "and we're likely to run out of that soon enough too."

"Do you have spices? Herbs? Even honey?" Patrick said, "A little can add variety, and variety may stem complaints."

"I'll speak to the quartermaster." The man clicked at the horses and drove them on perhaps twenty yards before stopping. Patrick could hear the groans, but no one refused the food.

After the gruel was done the children went back to play, but they quickly lost energy, sitting on the ground and stared into space.

"Justine," Patrick called, "I have an idea."

"Sure, Dad," she said, "what is it?"

"Have you ever played Rock, Paper, Scissors?"

"Sure."

"It might be a good game to keep the children occupied without wearing them out."

"I don't know if they know what scissors are."

"You could use knife instead."

"OK, I'll give it a try." She went over to Stone and dropped cross legged beside him. Patrick watched her show him the game. Stone caught on quickly. When Stone knew the game thoroughly, Justine and Stone started to juggle. Patrick had seen

Justine practice at home, but this was different. They juggled stones separately at first, then started to toss them to one another. Stone would pretend to drop a rock, catch it on his foot and toss it back in the air.

Children stood up and watched, some began cheering the more spectacular moves. Justine picked her stones out of the air while Stone juggled. He tossed one, two three rocks high in the air and caught them. One, two, the third one never came down and there were "oohs" and "ahs" from the children. Patrick saw him slip a rock into his pocket. Then Stone and Justine sat down and began playing Rock, Paper, Knife. The children crowed around as Justine explained the rules. Soon children as far as he could see were playing Rock, Paper, Scissors, only with their two fingers together to make a knife instead of scissors.

"It looks like a game we played when I was young," Davvad said, as he settled down beside Patrick. "It is easy to learn, but hard to win."

"It involves thinking like your opponent," Patrick said. "It is a very old game where I'm from. We have people who are masters of the game and spend their lives studying it."

"It's good the children have some occupation. Boredom leads to more complaint."

Patrick looked around. "Where is the firewood we carried in?"

"Some men in a wagon came last night and asked if they might use it. Since they promised to feed us hot food each day, I gave it to them," Davvad said.

"Perhaps the older ones could go and fetch more," Patrick said. "If they are collecting firewood from the refugees, they must be running very short."

"I fear the City is running short of a great many things, not the least of which is patience. None of the City people have seen any of the soldiers in white. It isn't that they don't believe the refugees, but seeing for themselves will shift their view. Right now, they are hoping that this is a very temporary situation."

"You've been busy this morning," Patrick said.

"I have a friend who lives in the City. His name got me past the fence. He is concerned, but not perhaps for the right

132

reasons. He is afraid that the people have forgotten the Goddess; I fear that they remember Her, but only to beg her for help.

"Is he the priest from Risha's wedding?" Patrick asked. "I was curious about what she said about the ceremony."

"Our weddings aren't so much a ceremony as a recognition of a choice already made. We are bound by our choices, not our words."

"Would you be able to arrange for me to meet him?"

"He has already asked to meet you." Davvad sighed. "I mentioned that you both came from the Goddess' Tree and he has it in his head that you are some kind of sign."

"That can be a dangerous role for a human being. What if we are the wrong kind of sign? Still I would like to talk to him."

"I will take you tomorrow."

Justine's Journal

Hi Mom, it was fun teaching that old game to the kids. We played it at camp. It felt good to be doing something. It is so sad in the camp. It's like those shows on TV where the kids are starving and just stand around. No one is starving, but the food is really boring.

Love you,

Justine

Chapter Sixteen

The next day Patrick was again wakened by the sound of children. They were playing Wolf or Guest. One of the little ones made a mistake that sent the whole crowd running down the road. He was sure there were more than yesterday.

"Stone has been dropping hints to the little kids," Justine said, as she handed him a steaming cup. "It's not coffee, but it's hot."

"It's not bad," he said after a sip. "Thanks, Justine."

"Why has Stone been dropping hints?"

"The best part of the game is when someone makes a mistake and changes their mind. Then we get to chase them and tickle them, but the older kids never make mistakes so it isn't much fun. Stone is convincing the littlest ones to make a mistake and get chased."

"What do the little kids get out of it?"

"Stone spends time with them. He plays the games with them the other big kids won't. So, when are we going to meet this friend of Davvad's?" Justine said.

"I didn't know that you were listening."

"Rock, Paper, Knife is a quiet game," Justine said. "I would like to know what they can tell me about Drasil."

"I'll have to ask Davvad if his invitation includes you."

"You know he isn't going to say no."

"You know, Justine, just because the Pax live by a code of hospitality and peace, doesn't mean that we can just barge our way in. That's what these soldiers in white are doing. They're taking advantage of the generosity of this land, and repaying it with violence."

"I don't want to impose," Justine said, "I just want to talk."

"I know, Justine, but we need to be careful, because it would be so easy to push into places we don't belong because the people of Pax don't want to say no." He waved at the camp. "This whole place is an example of that. Most of the people here are just assuming the City will take care of them, because that's what they would do if people showed up lost and hungry at their door. What they haven't done is imagined what it would be like if twenty people showed up and camped on their doorstep. That's why they aren't thinking about what they can do to help, because they would be insulted if their guests offered to help."

"Marisha lets me help all the time."

"Did she always?"

"Well, not the first few...oh." Justine put her hand to her mouth. "I told her that I liked to help, and I wanted to learn. I put her under guest obligation to let me help. I need to go and talk to her. Sorry Dad." She ran off toward the tents.

Patrick tried not to listen, but the gruel wagon had passed through and the children had moved to Rock, Paper, Knife.

"I didn't mean to insult you, Marisha," Justine was saying. "I really am used to helping my Dad."

"Sweetheart," Marisha said, "I was a little taken aback, but it is the host's obligation to make their guest feel comfortable, and to tell the truth, I appreciated the help. Cooking for my family is quite a task, and the girls are young yet for that much responsibility. Having you meant the little ones wanted the privilege of working in the kitchen too. It made more mess at first, but they're turning into little cooks."

"But I didn't want to hurt your honour!" Justine cried.

"There, there, you didn't. You honoured me with yourself and the truth. You taught me a great deal as well. Maybe guest and host should be more equal and trade back and forth rather than forcing the guest to be indebted to the host."

"I never thought about being indebted. I just like helping."

"I know you do, sweetheart, and you could be one of our family, but there are some who would rather be guests forever."

"So how do we change it?"

"Change what?"

"All these people here who are thinking that they are just guests and will insult the City people if they offer to help. The gruel man said they are already running short of grain."

"Ah, that is a much bigger question than the two of us can answer," Marisha said.

"But if no one tries, then nothing will change. Somebody has to start."

"You're young, Justine—"

"I know I'm young, but you remember the bruises I had when I came back? Let me tell you the story..."

"That's a great game you taught us, Patrick."

"Uh, thanks, Stone."

"Sorry, did I interrupt your listening?"

"Yes, but that is not a bad thing. I was being rude to listen in."

"It's how we learn. We listen in on our parent's discussions. If they really want us not to hear they go and stand in the rain to talk."

"I see, and do you let them listen in on all your arguments?"

"They complain," Stone said, laughing, "that they have no choice and try to send us out in the rain."

"So did you and Justine stand in the rain?"

Stone went red, then thoughtful. "No, the kitchen was strangely empty while we talked. Do you mind?"

"Mind what?"

"That I love your daughter."

Patrick let the silence continue while he thought. He remembered how Stone had led them from the village. He'd always listened to Justine and took her seriously. Stone began to fidget, and Patrick decided he liked and admired this boy.

"It isn't my place to guard my daughter's heart," he said finally. "It is hers to give or to keep, but that is true for you as well. If you choose to give your heart to Justine, then so be it. Just remember that she is young yet. Also remember this, if you deliberately cause my daughter pain, then we will have a very different conversation."

"I would never hurt Justine."

"Don't make promises you can't keep, son," Patrick said. "We all hurt other people, the ones we love the most. That's why we forgive each other. Just don't plan on it."

"I think I understand."

"Understand what?" Justine said.

"That your feelings are like a delicate flower that must be preserved," Stone said in a teasing tone.

She stuck her tongue out at him and wandered off to join

136

another group of children.

Stone looked at Patrick with a sad face, and he knew the boy had spoken lightly to keep the depth of his feelings from Justine. Patrick put his hand on Stone's shoulder in silent sympathy. Then Stone ran off on some errand of his own.

Davvad came up and waved at Patrick.

"Time to go."

Patrick went over to Justine.

"I'm heading out with Davvad. I'll ask his friend if he would like to talk to you too."

"Thanks, Dad." Patrick looked around at the litter on the ground. He bent down to whisper to Justine.

"See if you can invent a game that involves cleaning the place up. Garbage can harbour disease."

"Sure thing." She went back to the game, and Patrick followed Davvad away down the road. He looked at the other tents. Some were practically falling over and were surrounded by the detritus of a depressed people. Most of the adults just slumped in front of their tents. This close to Davvad and Marisha's tent most of the children were playing with the group that had attached itself to Justine and Stone. The children there were playing Rock, Paper, Knife endlessly.

"It's sad what we have come to," Davvad said.

"It is sad, but mostly because it is so unnecessary." Patrick gave Davvad a synopsis of Justine's talk with Marisha.

"Ah, Marisha mentioned this to me. We are used to being guest or host, and not mixing the obligations, but I can see that this is a problem here. We will talk about it further."

They got to the place where great kettles of gruel cooked over fires. There didn't seem to be much firewood left to heat such large kettles. One of the men came over to talk to Patrick.

"You're the one who wanted to help."

"That's right."

"We're getting low on firewood. We won't have enough to heat the meal for tonight. He brought out a couple of tiny bags and held them out to Patrick. What would you add to the gruel?"

Patrick stopped and sniffed at each bag in turn. The first smelled like mustard.

"I don't think this one," he said handing it back. The next was a lot like cinnamon." This would be good, but not too much." The last one reminded him of turkey stuffing. "This is nice, but for the evening meal."

The man shrugged and said "The quartermaster doesn't care as long as the people get fed. I'll try the sage tonight." He walked back to the makeshift kitchen and poured the contents of the little bag into one of the kettles.

Davvad looked at him with a raised eyebrow and Patrick grinned suddenly. They walked along the road and came to a gate that had been strung across the road. A couple of men in sashes stood by.

"I am taking friend Patrick here to Brother Raston." The one man shrugged while the other said what was obviously a well-practised speech.

"The City has already extended you guest rights. Please remember that each person is already contributing to keeping you comfortable and fed. If you're hungry or need something, come back to us so we can make sure there is enough for everyone."

"Thank you," Patrick said. "I will keep that in mind."

The man nodded and they walked through.

"The City operates under slightly different rules than we do," Davvad explained as they walked. "The country folk took to the Peace the first day, the rest of the three years was the City folk trying to be sure that no one was going to cheat them."

"So they use money?"

"Money?" said Davvad. "Oh yes, they use money, and count it, and horde it, but for all that, they are still bound by the Peace in their own way. Neighbours will borrow back and forth much like we do, but strangers to the City will be directed to the guest houses where they will be given food and shelter and whatever else they need. Those are maintained by the Priests, and everyone in the City gives according to their ability for their upkeep. Brother Raston runs one such guest house."

The City was busy and for the most part clean. Patrick saw young people with carts picking up what trash there was. There were stores, but while the ones that sold luxuries were still well stocked, the cloth and food markets were almost empty.

"Most of the residents of the City are eating gruel as well," Davvad said. "It would be impolite to eat better than their guests."

They came to a large building that Patrick would have taken for a hotel back home. There was a courtyard in front overrun with listless people. They seemed even more depressed than the people in the tent City. They sat or stood and watched while the people of the City went about their business. The young men who had accosted them on their way into the City stepped out in front of Patrick, blocking him from entering the courtyard.

"You bring this spy into our midst?" the leader said. He was taller than Stone, but he didn't look much older. Harder maybe. Patrick wondered how growing up in the City would change a person.

"He is my guest, and the guest of the City."

"We need to be more careful about who we allow as guests."

A man in frayed robes came bustling out.

"Pardon, pardon," he said, "I was busy with some question of space. A family were being very polite, but wanted more space to sleep."

Patrick looked at the young men who were still glaring at him.

"You wish to ask me questions?" he said.

"Someone needs to," the leader said.

"Now, Barsta, that is not polite," said the man in the robes.

"Brother Raston," the youth said, "we need to know..."

"There are better heads than yours trying to figure this out."

"Pardon, Brother, but I was talking to this man," Patrick tried to keep the annoyance out of his voice. He turned back to the young man. "The kitchens are running out of firewood."

"What of it?" another youth said. "They are the hosts. It is the City's concern."

"There is a forest not far from here," Patrick replied. "For every day that the kitchens don't run out of wood, I will answer one question. Only one, mind you, so you'd better think about it."

"We will need to ask if we don't understand something," Barsta said.

"Fair enough."

"Come, we have some work to do." Barsta looked at Patrick. "Where will we find you?"

"I can come here after breakfast each day." Barsta nodded. "Be welcome, then." He led the group of youth out toward the gate.

"I'm not sure that was a wise idea." Brother Raston said.

"Would you rather they hung around here and harassed everyone they thought looked different enough to be suspicious? Now they have something to occupy them, and they might even learn something. Besides, the kitchens really do need more firewood."

"You are a stranger here," Brother Raston began.

"And you are going to question me." Patrick interrupted, "Do you really begrudge the boys that same opportunity?"

"I'm a representative of the Goddess herself..."

"So are you not bound by her laws?"

The Brother puffed up until Patrick thought he was going to explode, but the explosion never came. Instead the man let out his breath and hung his head.

"Am I going to need to be schooled on this forever?" he asked apparently of the air around him. "I am Brother Raston, Welcome and be at peace in our home and hearth. Speak freely for the Goddess watches between us."

"I am glad of your welcome, Brother Raston." Patrick said.

"As am I," said Davvad. "Friend Patrick has a different mind than us, but I think we need to hear from him more than ever."

"The Goddess did send you to us," said the Brother as he led Patrick and Davvad to a tiny office.

"Pardon me?" Patrick said. "You think the Goddess sent us?"

"From what Davvad said, you came from her tree."

"That doesn't mean that she sent us. In the stories, I know, being sent by God is not always a good thing for the person being sent."

"Let's just say that she allowed you to come, so She must have something She wishes us to learn from you."

140

Patrick sighed.

"Ask your questions, and I will answer what I can."

Brother Raston poured out what looked like the same tea Justine had given him that morning and handed them cups. Patrick looked at him over the steaming tea. The frayed robes made him look older, but Patrick didn't see many wrinkles and the Brother's hair was dark and full. Patrick felt a discordant energy from the man. He thought of the interchange with Barsta and his friends. Brother Raston lived by the Peace, but it didn't seem to fit him comfortably.

"So where to start?" the Brother said. "Did you meet Her?"

"You mean the Goddess?" Patrick said. "No, we may have arrived through her Tree, but Justine calls the tree Drasil and says the being we met there was Drasil."

"Ah." The Brother took a long sip of the tea, and made a face. "It is much nicer with honey." He shook his head, "But that's neither here nor there. Have you heard of Yggdrasil?"

"I vaguely remember hearing the name. I think a country in our past had a tree called Yggdrasil in their mythology."

"Mythology?"

"It's what we call a religion when no one believes in it anymore."

"You come from a stranger place than I thought."

"The Goddess's Tree is called Yggdrasil in the oldest texts. In some versions, it is even older than the Goddess herself. So, that your daughter calls the Tree Drasil is indeed an indication that the Goddess is involved."

"I don't see that," Patrick said. "She was grieving and lonely and made friends with a tree."

"A tree that just happened to span the world."

"It was in her schoolyard."

"That must be a blessed school."

"Not particularly."

"So she just made friends with Yggdrasil. When did she first travel here?"

"Hmm, it's been at least a month or two. She was here before Risha's wedding."

"That was four months ago," Davvad said.

"Hmmm, time must be different here," Patrick said. "I'm sure it hasn't been four months since she told me about the wedding."

"She was there?" Brother Raston said. "I didn't see her."

"She would have been dressed like the other children. You probably wouldn't have noticed her in the mob."

"What an opportunity missed!"

"She wouldn't make much more of your questions then I do," Patrick said. "As far as she is concerned, the tree is Drasil. I never heard her speak much of the Goddess, except at the end of the story about Darsh."

"Ah, Darsh," said the Brother, "the author of our Peace."

"You have a different story?" asked Patrick.

"The old texts differ. In some versions Darsh is reunited with his family and lives to a ripe old age."

"And in the others?"

"In the others he is killed for his insolence and the land rises in rebellion to punish the murderers."

"Which do you think is the true one?"

"Well," Brother Raston said, "when someone breaks the Peace with violence they are sent out of the City and given to the land. On the rare occasions that someone returns it is assumed they were in fact innocent."

"That's a City thing," Davvad said.

Patrick wasn't sure. He remembered Justine's story about Thamos.

"What about after the Peace was concluded?" Patrick asked. "How was the Pax protected from the surrounding countries that would have seen you as easy pickings?"

"I'm not sure," Brother Raston said, "it isn't part of the scriptures. There may be some old scrolls that talk of it. It isn't really my strong point."

"I would think, in this current situation, it might be useful to know."

"All the Brothers are too busy with the refugees to spend time looking up obscure texts."

"Justine brought me here to do exactly that. It is what I'm good at."

142

"I'm sure I could get you access to the Library, but as I said, all the Brothers are busy with the people from the villages. They won't have much time to help."

"How many villages have been abandoned?"

"As far as we can tell, all the ones to the East and about half of the ones to the North and south. We have started to get a few people from the West, but none of them have met the invaders."

"So most of the country is crowded in around the City?"

"Yes, and we are just not equipped to deal with it. There have always been fires or droughts or storms that brought some people here for a time, but this mob is new."

"If the invaders are from Graffire, what does Rakkikt think of this mess?"

"It isn't any concern of theirs," the Brother said. "The Goddess will deal with it."

"They may not see it that way," Patrick said. "This is going to upset the balance of power in a big way. Let me tell you. If you think being invaded is bad, having two different countries fighting it out on your soil is worse."

"You know this from experience?" asked Brother Raston.

"I've seen it in the history of my people time and again."

"The Goddess didn't punish the offenders?"

"Our God doesn't get directly involved in these issues. I think He's afraid that it will lead to other problems."

"Interesting, what kind of problems?"

"Like being so dependent on God that we wouldn't work to solve our own problems."

"You must come from a strange land indeed."

"I'm beginning to think so."

"I will ask if you can have access to the library," Brother Raston said. "In the meantime, I'm afraid I have much work to do."

"I will be here tomorrow," Patrick said.

"Yes, right." The Brother turned to his desk and Davvad led Patrick back out to the street.

"I think you asked more questions than he did," Davvad said.

"You're right," Patrick admitted. "I didn't mean to upset him, but I don't want to be the messenger of any God or Goddess."

"Yes, Raston does tend to see the Goddess as the solution for every problem large or small."

"So what do you think?"

"I think, that until the Goddess shows up, we had better get to work and find a way."

"Now, that I can understand," Patrick said. "I really would like to get into those archives, but we also need to give some meaningful thing for people to do to help themselves or there is going to be trouble."

"Trouble?"

"Where I come from, this many people in one place without enough food or shelter is cause for concern. All you need is a couple of people to start complaining to start a landslide."

They left the City, waving at the men at the gate. As they were walking back to their tent they noticed something different. Children swarmed all over the place, straightening tents and picking up trash. The closer they got to their tent the greater the activity, until they got 'home' and found Justine and Stone sitting on the ground with their heads in their hands. They saw Patrick and Davvad and ran over to them.

"You asked us to get the children to clean up, and I remembered the cabin contests that we used to have at camp." Justine said, "So, I said the camp looked sad it was such a mess, and wouldn't it be delighted if we had a contest to choose the cleanest tent."

"And I promised them a really great prize if they had the cleanest tent," Stone said, "and now they want to know what the prize is."

"And we can't be judges because we live in a tent too and it wouldn't be fair," Justine said.

"So everyone is madly cleaning and tidying and we don't have any prize," Stone said.

"Or a judge," Justine said. "Please tell me you have something as a prize."

Davvad looked at Patrick and grinned. "A different stone

will start a different kind of landslide."

"I see that." Patrick said. "Justine, what happened to my shirt that I was wearing before I changed?"

"It's in a bag in the tent somewhere."

"How about you go and find it, without making too much of a mess in the tent."

Justine and Stone took off into the tent.

"I think I have the prize covered, but we still need a judge. Any ideas?"

"Perhaps one of the City officials will agree to act as judge," Davvad said. "I will ask." He turned and headed back down the road.

Justine came out waving his shirt.

"Here it is, but if we give it away, what will we do tomorrow?"

"We don't give it away; we give away the privilege of hanging it outside your tent. I haven't seen any cloth quite this bright white, so it will stand out."

Stone snapped his fingers and vanished. He came back with Patrick's stick. In a few seconds, they had the shirt tied to the stick and had a respectable flag.

"Good idea, Stone," Justine said, and Stone beamed.

"Now we just wait and see if Davvad can find a judge."

It wasn't that long before Davvad returned with a young man in tow.

"Patrick, meet Garad. He is a junior inspector of buildings in the City. He's been counting tents, but has agreed to judge our little contest."

"Thank you, Garard," Justine said, "we so need a judge who is wise and impartial."

"What am I judging?" he asked.

"I told the other kids that the tents would be judged first on cleanliness, second on appearance, and third on how they honoured their hosts."

Garad nodded at each item and his eyes widened a little at the last.

"I believe that I am prepared to take on this task," he said, "and what award do I give to the winner? We have no great reserves to give extra food."

"That's the best part," Patrick explained, and showed Garad the flag. "The prize is the honour of flying this white flag. As long as their tent is the cleanest they keep the flag."

Garad grinned. "A worthy prize indeed. Let me begin." He began touring through the tent area, muttering to himself. Then wandered off down the road.

"I hope he knows not to award the flag to us."

"I don't believe that will be an issue, today," Marisha said coming out of the tent, "but I would like it to be an issue tomorrow. We can do much better than this. Stone groaned, but Justine elbowed him.

"Set a good example."

Soon Boddi was picking up and tidying while Stone and Justine were sweeping and rearranging.

"Don't throw out the trash until I've looked at it," Marisha said. "I might be able to use it." The tents looked very different by the time Garad returned.

"I have chosen a winner for today, though your tent is much improved." He picked up the flag and walked back up the street. Patrick and the others followed him and soon there was a parade of whispering children and quite a few adults behind him.

He stopped at a tent that was immaculately square, the ground swept free of the slightest bit of trash. More, they had somehow found a board and written on it with charcoal. "In praise of generosity."

Garad made a ceremony of handing the flag to the oldest child who grinned as if she had been given gold coins.

The crowd soon dispersed with children planning what they were going to improve for the next day.

"I believe that I will come tomorrow to judge again. This has been a most pleasant hour. Thank you for the opportunity."

Patrick listened to Justine and Stone plotting all the way back, but he watched the amount of activity in their block of the tent City. All around them the children were cleaning and pushing their parents into helping them. At least in this part of the tent City, hope had returned.

When they got back to their tent, it was even straighter and tidier than before. Patrick sat himself on the ground near the fire and took out the little book.

He read past the creation story and saw very quickly the brother became the villain of the story. Naxic soon gave up on the struggle for improvement and concentrated on pain. Lyylen pled with him to follow the way of peace, but the people of the world understood pain. They fought with their enemies and the world around them. According to the story they were lost in an endless cycle of violence and despair. At least until the Goddess spoke to a man named Darsh.

The story of Darsh in the book was very much the same as what Justine had told him back in their kitchen over a plate of tortellini. He had decided with the Goddess's help that he was tired of violence and refused to fight with his neighbours. He had gradually been stripped of everything of value, including his wife and family. Only the persistence of his wife had reversed his fortunes and resulted in the Peace. There was a three-year meeting to discuss the terms of the Peace before it was established by the Goddess. Apparently from what Davvad said, it was a historical event. The book ended with the establishment of the Peace.

Patrick looked up and Davvad was sitting beside him. He handed the book back to the big man who placed it carefully in a pocket in his vest.

"What do you think?"

"It is a story that moves from history to myth and back," Patrick said. "I think it is more about what it means than what really happened. It talks about all the people meeting for three years to discuss the Peace, but if they did, who grew the crops and harvested them?"

"I told you the villagers and farmers decided on the first day what they would do. It was the City folk who took the rest of the time." Davvad sighed. "Brother Raston would tell you the Goddess fed them and kept them through that time, though there is nothing in the scriptures about it. I think that the people who accepted the Peace went back to their lives while representatives argued."

"Unfortunately that doesn't get us nearer to a solution to

this mess, does it?"

"No, and I don't believe that there is anything in the Agreement that really covers it either. There is provision for local disasters as Brother Raston said, but nothing for the whole country showing up all at once."

"So we are all making this up as we go along?"

"The City is doing a much better job of it than I expected," Davvad said, "but I don't expect it to last."

"How long have we got?"

"I would say until the food runs out, or the invaders arrive."

"I'd better get into that Library soon then."

"From your mouth to the Goddess's ears," Davvad said and shrugged. "See, even I am invoking the Goddess now." He got up and went over to help Marisha tighten a rope that already hummed.

Patrick sat deep in thought until the gruel wagon arrived. He could taste the sage in it. It was odd, but at least it was different.

Justine's Journal

Hi Mom, it was fun seeing the other kids cleaning for the contest. I didn't expect it to catch on so quickly. There isn't much fun in the camps so even cleaning up is better than nothing. Marisha really wants us to win the prize. Sometimes it's like she's another Mom. Do you mind?

Love you,
Justine

Chapter Seventeen

The sound of children playing woke Patrick and he lay a while just to listen. He didn't mind this sound as an alarm clock at all.

"Dad, if you want tea, it's made," Justine said from the other side of the tent wall.

"How did you know I was awake?"

"You stopped snoring," she said, though her tone added a "duh" on the end.

He crawled out into the main tent then went outside to get a cup of tea from Justine.

"Is it my imagination or are there way more children around?"

"More kids," Justine said. "There are some from over the other side of the camp. They said they like having something to do."

"They could play where they are."

"Someone has to start." Stone came over to them and sat down. "We started it, and our hosts haven't complained, so now it's spreading."

"Children wouldn't play to avoid offending their hosts?"

"Parents would tell them to be quiet so as not to bother the City people. But now that Garad is judging the tents, it's like the City people encouraging them to play."

The breakfast wagon came through and Patrick was sure there was cinnamon in the gruel. There was less complaining, in any case. When he walked toward the City he stopped at the kitchen to look at the huge piles of sticks there and nodded. At the gate, there were two different men, but they just waved him through.

Patrick wandered through the City. It hadn't changed. The change in energy outside was so dramatic that he had expected it to carry into the City.

The youth were waiting at the entrance to the guest house.

"We got the sticks for the fires. We get to ask you a question."

"Yes, you do."

"Where are you from?"

"The name of the City I lived wouldn't have much meaning for you. It is in a completely different world from yours."

"You mean you're not from Graffire?" one of the boys asked.

"Only one question." Barsta said.

"It's OK, Barsta," Patrick said, "I'll take it as a clarification."

"No, I don't come from Graffire or Rakkikt either. I came with my daughter through the Goddess Tree."

He could see them bursting with questions, but they held them back and Patrick nodded with approval.

"I will see you tomorrow."

"Tomorrow," Barsta agreed.

"I heard they are judging the tents; who has the cleanest and best kept," One of the younger boys said, carefully not asking a question.

"You heard true."

"Do you think they will come here?"

"Here?"

"To judge, we are guests too."

"I will ask."

"Tomorrow, stranger."

"Patrick."

"Patrick."

Brother Raston had no word about getting Patrick into the Library.

"You must realize the Library is more than just a collection of books. It is the repository of all the knowledge we have of ourselves and the Goddess. There is much more than the scriptures there, but it is still a holy place. The Brothers are undecided."

"You might want them to consider how the invaders will treat their collection."

"I will ask."

That afternoon the winning tent had a picture of the City done in rocks on the ground. Nobody grumbled, instead they went away planning even grander schemes for the next day.

Garad had taken twice as long to judge and a broader area of the tent City wanted to be included.

"The guest house wanted to be included in the judging," Patrick told the man.

"Which one?"

"The one that Brother Raston runs."

"How am I to judge between tent and guest house?"

"Maybe challenge the other guest house?"

"I will need to talk to my superiors about this. Were you the one who sent the boys out to get wood?"

"How did you know?" Patrick asked.

"It seemed the kind of thing that you would do," Garad said.

"It seemed safe enough for now, no soldiers have been seen this near the City."

When Patrick was walking back to the gate he saw another fair skinned man among the bronze coloured Pax. The man wore a leather vest been tooled to look like it was covered with strange birds. He wore boots instead of the sandals most of the Pax had. Patrick went up and introduced himself.

"I am Patrick. I'm a stranger to this land."

"I bid you welcome, be it you come in peace," the man replied. He looked at Patrick with clear blue eyes. No smile there, but neither was there a frown.

"I don't want to be rude, but I didn't know there were others as light skinned as my daughter and I here."

"I am a Wester, from the mountains. We are considerably lighter skinned than most of the Pax. Yet we hold to the same peace."

"I do not doubt it," Patrick said. "It isn't the colour of a person's skin that matters, but the colour of their heart."

"I like that saying," the man said. "I am Pauli." Now he smiled, and Patrick felt Pauli's welcome become more than just words.

The men clasped hands briefly.

"I must be away. I have some relatives in the camp and said I would visit, but come by the Street of Leathersmiths and ask for

Pauli, and we will talk further." The man bowed and disappeared into the crowd.

The next morning the boys asked what Patrick knew of the invaders. He told them what he had seen, but they were disappointed he had only seen them from a distance.

Once again Brother Reston had no good news from the Library. He was running on about trying to sort out some confusion in the Guest House so Patrick left him without argument.

"I am looking for the Street of the Leathersmiths," he asked Barsta. "Perhaps one of your group could show me the way?"

"You are looking for the Westers?" the boy said.

"Yes," Patrick said, "what can you tell me about them?"

"They're from the mountains," Barsta dodged through the crowds as he talked. "They are the same and different from us. They live by the peace, of course, but they dress in leather and fur and talk funny."

"Why is that?"

"They're Westers." Barsta shrugged. "They've always been like that. We don't have many in the city."

"So if you knew about Westers, why did you challenge my daughter and me?"

"There is something different again about you. You aren't like us, but you aren't like the Westers either."

"So do you trust us yet?"

"You're under the peace."

"True, but do you trust us?"

The boy stopped and looked at Patrick.

"You're helping," he said. "That's good enough for me."

"Then why continue the questions at the door every morning?"

"The guys are getting bored. They need something to do. Picking up sticks and thinking of questions is as good as anything else for them to do."

They arrived at the street and Barsta waved around.

"Just ask anyone here who you are looking for. They'll tell you. I've got to get back."

"Thanks, Barsta."

He waved and melted back into the crowd. Patrick looked around and took in the busy street. About half the people were the bronze shaded Pax, the other half ranged from blonde to red head. Patrick went up to a woman with fiery red hair and asked for Pauli.

"Right, Pauli," the woman said, "it would be easier to just show you myself. I am Kayta." She walked along the street. Where Barsta had twisted and dodged through the crowd she moved with its rhythm. They arrived at a store. Its window filled with leather goods from what looked like purses to belts to nets of leather that had Patrick wondering what they were for.

"Pauli," she called, "you have a visitor." She turned to Patrick. "Just wait a minute and he'll be out."

Patrick watched as she flowed away through the crowd.

"Hello, Patrick," Pauli stepped out through the door. "Be welcome in my home and business."

"Why did she ask me to wait?"

"You asked for me, that made you a visitor, not a customer. It's polite for me to welcome you at the threshold. Kayta is a stickler for custom."

"Right," Patrick followed Pauli through the doorway. "Then why didn't she welcome me?"

"If you were here, you already had the peace of the City. She didn't need to welcome you again. We'd do nothing but welcome folks if we did that. It's different if you cross the threshold into a private home."

The shop was a combination store and workshop. Awls and thread lined one bench while punches and other tools hung on hooks over another. More bags and belts hung on the walls. Pauli led him through another door to a comfortable room with a table and chairs. A stove sat in the corner, but Patrick didn't feel any heat off it.

"I apologize, but I cannot offer you tea. With the shortage of wood in the City we only have one hot meal a day. I can offer water."

"Water will be very welcome."

"So Patrick, what brings you to the Pax? You have the look

of a Wester, but your accent is different. I heard from my cousins that you are in the camp on the south of the City. My cousins are on the West, but they heard about a girl who looks like a Wester who is turning the camp upside down."

"My daughter," Patrick said and smiled.

"News travels fast among the Pax. My cousins' children are already asking if they might join this competition. They are also playing a very old game almost without ceasing. I haven't seen their section of the camp looking that lively since they got here."

"I am glad my daughter's influence is so positive."

A woman walked in through the back door and nodded to Patrick. She refilled his glass.

"The children are helping their cousins. Marta said she would walk them home." She poured a cup of water and sat at the table with them. My name is Krysa."

"Patrick."

"It is an honour to have you in our home."

"The honour is mine," Patrick said. "I'm a stranger here. I am pleased to be made so welcome."

"It is who we are Patrick. If we are not the people of the peace, then who are we?"

They talked until three children ran shouting into the room. The sun was much lower in the sky. When they saw Patrick, they stopped and lined up.

"Be welcome in our home, and come and go in peace," they said together.

"I'm afraid that I must go in peace now," Patrick said. The children moaned, but the oldest bowed.

"I can show you to the gates." He looked at his mother. "Please?" His mother smiled and nodded.

"Why don't you two tell me about what you did with your cousins?" Patrick heard her say as he followed the boy out of the shop.

"Come right back," Pauli said, "I don't want you to be late for dinner."

"Yes, Father." The boy walked beside Patrick and chattered on about the city and his friends and his cousins until it all blended together. It reminded him of when Justine was younger and would talk endlessly the same way. The City was a mix of stone and wood. Some of the streets were wide and straight, but tiny alleys shot off at old angles. Patrick saw one where the upper stories joined above the alley, but he could see light from a courtyard at the other end. It brought home to him how little he'd seen of the City. He walked from gate to guest house, but didn't explore at all.

They'd arrived at the gates. The boy bowed again then took off like an arrow. Patrick had been so busy looking around that he hadn't thought to ask his name.

When Patrick got back to the tent, he learned the winning tent had sung a song in honour of the City. The adults had sung with the children. Garad was so touched that he didn't mind that he had taken almost four hours to visit all the tents that wanted to be judged.

The next morning there was flat bread along with the gruel.

"Someone came up and told us we could cook the bread on the outside of the kettles while we cooked the gruel on the inside. An army of women came and ground flour to make it too."

Justine looked at him and Patrick just shrugged.

At the guest house, the boys hadn't decided on another question, but they did tell him that a City official had come by to announce a contest between the three guest houses, on the same terms as the tent contest.

"Ah, we aren't interested in some silly contest," Barsta said.

"Well, I'm sure the other houses will be delighted to win."

Brother Raston came out and the boys scattered. Patrick laughed when he saw some of them surreptitiously picking up the clutter around them.

"Good morning, Patrick," the Brother said. "I got word yesterday that you are to be given access to the archives. I will walk you there."

Brother Raston led him back out into the City without another word.

Patrick noticed the buildings grew larger and more luxurious. He wondered about how the City's economy worked around the guest rights? How did the wealthy keep the poor from showing up at their doorstep for an extended visit? He guessed the guest houses were part of the answer, but was sure it was more complicated than that.

Brother Raston set a stiff pace and the tension in his back suggested he wasn't interested in conversation. Patrick did have much time to look around either.

They reached a building that looked like a warehouse with pillars all along the front and a carved fresco along the roof line. Brother Raston took him inside.

A woman in robes considerably less worn than Brother Raston's came out to meet them.

"Ah, thank you Brother," she said. "I have been looking forward to this since you mentioned our friend might be visiting."

"Patrick, meet Sister Hersh," She reminded Patrick a little of Ms. Ballanteen. The Sister looked like she'd be as comfortable on the floor with children or with a book in hand. She exuded competence and welcome.

"Welcome and be at peace in our home and hearth. Speak freely for the Goddess watches between us."

"Thank you, Sister Hersh, I am honoured by your welcome."

Brother Raston had already turned to leave. Patrick followed Sister Hersh into the Library.

"Sister Hersh," he said.

"Please, call me Hersh, or just Sister. There are so many of us here we could spend all day on the niceties and never get any work done."

"Hersh," Patrick started again, "I seem to have upset Brother Raston somehow and I don't wish to upset you." He told about his conversation with Brother Raston and his talks with the youth.

"Brother Raston is a good man," Hersh said carefully, "but he is very tied to his own idea of our relationship with the Goddess. He believes explicitly in all the scriptures, even the passages that seem to contradict themselves. Thus, he is always seeking answers that will explain Her. I am sure he put great hope in you coming from the Tree."

"I'm afraid that I come with more questions than answers."

"That would trouble him indeed." Hersh stopped and

looked at Patrick. "Don't get me wrong, Raston is a good man. He is likely chastising himself even now for his rudeness, and will try to find some way to get back into your good opinion." She started off again, leading Patrick to a set of black wood doors that gave an impression of being immensely old.

"This is the library proper." Hersh said. "The outer shell was built a couple of hundred years ago by the Final King."

"Final King?"

"He was a very devout man and put a great deal of effort into the peace. He was responsible for the idea of the guest houses. He wasn't very popular with the wealthy families since he forced them to contribute to making sure everyone had sufficient food and shelter. He also instituted schools that tried to ensure at least a basic education for everyone."

"What did people do before the guest houses?"

"There is provision to tell a person on your door step that you are very sorry, but you have no room and insufficient food for your own household. Then the person is obligated to leave and find other shelter."

"I imagine that would be hard to take if you were being turned away from a grand estate."

"Oh yes," Hersh grinned, "but the rules of the peace say you can't argue. The host loses face, but keeps their wealth. The King wanted to take that option away completely, but it would have been impossible. The compromise was the guest house. Unfortunately, he died before they were put into use."

"Why did you call him the Final King?"

"He had no children and had been an only son. The City Council stepped in as Regent until a suitable heir could be found. Everything ran so much smoother without a King on the throne they just never got around to replacing him."

"Convenient."

"The Brothers of the Goddess have a seat on the Council, and the other seats are filled by lot from a pool of candidates chosen by the people of the City. Since there is no direct compensation for being on the Council most people are content to allow the people who want the job to have it."

"If it's worked for two hundred years, it must be a

reasonable system."

"Oh, yes, it works well. The City's response to the refugees proves that. There are complaints from some quarters that the influx will bankrupt the City, but there are fortunes being made too."

"That sounds a lot like where I come from."

Hersh laughed.

"Let's go in." She knocked on the doors and they were opened from the inside. Another Brother waved them in and closed the doors behind them. "There is a Brother or Sister here at all times. We take turns at the doors," Hersh said in a lower voice. "The outside shell was built to protect the library and regulate the temperature and moisture. Our offices and a school, even a dormitory are all in the outer shell. All that is in here is books and scrolls.

Patrick's eyes adjusted to the dimmer light and he looked around. He was in a warehouse sized building that was filled floor to ceiling with shelves of books and scrolls. The occasional table was set in the aisles. Dim lamps glowed on each table.

"I really hope that you folks have a good catalogue system."

Hersh chuckled. "That's what I'm here for." She picked up a lamp from the nearest table. "What exactly are you looking for?"

Justine's Journal

Hi Mom, we didn't win the flag today either. Everybody wants to be part of the contest. There are children from all the way on the other side of the City who came to play! I'm trying to sort out this whole guest and host thing. It is a lot more complicated than I thought and not much like home. At least it is more fun than sitting around trying to be quiet. That's just depressing. Stone has an idea for tomorrow. Just wait until you see it!

Love you,

Justine

Chapter Eighteen

The sound of singing woke Patrick and sent him crawling out of the tent. Stone and Justine had lined up a troop of children and had them practising the song that had made its way through the tent City since it won its writers the white flag. In the week since he'd been going to the library the competition had spread through the entire camp and there were dozens of judges who scoured the camps constantly to determine which section, block and tent would host the flag for the day.

Justine and Stone were determined to bring the flag home for at least one night. This chorus was obviously their latest scheme.

"Morning, Dad," she said, "tea's in the pot."

"Choir sounds good," he said as he poured a cup.

"Really?"

"Yes."

"We're going to the gate to sing the song for the City folk. It seems a pity that they haven't heard it."

"Ah," Patrick sipped at the tea, "good luck."

He walked with the choir to the gate where the man waved him through then stared bemused at the mass of children.

Patrick waited on the other side of the gate to see what would happen. Justine hummed a note and the children burst into their song with great enthusiasm and a fair bit of unintentional harmony. The words came through loud and clear. Patrick thought their lavish praise of the City's generosity a little over the top, but he was sure he saw one of the men brush away a tear. The guard conferred with his partner. When the song had finished, he went to talk with Justine and Stone. Soon after, the children formed up in lines and marched into the City singing their song of thanks.

Patrick followed behind the children, curious about how the City would react to this invasion. People listened then smiled or teared up. They waved at the children. When the band reached the guest house, Barsta and his crew were at their usual spot. They began a complicated clapping rhythm that merged with the song.

Then, as if it was the plan the entire time, they fell into step with the choir adding their rhythmic accompaniment.

Barsta dropped back to whisper to Patrick.

"We've been hearing this song all over the camp. I figured it was only a matter of time before they brought it into the City. We can't sing very well, but the rhythm is fun."

Patrick left them to go to the library. Hersh met him at the door.

"I hear we've been invaded again," she said with a smile. "I hope they make it this far."

"We could go back and find them. I think they were headed toward the Council House."

"Great idea," Hersh said. "I know a short cut."

She led the way at a brisk walk and weaved through back streets to come out in a large square just as the children entered the other side. The square was full of people, but they parted to let the choir, which to Patrick's eye had grown considerably, up to the front steps.

Several men and women came out of the huge doors that opened out of the immense building. They were dwarfed by pillars that were wider than three men standing shoulder to shoulder. More carving ran along the roof line leading to a woman whose feet were set on mountains and sea. *The Goddess*

The children finished the song and started up again, singing the whole thing through. Barsta and his gang must have been exhausted, but they kept up with their clapping until the end. When they finished, there was silence in the square, then the whole crowd burst into cheering.

"Well, well," one woman said who stepped forward, "this is an honour." Her practised voice soared over the crowd as it quieted. "Be welcome, friends, be welcome. May I know who you are?" Justine and Stone must have introduced themselves and their group because the portly nodded, and waved at the choir then walked down the step to clasp hands with Justine, Stone and Barsta. The children cheered, then took up their song again and headed out the way they came in.

"Well done," Hersh said. "Our Council Chair was genuinely touched. There is no other explanation for her voluntarily going up and down those steps. Ah well, I needed to see that." She led Patrick back to the library.

In the dimness of the great library Patrick returned to the scroll that he had been studying. Hersh knew the general area that probably dealt with Pax's relationship with her neighbours after the peace had been sealed, but there were hundreds of dusty books and at least as many scrolls. Patrick would pick out a selection and skim through as quickly as he could. He was closing in on his goal, but it was taking him a long time. This scroll had hints of a calamity, but since it didn't appear to affect the Pax it was only mentioned tangentially. It was still the closest that he had got to answering his question. What had happened to prevent other countries from invading and taking over once the Pax had disarmed themselves?

What he did find, and had found in other scrolls was reference to people who had gone out to other countries to teach about the peace. It was a dangerous job from what he could tell. There was no rule of peace and hospitality to protect them outside their own borders.

"Any luck?" Hersh asked. "It is lunch time, and everyone works better on a full stomach."

Patrick followed the Sister out to the shell and to the mess hall where he had been joining the other Brothers and Sisters for a midday meal of gruel and bread each day.

"Are there still people who go out to teach the peace?" he asked Hersh as they sat down.

"Not in my memory," the Brother across the table from them said. "People are content to stay at home and live quietly. What the scrolls don't mention is that many of those teachers who did return came back with disturbing ideas and questions. The Council stopped encouraging them about a generation back."

"That sounds right," another Brother said. "The last one came back with the idea that we should be making political alliances with the Rakkikt to open up more trade. That would cause more trouble than it's worth. We don't trade much with them, never needed to. The Goddess has given us everything we need between mountain and sea. There is nothing we need from the North."

162

After they had finished their meal Patrick and Hersh returned to the library.

"I hadn't realized we'd become so turned in on ourselves." Hersh said.

"It happens easily enough when you don't need anything from your neighbours."

"Now we might need something and we don't know them well enough to ask."

"You don't have envoys or ambassadors from Graffire or Rakkikt?"

"Not since the time of the Final King." Hersh sighed. "The Council didn't see the need to spend the money on maintaining the relationships to East and North. I wonder how we could convince them that it is worth the effort now."

"You probably should get a message to the Rakkikt and invite them to come and talk. They will be very interested in Graffire's invasion."

"I wouldn't know where to send to," Hersh said.

"If they are anything like the people of my world, they will have people here already."

"How will we find them?"

"Just arrange for a public invitation, and I am sure they will get the message."

"I still have a hard time believing that strangers could hide in our midst without us knowing."

"When Justine and I arrived at the City, I thought we were the only fair skinned people around, but there are plenty of variations. The Westers are almost as light as we are. Even in the City there is enough difference for someone to find a place. If they followed the peace, then people would accept them just like they have accepted me."

"I guess," Hersh shook her head. "Let me take this to the others."

Patrick nodded and went back to his reading.

Late into the evening he finally gave up and went back to the camp. His shirt flew proudly in front of their tent. Justine and Stone were so excited that they kept hugging each other.

"How goes the search?" Davvad asked.

"Slowly," Patrick rubbed his eyes. "I feel that I am getting closer, but there is a big piece still missing."

"The Goddess will show you what you need in time."

"I didn't take you for a religious person," Patrick said.

"I don't see the Goddess as the solution for problems that I can solve on my own, but nonetheless She uses her people to move her purpose forward."

Patrick shrugged. "Well, unless she makes one of the scrolls glow for me, I will have to do it the hard way."

Davvad shrugged too and poured Patrick more tea.

The next morning when the food wagon came by people were talking excitedly in its wake. When Patrick got his portion, he could see why. Raisins were mixed into the gruel.

"The word is there will actually be meat tonight," the server said. "The Council has encouraged people to open up their private cellars to share the food."

Patrick looked around the tent City. When he and Justine had arrived, the people were listless and defeated. Now they carried themselves with some dignity. People were turning out to help take care of the camp and the City. They didn't look defeated anymore.

He headed off to the library and saw a poster that was new. He went up to read it and laughed. It was certainly direct enough.

To any visitors from Rakkikt, Welcome and be at peace in our home and hearth. We would like to speak to you. Find us at the Council House. The Council.

He headed off to the library to learn if there had been any response.

Hersh hadn't heard anything, but she was pleased that the signs had gone up so soon.

"I think the Council was just happy to have something to do, especially if it meant bring someone else with more resources to the table. They have asked for a chance to meet you."

"I'm not getting very far with the research," Patrick said, "I could use a break."

"Let's go then," Sister Hersh said and led him toward the Council Hall. "They'll be glad of an interruption. All they've had to talk about for weeks is how to host the Camp."

Her prediction proved correct, and Patrick was shown into the Council Chamber without any wait. It was a surprisingly utilitarian room. They sat around a large table with an oversized chair at one end. They set a smaller chair for Patrick at the other end.

"Welcome," the Chair said. She looked even bigger up close. "be at peace in our City and our Land."

"You honour me with your welcome," Patrick said.

"Is it true that you came through the Goddess Tree?" a man dressed in Brother's robes asked.

"Yggdrasil," Patrick said. "Yes, Yggdrasil brought us here."

"Us?" one of the other counsellors leaned forward to examine Patrick more closely.

"Brother Raston mentioned that his daughter came with him," the Brother said.

"That's right," Patrick said. "Justine, she was one of the children leading the singing this morning."

"A fine tribute to our City," the Chair said, "I was truly touched. It reminded us of everything that is good about Pax. Since you come from so far away, perhaps you have some suggestions to offer."

"It really isn't my place to give advice—"

"Come now," the Brother said, "you came through the Goddess Tree to help us. Why else would you have come at this troubled time?"

"I did wonder if anyone had talked to the leader of the Graffire army." Patrick said, "You have signs up looking for Rakkikt who are living among you. Maybe you should send someone to ask what the invasion is about. There may be a way to resolve it peacefully. What did you do last time this happened?"

"This has never happened before," the Brother said. "I have seen nothing in the library that mentions anything like this."

"But surely the countries around you would have seen the Peace as weakness—"

"The Goddess protects our land," the Brother said with a finality that made Patrick grind his teeth.

"Still, the idea of sending some people to talk to the Graffire is a good one," a woman councillor said. "It's foolish to just sit and wonder why they've come."

"Do the rest of you agree? We send a committee to talk to the Graffire army?" The Chair looked around then nodded. "Perhaps you can lead the delegation Brother Haspan?"

"I will ask the Goddess to guide my words," the Brother replied.

Before Patrick knew what was happening a dozen names had been proposed from prominent families.

"How are we to find the Graffire? One of the other counsellors who had been appointed to the delegation asked.

"It seems to me that most of the people from the camp came from the East, toward the Graffire border. If you follow the road east, you will probably find some soldiers. They will be able to take you to their leader."

"If their army is to the East," the Chair said, "perhaps we can send people out to the West to find more food. There must be some left in the villages that are abandoned. We are running short of food for so many people. There is almost no reserve left." She stood and bowed to Patrick. "Thank you for your wisdom."

They let Patrick go after each of them bowed to him. He heard them return to wrangling about details as he closed the door behind them.

"So?" Sister Hersh said.

"They are going to send a delegation to meet with the Graffire army. Perhaps we can work out a peaceful solution to this mess."

"That would be wonderful," Hersh said. "Wonderful indeed."

Early in the morning a delegation of eight men and women from the City rode out on the road East. The Chair of the Council whispered to Patrick that another wagon had gone out to the West to look for more food.

"We may be a people of peace," the Chair said to the curious crowd that had gathered, "but we are not a weak people. Trust the Goddess and all will be well."

People wandered away buzzing with conversation about the bold move to talk to the invaders.

"It was the man from the Goddess Tree who suggested it,"

Patrick heard. "How can it fail?"

A shiver went down Patrick's spine. He remembered his warning to Brother Raston about messengers from gods. They hadn't heard anything from the soldiers in white for a while, but Patrick was sure that the invaders had their spies in the camp. He wondered what they would do in response to this delegation. Surely they would listen?

Nobody had heard from the delegation or the food wagon for days and Patrick tried to ignore the worry settled in his stomach. He dove back into his research at the library.

He had read his way through another bunch of scrolls that didn't quite mention what had happened in the last invasion. He was sure that there had been one in spite of what the Brother at the Council said. Hersh hadn't appeared at noon so he worked through. It was late in the afternoon when he stretched his neck and saw a glow a ways off to his right.

"Oh no," he said, "you've got to be kidding." With some trepidation, he walked over to where he found one of the lamps sitting on the floor by the shelves. He breathed a big sigh of relief. No Goddess, just a forgetful Brother. He picked up the lamp to return it to his desk when he noticed a book lying precariously on a pile of scrolls. As he looked at it, it slipped and without thinking he caught it. The book fell open. Patrick sat abruptly on the floor and began reading the book.

There was no title on the cover; it appeared to be a diary of some kind. The entry that had caught his eye was simply "Today the Goddess destroyed Hamlan for breaking her peace." He flipped back and found the details of an invasion from the West. The people of the Pax were easy victims. They were pushed out of their homes or slaughtered. Until some event triggered an uprising of the land. Creatures of every kind attacked the Hamlan army and harried them across the border. None of the leaders of the invasion survived and only a tiny fraction of the invasion force. The writer of the diary was one of the few who lived to write of the catastrophe. The entries following the invasion talked about how the crops had failed and the people of Hamlan starved, when the neighbours they had invaded invited them to join in the peace. Hamlan became part of the peace and the horrors of the invasion were forgotten.

"I'm sorry I doubted you," he said to the Goddess. "I'm not sure what to do with this." He was sure he heard a huge sigh, then he felt the urgent need to get out in the sunshine. The Brother at the door was scandalized Patrick still had the book in his hand.

"Give it to Hersh, tell her to read it." He pushed the book into the man's hands before he ran out the door and into the daylight. At the bottom of the steps the urgency left him and he turned to face the library.

"I don't know whether I'm relieved or terrified that you are taking a direct hand in things."

A beam of sunlight broke through the gathering clouds and illuminated one portion of the carved fresco. It showed a lone tiny figure facing what looked like an invasion of demons.

"I think terrified is the right choice." Patrick said. "I have no desire to face an army by myself." The clouds closed and left Patrick feeling alone and afraid. He turned and walked away from the library as fast as he could, but it wasn't fast enough. He ran until his lungs burned; past the gate until he reached the edge of the tent City.

There was a wagon approaching. Following it were eight men in the white uniforms Patrick remembered from his first day in this place. His heart sunk to his feet as they reached him and stopped.

The lead soldier stepped up to Patrick.

"The Emperor of Graffire has claimed all this land. He will tolerate no more theft of his goods and he is not interested in your weakling talk of peace." They cut the horses free from the cart and led them away again. Patrick felt himself compelled to lift the corner of the tarp.

By the time he'd stopped vomiting in the grass at the side of the road, others had arrived. They looked in the cart and start screaming and wailing.

The cart was full of heads that were once people of the Pax. There was the Brother who led the delegation and the other seven men and women. Others Patrick was sure were the men who had been sent out to gather more food for the City. The invading army didn't want the people fed and content. They didn't care

168

about peace. This was a message. There would be more fear to come.

Justine's Journal

I'm scared again. It was just starting to go right and people were happy, then that wagon had to show up. Why did Dad have to be the one who was there? I wish he was here. I wish you were here.

Love you,

Justine

Chapter Nineteen

Patrick woke with a stiff neck and the taste of bile still in his mouth. He grabbed the pitcher and poured himself a cup of water, but he couldn't wash out the taste. After weeks of sleeping on the ground the soft mattress had been terribly uncomfortable. He had a sudden vision of Lee sleeping in his bed while he slept on the floor beside her.

Where did that come from? He had been too busy to think of her in ages. He put his head in his hands as the memory of that wagon pushed any thought from his head. He was well out of his depth.

"Friend Patrick," a young man knocked on the door, "if you are awake, the Council would like to see you."

Patrick looked the clothes set out for him, a much finer version of what he had been wearing. He tried another glass of water with no improvement.

"Lead on."

The arrival of the wagon had sent waves of fear through the tent City. Everybody who hadn't seen a family member that day was afraid that their heads were in the wagon. The gruesome cargo had been covered up again and taken to an empty warehouse in the City. Patrick had been asked to report to the Council. Fortunately, he had seen Barsta and sent a message to Justine and Davvad that he was all right. People who had just been laughing and cheering a marching band of children shrank in fear from the wagon that was being pushed by grey faced men.

Once the thing was secured it was obvious that Patrick wasn't going to be able to make a coherent report of the incident. Every time he tried to talk, he choked up and started vomiting again. One of the Councillors had finally suggested that he stay and rest the night and speak to them in the morning.

Now Patrick followed this young man to the Council Chambers.

A young woman put tea beside him.

"I've added a root that should help settle your stomach," she said. "If it displeases you I can fetch something different."

170

"No, thank you," Patrick said, "this should be fine." He took a sip and felt a gentle warmth flow into him and relax his clenched muscles.

"We much regret this incident, Patrick," the Chair of the Council said. "It would be helpful if you could tell your story. We won't interrupt, but we may ask questions when you are done." Patrick took another long sip of the tea.

"I was working in the library, and had found a book that explained much of what I wanted to know." Patrick wasn't sure he wanted to try to tell them how he had found the book. "I felt the need for fresh air and went outside. The fresco at the library had a different meaning in the context of that book and it upset me. I needed to get out of the City to where I could breathe and think through the implications."

He took a deep breath.

"That's when I saw the wagon, which was curious since it came from the East. I saw the soldiers accompanying it and I froze. I couldn't move until after the leader spoke to me.

"He said 'The Emperor of Graffire has claimed all this land. He will tolerate no more theft of his goods.' Then they walked away. I looked under the tarp and you know what I found." Patrick took another sip of the tea and tried to steady the shaking of his hands.

"You were seen running through the City," one Councillor said. "That is more than just needing fresh air."

"You haven't read the book yet, or looked at the fresco in its light. I felt I needed to escape."

"What did this book say that was so upsetting?"

"Have you heard of Hamlan?" Patrick asked.

"Certainly, that's the western province," another Councillor said.

"It wasn't always," Patrick took another sip and looked at the Council. "At one time Hamlan was a kingdom in its own right. Shortly after the peace was signed, they invaded the Pax. Their King thought that the Pax would be an easy target once they had sworn off violence." He stared at the table in front of him. "There were people uprooted and killed, just like this time, but something happened and the land itself fought against the invaders and destroyed them. The crops in Hamlan failed and the people ended up begging to join the peace."

"So the Goddess acted to protect her people," a new Brother at the table said.

"Not without a price," Patrick said. "Go look at the fresco and you will see a single figure facing an army of what look like demons."

"Yes, that is a representation of Darisha facing the people who would take her husband's goods."

"I think it is Darisha meeting the invading host on her own. I think she welcomed them to the Pax and they killed her and that is what set off the land."

"Stories," said one Councillor, "we don't have any real record that Darsh and Darisha even existed."

"Now the scriptures are clear..."

"Scriptures aren't history, Brother."

The table dissolved into discussion. Patrick just sat hopeless and drank his tea. He knew why the Goddess had shown him the book and the fresco. She hadn't brought him through the Tree to give advice from a safe distance. She expected him to go and welcome the invaders and die in the process so she could send her wrath on them. Patrick didn't want to leave Justine alone, though Davvad and Marisha would care for her like one of their own family. Maybe she would even grow up to fall in love with Stone and become one of the family.

Patrick didn't know why the Goddess hadn't already acted. Certainly, enough of her people had died. He was sure there was something he had missed.

"If this story of Hamlan is true, why hasn't the Goddess already acted?" some said, echoing Patrick's thoughts. "She sent us this person through her Tree and all he has done has got more of our people killed. We must have angered her. We're cursed!"

The Council Chamber erupted into noise again.

There was a knock on the door and the babble ceased and a young man opened the door.

"There are people here who wish to speak to the Council."

"We are busy. Can they return later?"

"They say they are from Rakkikt."

There was dead silence for a moment before the Chair heaved a deep sigh.

"Bring them in," she said.

A man and a woman in clothes not much different than what Patrick's walked into the room.

"Be welcome," the Chair said. "I don't mean to be rude, but do you have proof of who you are?"

"Certainly, honoured sir," The taller of the two said. He handed the Chair a sealed letter. The Chair looked at the seal and passed the letter to the Brother who also examined it closely.

"It is the seal of Rakkikt, if my memory serves me," the Brother said finally. "May I?" the Chair nodded and the Brother broke the seal to read the contents.

"Greetings to the Council of Pax, from Harild King of Rakkikt. Those who bear this letter are trusted members of my court and have the right to negotiate in my name."

"Very well," the Chair said, "please be seated and bring us what message you may have."

"Thank you, honoured Lady." They sat and waved off the young woman's offer of tea or water. "We come to bring you the offer of military support from King Harild. We can field enough men to push Graffire back to his own borders."

"And the cost of such support?"

"We would expect some favourable trade concessions, but for the most part we would be content to have Pax intact and peaceful between us and Graffire."

"You mean you'd rather fight them here, than at home," Patrick said.

"Friend Patrick," the Chair said, "please don't be rude to our guests."

"Not rude, but blunt spoken," the woman from Rakkikt said. "We value such honesty."

"Yet he is not a member of the Council and perhaps has other things to do, now that he has reported to us."

"Just remember," Patrick said, "it is much easier to invite someone in, than to get rid of them once they have made themselves at home."

The Chair frowned and Patrick nodded to the two visitors

and left. He heard as he left one of the Councillors ask, "Just how long would it take for such support to arrive?"

He wandered out of the Council offices and found Hersh waiting for him on the steps.

"I was told you would be most of the day in Council."

"I spoke my mind a little too freely it seems and was invited to leave." Patrick shook his head. "Two people from Rakkikt came offering help."

"Surely that is good news?"

"Not if their help involves fighting a war over your country. They are very concerned that Graffire will take the Pax and leave them next on the list of conquests. It is much easier to fight here, than on their own borders."

"I see," said Hersh, "but it doesn't sound like you to speak out of turn."

"They gave me some special tea to relax my stomach and it seems to have relaxed my judgement as well."

"Ah, it can have that effect on some people," Hersh said. "It will wear off shortly."

"Thank goodness. I feel like I'm carrying all my thoughts on the outside of my head."

"Let's walk a bit and that should clear the last of it from your system. That was quite a book you sent me. It shows we need to preserve our history better. I can't imagine how something like an invasion and the destruction of any entire people could be forgotten."

"Because it is a lot more comfortable not remembered. I expect after the shock wore off that the only way both sides could move forward was to pretend it never happened. Then you don't have one group being the remnant invaders and the others, the ones whose land slaughtered an army."

"I see. I'm not sure how it helps us now."

"The Goddess expects someone to go and welcome the invaders on behalf of all Pax. When they are killed, the land will rise and crush the invaders and the Goddess will add another country to the peace."

"You sound She planned all this."

"She brought my daughter here, and through her, me. She

showed me this book and lit one section of the fresco, the part about Darisha and the demons. I think She intends for me to be the one to go and die."

"Why you?" asked Hersh, "Why not me, or the Council?"

"I don't know. Maybe you are so close to the peace that it would never occur to you that there is a curse attached to it."

"A curse?" Hersh stopped and stared at Patrick.

"What is the oldest form of the welcome?"

"Welcome and be at peace in our home and hearth. Speak freely for the Goddess watches between us."

"The Chair just says, 'Be welcome,' even Davvad just stops after home and hearth. I expect the original welcome had something in it about if the guest or host broke the peace that the land would consume them. Maybe the Goddess won't act unless the full welcome is given."

Hersh opened and closed her mouth several times before sighing. "I fear you are right. I know where to find out. If you are OK to find your way home from here, I will go and look."

Patrick nodded and Hersh ran off through the crowds. He walked in a daze through the streets and didn't come to himself until Justine threw herself into his arms and he was home.

Justine's Journal

Dad's back! I don't know what to do. I've never seen him look so scared. I don't know what to do. Could you ask God to tell me?

Love you,

Justine

Chapter Twenty

Patrick woke with Justine's hand in his and silence outside the tent. She hadn't let go of him since he returned the night before.

"Mmmhphf" she said and opened her eyes. "Daddy, I want to go home now."

"Me too," he said.

"But we aren't going, are we?" Tears leaked from her blue eyes. "Our friends need us too much."

"Sometimes the only thing to do is the hardest thing." Patrick looked at her, "Even if we could get back to Drasil. How would feel about leaving them in this mess?"

She sighed, "Stone is back to wanting to start an army. I told him to go look at the heads in the warehouse first. I don't think he likes me anymore." She started crying and he pulled her close and hugged her.

"I am sure Stone still likes you, but he is as scared as everyone else."

She cried for a while, then crawled out of their corner. He could hear her splashing water on her face. He followed her and went outside. The weather had changed while they slept. Grey clouds covered the sky and a cold wind slapped at the tents. Nobody was moving about much; they were all trying to stay out of the wind.

Davvad stood looking at the sky.

"The Goddess is angry." He shrugged at Patrick. "It is something my father used to say when a storm was coming. It seems appropriate now."

"That's an understatement."

Marisha came out with tea, then went back into the tent.

Three figures walked toward them with their head down. Two wore the robes of the Brothers and Sisters of the Goddess. The other was Barsta.

"Here," Barsta said and turned to go.

"Thank you Barsta," Brother Raston said. "Go in peace." The young man shrugged and trudged off.

"Come into the tent and get out of the wind. Welcome and be at peace in our home and hearth." Davvad led them into the tent where the children were playing Rock, Paper, Knife.

"Go, children, and see if Risha needs help." The children rolled their eyes, but left quietly. Justine came and took Patrick's hand and sat beside him. Marisha passed the Brothers tea and sat beside Davvad.

"You didn't come all this way to drink tea," Patrick said.

"No, you are right," Hersh said. "I checked what you said to me last night. You were correct. I found the scroll from the end of the meeting to set the peace. The full welcome is as you said. "Welcome and be at peace in our home and hearth. Speak freely for the Goddess watches between us. May she send the land to consume us if we break peace with one another."

"There needed to be a balance to the peace," Patrick said. "Some incentive for people to keep the peace until it was a habit."

"I have lived in the peace all my life," Davvad said, "and I have never heard this, or thought it. A guest is welcome in my house."

"And if the guest brings violence? If they do you harm?"

"That is a risk of welcoming people. They should not die for it."

"Thamos," Justine said, "he broke the peace."

"Poor boy," Marisha said, "he didn't deserve to die."

"It doesn't say anything about deserving or not," Brother Raston said. "You follow the Goddess' law or you perish."

"Yet though the Goddess blessed it, it was the people who wrote the code," Hersh said. "We have the scrolls that record every day of that meeting."

"Did it really last three years?" Justine asked.

"Every day of it," Hersh said with a sigh. "They were so afraid that someone would take advantage of them."

"So what does it mean for us?" Davvad asked.

"It means that we need to warn the Graffire army before the Goddess destroys them," Patrick said.

"What?" everyone but Justine said.

"Do you really want to live with an entire people being destroyed?"

"They broke the peace," Brother Raston said.

"Did anyone tell them the consequences?" Patrick asked. There was silence. "I didn't think so. They may be all terrible people; they may all deserve to die a horrible death. Their country may deserve to starve when the crops fail, but they still need to be warned. They need to have a choice. Besides it isn't really about the Graffire, but about the Pax. Do you want to be a people who allowed this destruction?"

"The Council must hear of this," Hersh said.

"Do you think they will listen?" Brother Raston said.

"You must make them listen." Patrick said. "They aren't going to listen to me after I got a wagon load of their people killed."

"That wasn't your fault, Dad," Justine said.

"They were following my advice, and I didn't have all the information."

"We will go now," Davvad said.

"Yes, they may listen to you," Brother Raston said.

"I will return to the Library," Hersh said, "and see if I can get the Brothers and Sisters to read the book. Maybe if enough of them see, they can influence the Council."

As they walked through the cold wind back into the City, Patrick asked Davvad why the council would have any reason to listen to him.

"I was born in the City," Davvad said. "I grew up knowing all the complexity of rules that the City folk bind themselves with. I became a judge between people who disagreed, but needed some way of resolving their issue without breaking the peace. At first it was just my neighbourhood, but then it was the whole district and finally the entire city was coming to me to decide whether they should be allowed to build a fence or a second story on their house.

"As I moved up I found the disputes were more about property and less about the peace of the Goddess." He stopped and stretched. "I decided to try out for the Empty Chair in Council."

"The Empty Chair?"

"The seat left by the Final King. The Council of Regents

has never filled it. Yet they are required by law to accept applications from any who feel they have a claim to the seat. My family had as good a claim as any. I had an ancestor who was a cousin of the King. There are many tests. I had to recite my family tree back to the original claimant for the throne. I had to prove my knowledge of the law and history of Pax. My dedication to the peace needed to be without reproach. Raston, who had just taken the robes of a Brother of the Goddess was my biggest supporter. He was sure that it was the Goddess's will that the Empty Chair be filled."

"You tried out to be King?" Patrick tried to keep his amazement out of his voice.

"Not quite," Davvad said. "I would have had to be offered the Chair, then after a year be ratified by the Council of Regents, then after another year by all the people of Pax with seven out of ten adults voting in favour."

"Tough process."

"I never made it that far. The Regents were afraid that I would upset the careful balance they had maintained for two centuries."

"Right, Hersh mentioned something about this. The Final King built the shell around the Library and instituted the Guest Houses."

"Yes, and while the people loved him, the rich had cause to be concerned. They were relieved when he died without an heir. The Pax was much easier to run without the King coming up with new reforms every year."

"If it ain't broke, then don't fix it."

"That sounds like a saying from your world, but we have a very similar one. The Council found cause to stretch my application on for a year, then two years. At the end of the third year I was one vote short of the empty seat. I met Marisha while wandering through Pax trying to find a way to get that last vote. She told me I could have the Empty Chair or her. I chose her and sent a letter to the Council saying that if they couldn't fill one seat in the time it took the entire country to agree on the peace, then I was no longer interested." He sighed deeply. "I settled in Marisha's village and never went back to the City. Raston never quite forgave me. He came often the first few years to sit at the foot of the Goddess Tree hoping for a vision or something. It never came, and he stopped visiting. I found that I enjoyed being a farmer and raising a family.

"Thus it stayed until one day out of the blue a strange girl appeared in our village. She wore odd clothes and talked of the Goddess Tree as Drasil. She learned the peace like she had always known it. Justine made friends with Stone and the others and soon felt like a part of the family. I knew some great change was coming, or why else would the Goddess send us such a visitor? Yet I just watched and waited."

"What else could you do?" Patrick said, "I am honoured that you welcomed Justine."

"She told us about you and your wisdom. She would say some wise thing, and when we asked, she would tell us it was something you said. I was filled with hope when she said she was going to bring you here. I waited as long as I dared, but I needed to keep the peace and go with Marisha. I am sorry I wasn't there to welcome you properly."

"Stone was there and made us welcome."

"Yes," Davvad said, and chuckled. "We had a few words about that too, but I am glad he did. He is a good boy for all his impatience with the peace."

"Justine likes him, though not as much as he would like."

"She is good for him. She makes him think in new ways, she makes all of us think in new ways. I would never have thought to rally the villagers in the tents the way she did. I have seen the way that he looks at her when he thinks she isn't looking."

They arrived at the gates and were let through. The guard at the makeshift gate had been doubled, but the guards didn't look too sure of themselves. Almost no one was on the streets of the City as they walked the same route that the children must have taken only two days before. There were lamps lit in the Council Chamber and Davvad led them straight into the chamber that Patrick had been dismissed from the day before.

The Chair looked up at the interruption and frowned.

"What is this about?" she asked.

"We have some information that the Council should hear,"

Davvad said.

"We are busy," the Chair snapped at him, "and there are proper channels."

"There is no time," Davvad stood behind the empty chair. "What is easy is not always what is right."

"We've heard this before," another councillor said.

"You didn't listen then either, as I recall," Brother Raston said.

"Careful, Brother," one of the others said.

"The Goddess is planning to massacre the Graffire army, if the Rakkikt army interferes they may be caught up in the destruction too."

"No one would mourn the loss of the Graffire. They brought it upon themselves when they invaded. However, I expect their destruction to be at the hand of our friends the Rakkikt."

"When was the last time a war was fought in these lands?" Patrick asked.

"There has been no conflict here since the Peace was signed," one of the councillors in the robes of a Brother said.

"Not quite," Patrick said. "Remember, Hamlan was once a country in its own right."

"Nonsense," the Brother said, "I spent the night in the library. None of that is in the scriptures."

"Your scriptures stop with the signing of the Peace. You need to read the diary I left with Sister Hersh."

"But we have no tales, no stories of an invasion."

"Would you tell stories that would humiliate members of the Peace? You hardly talk about the people who used to go teach the Peace in other lands, and that was only a generation ago."

"So you think you know our history better than we do?" asked the Chair.

"To be honest," Patrick said, "yes, I do. I spent weeks in the Library researching this very thing. This is what I do. You never thought to ask the question."

"So what would you have us do? Tell the Rakkikt not to come, give our land away to the Graffire?"

"I think it is too late to tell the Rakkikt not to come. They would come anyway. If the Pax falls, they would be next. They have to stop the invasion here where it won't do as much damage to their country."

"And the Graffire?"

"They should be warned," Patrick said.

"Why?"

"Because it is the right thing to do. Not everyone in that army is at fault for the invasion. Most are doing what they are told, because to refuse would mean death."

"They have a choice. They follow whoever is leading that army. They have driven people out of their homes, and killed people who were just trying to find food to feed their own. If it means their death, then so be it."

"This isn't about what kind of people they are, but what kind of people you are. Are you a people who will allow a massacre?"

"They broke the Peace, not us," the Chair said. "It is not our responsibility! We aren't going to send any more people to be killed."

"They need to be made welcome with the full formal --"

"Enough!" the Chair stood red faced. "Enough I say. We are through arguing. If you want to go warn the invaders, go ahead. I expect they will send your head back to us soon enough. If I knew how to undo my welcome, I would do it!"

"I think those words do the job," Patrick said.

"You may keep the Peace in word, but you have lost the Spirit." Davvad said.

"At least go and talk to Sister Hersh," Brother Raston begged. "She has seen the book."

"We will not make policy based on fairy tales and old stories," the Chair shouted. The other Councillors looked shocked, but said nothing.

Patrick turned and left, Davvad and Brother Raston followed him.

Justine's Journal

I don't know why Dad wants to warn those terrible people from Graffire. Well, maybe I do. I think it is what Jesus would do. They may be bad people, but they are still people. I don't know what to do. I want to help, but I'm just scared. This is even worse than Kelly's dad. Please can I go home now?

Love you,

Justine

Chapter Twenty-one

Patrick woke to the sound of the wind howling through the ropes of the tent. He could see his breath in the air. Justine was curled up against him. He got up and gently tucked the blanket around her. He dug around in the bag until he found his sweater. He thought about putting it on, then wrapped it around her too.

Marisha had a tiny fire going in a corner of the tent. The smoke that refused to go out the gap between wall and ceiling stung his eyes, but the warmth of the tea was welcome.

"Morning, Patrick," Davvad said. "I fear that if the army doesn't destroy us, that this weather will. Most of my people are not prepared for such cold."

"Are such changes in weather common?"

"Not common, but not unheard of either."

They drank their tea in silence. Justine crawled out of their corner wearing Patrick's sweater. It was almost long enough to be a dress on her. She had the sleeves rolled up to her elbows.

"Tea's on," Patrick said. Marisha handed her a cup.

"How did it go at the Council last night?" Justine asked.

"Not good is probably being generous," Patrick said. "Committees don't do well in a crisis."

"So now what?"

"Someone still has to go to the Graffire and warn them for all the good it will do." Patrick took a long sip of his tea, then sighed. "The Council generously gave me permission to do so. I think I knew it would come to this as soon as I read that book. The Goddess has been moving me around like a piece on a board. She brought us here, showed me that book and the fresco. Her plan isn't done yet. I'm not interested in fulfilling her plan. I'm interested in saving a lot of lives. Talking to the Graffire is the only way I can think of accomplishing that.

"I don't want you to go, Daddy," Justine said. "I don't want to lose you too."

Patrick went over and knelt beside her.

"If anyone else could go, I would let them."

"I will go," Davvad said.

"No, friend Davvad," Patrick said, "for good or ill, the Goddess seems to have chosen me for this task. I was the one she showed the book to, and sent out to meet that wagon. Someone needs to offer the full formal welcome to the Rakkikt forces when they enter the country."

"I will travel north to meet them," Davvad said.

Stone came into the tent, his face white.

"I saw the wagon in the warehouse," he said. "I told them that I wanted to raise an army, but that a wise woman had told me to look at the heads first. I couldn't stand." Tears rolled down his face. "I cried like a little child. They let me out and told me to tell anyone else who wanted to start an army that real soldiers were coming from the North to drive out our enemy. When did we start trusting more in soldiers than in the Goddess?" He went into the corner and curled up in a ball. Patrick could see his shoulders shaking. Justine looked at her father, then walked over and sat beside her friend. Patrick could see her stroking his hair and heard her talking quietly to him.

"I will walk east until I meet the soldiers," Patrick said quietly "and I will give them the warning. If I don't return, then take care of Justine for me."

"She will be as a daughter to us," Marisha said.

Patrick walked over and sat beside his daughter. He looked at her for a long time.

"I'm sorry, but I must do this," he said finally.

She nodded and looked at him. "I know." She went back to whispering to Stone.

Patrick stood and looked around, but there was nothing else to say. He ducked out through the flaps and the cold wind grappled with his clothes, chilled already. He thought about his sweater, but he wasn't going to take it away from Justine. Setting his face, he walked toward the road. He didn't pass anyone, and no one stopped him when he turned east down the road.

The walk along the road reminded him of the agony of sore feet and carrying firewood to the city. Now the only thing that ached was his heart. He wished he could trade the heartache for sore feet. Perhaps he felt the Goddess pushing him, but he wasn't sure if he was doing what She wanted. He didn't care. He was doing what he needed to do.

Patrick wished he could send Justine home where it was safe. They had convinced themselves with games and songs there was no problem, but the soldiers were serious. Now they were in worse danger. Why didn't they just go home when they had the chance? Maybe the Goddess had been playing with his mind from the beginning, or maybe he was just a fool. He certainly felt like a fool walking into the cold night by himself.

He thought for some reason of Pastor Daniel's sermon at Ingrid's funeral. 'No father wants to lose a child.' That was what he was most afraid of here. That he would lose Justine.

"Watch over her, please." Patrick hoped God could hear him from this place. He didn't trust the Goddess. Once he'd thought the problem was a God who didn't understand him, but the truth was he didn't understand God. The Goddess on the other hand he understood all too well. She was all too like humans in her manipulation of others.

It was black as night when he reached the trees, but it was too cold to stop so he kept walking along the slightly lesser darkness that was the road. He half expected an arrow to fly into his chest, though he hadn't seen any of the soldiers in white carrying a bow. He shivered uncontrollably and was barely able to put one foot in front of the other.

Somehow he kept walking through the night until he saw a light ahead. As he got closer he saw that it was a fire, and two men in white uniforms stood beside it warming their hands.

Patrick walked up to them and tried to still his chattering teeth.

"You won't find any welcome here," one said.

"Go back to where ever you came from," the other said.

Patrick just shook his head; he couldn't force any words past his teeth.

"Well, don't say we didn't warn you." The first one said as strong arms took hold of Patrick. He was quickly tied with coarse rope.

"Better take him to the surgeon first. We don't want him dying before His Highness gets to talk to him."

"Poor blighter," the second guard said, "he'll wish he was

dead soon enough."

Patrick was carried to a stifling hot tent and left on a cot. One end of the rope tying his wrists was fastened to bed. He laid shivering and trying to convince his body now he was warm, it should cooperate, but even in the heat he felt cold to his very core.

A man in a white uniform with a red patch came in and looked at him.

"I'm not sure you're worth saving," he said, "but I have my orders." He cut the rope from Patrick's hands and waved at another man who had followed him in. "The baths, at least until he stops shivering. Give him hot water to drink if he can get it down without choking. We must get the temperature of his blood up if it isn't already too late. If he's still alive, bring him back here, put him to bed. You'd better stay and watch him." He walked out without looking back.

The other man picked him up as easily as Patrick used to carry Justine and walked out of the tent. Patrick barely noticed the cold. Almost immediately he was put in a hot bath and a scream was forced out of him, but the fiery heat moved inward and he gradually stopped shaking. A cup of steaming water was handed him and he drank it down. He was almost warm when he was plucked out of the water and carried back to the other tent.

"C c can I h h have d dry c c c clothes?" Patrick stuttered.

The man looked at him a moment and went to a trunk. He pulled pants and a shirt from it and tossed them to Patrick who forced his hands which now limp as cooked noodles to strip the wet clothes and put on the dry ones. When that task was finished, he fell into the bed and slept.

He woke a couple of times through the night. Once when the first man came in to look at him and told his assistant to put a blanket over him. The second was when the blanket shifted and the assistant carefully, even gently wrapped it back around him.

Morning arrived with pain shooting through his limbs. Patrick had to clench his teeth to keep from screaming in pain. He got up and walked around the bed, while the big assistant watched from a chair off to one side. The pains slowly subsided and other than feeling very weak, Patrick was fine.

The first man came in and nodded when he saw Patrick up

and about. He carried himself more like a soldier than a doctor. The lines on his face emphasised his frown of disdain.

"You can call me Surgeon. Ask, if you need something. My assistant here doesn't talk, but he understands well enough."

"Doesn't he have a name?"

"No, why would he need one? He does what he's told and so he can live another day. What does someone who lives one day at a time need with a name? If you are fortunate you will understand this someday." He glanced at the big man. "Feed him, then stay and watch." The surgeon left the tent again. The big man brought a bowl of gruel to Patrick. The mute slave was neither the bronze of the Pax or the olive complexion of the invading army. He reminded Patrick of the First Nations people.

"Is that all anyone eats around here?" Patrick asked. The man shook his head. Patrick ate the entire bowl and felt tired again, but there was another urgency making itself felt.

"Uh, I need to use the bathroom, take a piss?" The assistant pulled back a curtain to reveal a bucket. "Well, it could be worse," Patrick said. He made use of the bucket then went back to the cot. He was asleep before his head touched the mattress.

"He looks weak. They all look weak. It comes from worshipping a Goddess. A real man should worship a proper God." Patrick opened his eyes to look at a man dressed in white with a thin band of gold on his head that gleamed against his black hair. The man was much younger than the Surgeon, probably younger than Patrick. Patrick opened his mouth to speak, but the man struck him. "Do not speak unless you are required to. I know you have lots to tell me, but I will hear it in my own time and in my own way." Patrick bit down on his tongue to keep his words from spilling out.

"Good, you begin to learn your place." The man turned to leave. "Bring him to me tomorrow at sunrise."

"Yes, Your Highness," The surgeon bowed low. After the Prince left, the big assistant clambered to his feet.

"Watch him, feed him if he hungers." The surgeon left without looking back.

The assistant handed Patrick another bowl of the thin gruel.

188

"Thank you." The man's eyes widened a bit and he shook his head. "I'm not supposed to thank you?" The man shook his head again. "I don't want to get you in trouble," Patrick said, "So I will thank you in here." He tapped his head. The big man smiled an instant before he went back to his chair.

Patrick alternated between sleeping and walking around the tent. If he stayed away from the door flap, the big man simply watched him. He had another bowl of the gruel before he climbed into the cot and slept.

Justine's Journal

Dad went to warn the Graffire army. I can't believe it. I didn't even say goodbye. I know how much you love him, but can you let him come back, please? Please, please, please. I'll do whatever you want, God, if you just bring my Dad back.

Chapter Twenty-two

He was wakened by the surgeon and handed a bowl of gruel. There was some bitter tasting herb in it, but Patrick choked it down.

The surgeon just watched until Patrick had finished, then led him out of the tent. They were surrounded by a camp which looked almost as big as the one around the City, The refugees had made their tents into makeshift homes These tents stood in rigid lines and all looked identical. It was clear to Patrick the only purpose of this camp was military. Soldiers in white bustled about their work paying no heed to the surgeon and Patrick. He noticed a few others who worked in the background. The soldiers, like the surgeon and Prince were more olive toned than the Pax. These others were much more diverse though they were dressed in grey or brown. Their eyes flinched away from the surgeon. *More slaves. What have you got me into?* He silently asked the Goddess, but got no answer. He was on his own here.

The surgeon took him to a tent blood red in contrast to all the white that surrounded them.

"The Blood Tent," the surgeon said, "punishment and fear are its purposes. You will feel both before the day is out. If you still live, I will see you at dusk." He pushed Patrick through the opening.

The tent was dark and it took a while for Patrick's eyes to adjust to the light. What he saw made him close his eyes.

"None of that," said the Prince, "open your eyes or I will cut the lids from them."

Patrick opened his eyes and tried to slow his heart.

"You have much to tell me."

"Yes," said Patrick, "there is no need for this."

"I will pretend, this once, that I gave you leave to speak." The Prince sounded bored. "Speak again, and I will cut out your tongue."

That would do you a fat lot of good. The Prince frowned as if he could hear Patrick's thoughts. Rough hands seized him and dragged him to a table where they fastened his hands and feet to the corners.

190

"In the old days, you would be nailed to the table, until I allowed you release," the Prince said, "but sadly much knowledge has been lost and I would not be able to keep you alive long enough to be a suitable offering to the God."

"So, what weak begging for mercy shall I hear from your lips?" When Patrick didn't say anything, the Prince struck him. "Speak, fool!"

"The Goddess sent me to warn you." The Prince's gloved hand covered Patrick's mouth.

"You are not begging," he said, "I will only hear begging." He uncovered Patrick's mouth.

"She will destroy you." Patrick said before the gloved hand covered his mouth again.

"Begging," the Prince said. "I will hear your pitiful threats when I wish to."

"Then you will die," Patrick said.

"Perhaps you need a lesson," the Prince said. He fitted a device to Patrick's left hand and began twisting the wheel on the side. His hand was being crushed between two plates of steel. Sure he felt the crack of bones breaking, before the Prince suddenly spun the wheel the reverse direction. The relief of the pressure was almost as bad as the pain itself. "Now you are learning," the Prince whispered in Patrick's ear, "that all the world is pain."

"Your world," Patrick said, "not mine."

The Prince moved to strike him again but instead caressed his face, then gripped his cheek and twisted viciously.

"All the world is pain," the Prince hissed.

"I don't live in this one," Patrick said, "I came through the Tree."

"Ah." The Prince studied him. "Then let me see if I can convert you." He spun the wheel on the press and crushed Patrick's hand again. "The Goddess would have you believe that peace is possible. That people can just share what they need. Look at them, they are weak, miserable, fearful."

"Yeah, they were so fearful that they were singing and dancing, until you massacred their friends and family."

"Pain can do strange things." The Prince picked up a device

191

and fastened it to Patrick's other hand. The wheel was on the top of this one. When the Prince turned it, a spike drove down into his hand. At the same time the Prince tightened the wheel on his left hand.

"Which is worse," the Prince asked, "the pain in your left," he tightened it another turn, "or your right?" The spike might have gone right through his hand.

"Actually, listening to you trying to justify murder and war is far worse," Patrick said. The Prince laughed and left the torture devices on Patrick's hands. He brought over a red-hot poker and put it so close to Patrick's chest his shirt smouldered. He felt the red heat and wanted to scream, but something else took over.

"The need to cause pain is a sign of weakness," his voice said.

"Weakness is the fear of pain."

"Avoiding pain is not weakness, embracing it is not strength."

"All creatures fear pain; control pain and control the creatures."

"Why control them when we can give them lives and let them control themselves?"

"Because they don't control themselves!" The Prince was frothing at the mouth, but the voice still poured out of his mouth. "They get lost, they forget, they wander away."

"They won't worship pain."

"But your peace has made them weak. They just sit and wait for you to come and rescue them again. Then they will forget. They are made to serve us."

"No, Father put us here to serve them!"

The Prince arched over backwards and fell to the ground, the poker painted a streak of pain across Patrick's chest before falling to the floor. Patrick breathed until the pain receded.

"Wouldn't it have been polite to ask before you took over my life?"

A faint light appeared in the tent and Patrick's pain receded.

"Would you have said yes?"

"Hell no! This fight is between you and that thing, why let

192

me do all the suffering?"

"Yet you chose to walk this road."

"Because I wasn't going to let you destroy an entire people without giving them warning."

"They are your enemies."

"They aren't my enemies. You created this situation."

The Prince stirred on the floor.

"What will happen will happen."

The light vanished. The Prince pushed himself to his feet and staggered from the tent.

"Oh God, what have I brought Justine into?" Patrick said, "Please hear me. All I ever wanted was for her to be happy. What do I do?"

Love.

The word dropped into his thoughts like a stone.

"But they're going to kill everyone. They're going to kill Justine!"

Love.

This time the word bubbled up from beneath his fear.

"I'm so scared, I have never believed in You like I should. What's going to happen to me?"

Love.

The word was accompanied by a vision of a man nailed to a cross. Yet he looked at Patrick with eyes holding no blame, only compassion.

"If I must die, then I will die, but take care of Justine." Patrick let the tears flow from his eyes. "I am yours." A touch brushed his heart not affecting the agony in his hands, but healing a wound deep within his soul.

Love.

The word came to him one last time like a light in a dark room. He saw his anger and pride and fear. They were nothing in the truth of that light. It was out of his hands now. Strangely at peace, he stared into the darkness of the tent and prayed for Justine.

Hours later the surgeon came and removed the presses from Patrick's hands. The big assistant carried Patrick back to the cot and laid him gently on it. There might have been pity in the slave's eyes as he tucked the blanket around him.

The next day the Prince came and collected Patrick again. This time he was hung from his hands and feet and stretched until he was sure his arms were going to come off.

"I sent emissaries into this land offering strength and honour instead of this weak peace. My emissaries didn't return. I sent more, and they too vanished into the lie that is this peace." The Prince walked around the tent as he talked. Occasionally he caressed one instrument of torture or another. "Once it was clear that this peace was a lie and a sham I had no choice but to call up my army and bring honour to this wretched land." He stopped and glared at Patrick. "I want this land for my Empire. I will be greater than my father. I will teach the sacred pain to these people and they will bemoan their weakness."

"You will die," Patrick gasped, "and your country will fade from memory. You don't have to do this."

"So this weak people will suddenly become true warriors again and slaughter me and my army?" The Prince struck Patrick so he thought his arms would pull right off. "No, they will beg me to stay and rule them. They will give themselves to me or they will die. It is the way of the world." The Prince walked out of the tent. Sometime later the big slave came and collected him. He was fed gruel and tucked carefully into bed. The big man looked around to see that they were alone, then tapped his head. Patrick nodded then collapsed into sleep.

The next day the gruel had an odd taste. Soon Patrick's head was spinning. The big slave put a finger to his lips. When Patrick was strapped to the table he only felt the ropes as a distant discomfort. The Prince wielded a knife like a pencil on his chest scribbling lines then rubbing black powder into the cuts. All Patrick felt was a distant coolness. The Prince was furious at his lack of response and went stomping from the tent screaming for the Surgeon. The Surgeon came in and poked and prodded at Patrick.

"He seems to have been drugged, your Highness."

"I know he's been drugged!" The Prince slapped Patrick, "I want to know who!"

"I am the only one treating him. My medicines are locked

194

up. No one could have given him the drug."

"Well, someone did," the Prince said. "I suggest you find them before you find yourself on this table."

The Surgeon paled, then bowed and walked out of the tent. The Prince threw the equipment around, then left the tent as well.

The big slave came and collected Patrick. When he carried Patrick into the tent there were two soldiers in white standing on either side of the door. The slave dumped Patrick on the bed, then tossed the blanket over him. He squatted in the corner with his head down while Patrick slept.

He was wakened by a slap. He opened his eyes to see one of the guards standing over him.

"Time for dinner," he said and handed Patrick a bowl. The Surgeon was watching from the door. Patrick forced himself to sit up and tried to hold the bowl while he used the spoon. He spilled more gruel on himself than he got in his mouth.

"Feed him you fools," the Surgeon said. "The Prince will be angry if he weakens."

"Yeah, and if he is drugged again we'll be blamed."

The Surgeon walked over and kicked the slave. The big man crawled over and began spooning the food into Patrick. Patrick was sure the man winked at him. The next day the soldiers and the surgeon repeated their argument and the slave ended up feeding him. Again, he tasted the drug in the gruel.

This time when the Prince went out red faced and screaming he came back with the Surgeon and the two soldiers being dragged by more soldiers. The three were strapped to different pieces of equipment then the Prince began torturing them. The drug could dull the physical pain, but it couldn't stop the screams and moans from bringing tears to Patrick's eyes. The Prince saw the tears and sneered at him.

The screaming went on for a very long time.

Justine's Journal

All I want is my Dad back.

Chapter Twenty-three

Patrick woke still strapped to the table. The sounds of breaking camp came from outside the tent. The big slave came in to collect him. The man looked at the bloody corpse that was once the surgeon and nodded. He lifted Patrick from the table and took him to the Surgeon's tent. Patrick saw the soldiers in white formed up in tight formation. The two guards who had met him at the edge of camp came to the tent.

"We have the pleasure of guarding you," the one said. "Don't try to escape. We won't be gentle."

The other one didn't say anything, but he handed Patrick some warm clothes. The big slave helped Patrick put them on. The army was already in motion by the time he was dressed and his keepers pulled him into line and marched off with him in between them.

After a while the motion loosened the pain in his hips and Patrick could walk almost normally. Whenever he faltered his guards dragged him along until he got to his feet again. They marched until he could see the City in the distance. The army formed up and waited. The air grew even colder and the wind became almost strong enough to push the soldiers off their feet. The sky loomed over them all, black with thick clouds.

The Prince came up to him.

"Now you will see the end of your peace. Nothing in this weak land can damage my forces. Even that poor army waiting beside your City will be crushed. My emperor will reign supreme and everyone will fear him."

Patrick just shook his head. The Prince stalked off to the front of the army.

"Whatever happens," Patrick said, "don't draw your weapons."

"The Prince will have our guts on a stick if we don't."

"In a short time, I expect the Prince to be the least of your problems."

The pair pushed him forward.

"If it's going to be like that I want a front row view," one said.

The entire white army marched forward in slow cadence. The only sounds were the tramp of feet and the howling of the wind. The march went on for hours. Patrick walked just behind the Prince and his bodyguard.

They stopped near the edge of the tent City. Soon a delegation from the City appeared. The Chair of the Council was there, and the two envoys from Rakkikt along with another man in shiny steel armour. Oddly, Brother Raston was also there. When another small figure stepped out from behind the Brother, Patrick moaned.

It was Justine.

Justine stepped forward carrying a cup. The wind whipped at her dress and tugged at her braids.

One guard put his hand over Patrick's mouth, but fear was already holding him frozen in place.

She walked up to the Prince and curtsied, and offered him the cup.

"Be welcome in peace, O Prince." Patrick could hear her voice clearly, "Be welcome to our hearth and home and land. Speak freely for the Goddess watches between us. May the land rise and consume us if either of us breaks the peace."

Even frozen in fear, Patrick's heart swelled in pride. Though he wished her worlds away from this cold and dangerous place, her beauty gave him courage. Her spirit shone like the sun through a gap in the clouds.

Patrick wanted to run to her side and hug her. He smiled, then the Prince dashed the cup to the ground and crushed it under his foot.

"Peace!" he screamed. "Peace! I don't want peace. I want blood and fear and GLORY!" He whipped out his sword as he screamed. Justine backed from him and tripped. The man in armour stepped forward and was reaching to help Justine to her feet when the Prince stabbed him through the neck and kicked him backwards.

"NO!" Patrick screamed, the arms of his guards holding him back. The Prince whipped his sword in a flourish, and turned to look at Patrick.

He smiled.

Then he stabbed Justine through the heart.

Patrick thought the sword went into his own heart, it hurt so much; the pain left no room for anything else. The world stopped, frozen in place with his heart shattered while an insane Prince held a sword pinning his daughter's heart to the earth.

The world went black, then a spear of pure incandescent fury struck the Prince. The lightning held the Prince in its grip and he twitched and danced as he had in the red tent when his god had possessed him. Then it dropped him to the ground.

"Now what?" one of the guards asked.

"Now you all die," Patrick shook himself loose from their grip. The lightning struck other places leaving men twisted and smoking. The earth split open and pulling screaming soldiers into its depths. The wind howled into a funnel and began tearing the ranks of white uniformed men to shreds. The land had gone mad. People from the City were fleeing or frozen in fear. A people who refused violence watched their land murder the invading army. The soldiers from Rakkikt crept forward. They carefully kept their hands away from the swords on their belt. The wind blew them back. Patrick heard the bang and crash of their armour as they tumbled away from the centre of the land's rage.

Soldiers in white bolted for the woods, but the wind and the ground conspired to hold them fast while the tornados and lightning slaughtered them.

Patrick ignored it all. As if he was in a bubble separated from the rest of the world. He reached Justine and knelt beside her. He picked her up and cradled his daughter in his arms.

The first time he had ever held her, he'd known this person would own his heart. He remembered trying to explain her mom would never come home; holding her when she cried for grief or pain, the night at the hospital, the day with the mayor. He remembered the bright and shining light of her life.

He put his head back and howled his loss to the heavens and his voice drowned out the thunder and wind. He wanted them all dead, all dust.

"Daddy," came an impossible whisper from Justine, "Daddy, it's wrong. Make it stop." She opened her eyes for a brief moment, then smiled. "Hello, Mom." Her eyes closed again and she was gone.

Make it stop, she'd said. He saw lightning slaughtering soldiers, wind shredding them, the earth crushing them. He looked deep inside himself and found the part that took glee in this destruction, and crushed it. He pictured Justine with her smile and filled his soul with that picture.

"GODDESS," he roared. "Goddess, you have broken the peace!"

An immense power reached through him and he welcomed it. *Be at peace in my heart and soul.* It reached out and took hold of the lightning. It stilled the wind and calmed the earth. Then it brought the Goddess to stand before him. Beside the Goddess stood the God glowering like a bully caught in the act. The world about them had frozen in place.

"Goddess," Patrick said, "you have broken the peace. You invited my daughter here just to kill her, you brought me here to hand me over to torture."

"I never offered her the peace," the Goddess said. "She came of her own free will."

"Your people granted her the peace, they welcomed her, loved her, made her part of their family. You have broken the peace."

"I have won," the God gloated. He turned to his sister. "You will be cast out and I will rule this world."

"You're a miserable excuse for a God," Patrick said. "You think pain is the way to rule, but pain exists to warn us of something wrong in us. You should be teaching wisdom, health, love. Instead you wallow in the worst of what your people do and urge them to worse yet."

The being that inhabited him spoke.

"My children," She said, "What have you become?"

The God and Goddess went to their knees.

"Mother," they said.

"I picked this world from Yggdrasil for you so you could grow, not squabble over it like children. You have wronged this visitor from another world, you have wronged his daughter. More, you have shattered the people I gave for you to serve and love. Since this man has called you to account, he will name your penance."

"I think," Patrick said to the God, "perhaps it is time for you to learn something of pain for yourself. Go and learn what lies beneath the pain and then you may be fit to rule your people. Live as a human for a thousand years."

The God's face reflected shock, then fear, then he was gone.

"Are you going to banish me too?" asked the Goddess.

"No, your problem is your impatience," Patrick said. "You will follow your people and learn from them. They must find their own peace, and not one enforced by fear. Their love must be a choice, not compelled. You tried, but you wanted it to be easy. Peace is never easy. Love is never without a price. For a thousand years, you will be bound to the library, but unable to command, only ask."

The Goddess bowed her head in submission, then she too vanished.

Patrick looked inward.

"And what of you?" he asked, "Did you not allow this?

"I did," the voice inside him said, "and yet, would you have me compel my children? Would you make me less than you who trusts his daughter with his life?"

"No," Patrick said. "I would not, but in my world, my God did his own dying. He died for us, for me, out of love, not because someone manipulated him."

"Ahh," the voice sighed, "maybe someday I will learn such courage."

"Until then leave me to my grief."

"Grief is not forever," said the voice, and the world started moving around Patrick again.

"Not forever," said Patrick, "but it is now."

He picked up his daughter's body and carried her back to the City picking his way through the blasted landscape of the Goddess's anger.

The rain started before he reached the City. It washed the blood from Justine's dress and mixed with the tears on Patrick's face. Stone met him and Patrick could see his tears through the rain.

"If you want to hate me," Stone said. "I'll understand. I didn't want her to go, but she insisted."

"She was like that," Patrick said. "She did what she thought was right."

Stone walked with him until he met with the Chair of the Council. The woman looked older, less sure of herself. She fell to her knees before Patrick.

"You were right."

"Yes."

"She saved us," the woman said.

"More than you know," Patrick said.

"I'll resign, we'll all resign. We were fools."

"You don't get off that easy. Live, learn, rebuild, use the chance she gave you."

Others gathered as Patrick stood. Marisha took her from Patrick.

"I will look after her," she said. Patrick let her go reluctantly. She seemed like such a light burden to be causing so much pain.

He went to follow after them.

"What do we do with the soldiers that surrendered?" asked one of the envoys from Rakkikt.

"If they will follow the peace," Patrick said, "let them stay. If they don't, send them home. Make sure you give the slaves a chance to stay. No one else must die."

People kept asking him questions and Patrick kept answering until Davvad picked him up and carried him off to a room in the Council House and laid him on the bed.

"Sleep," Davvad said, "or if not sleep, then rest."

Chapter Twenty-four

Patrick woke to the sound of rain on the window. He was back on the soft mattress in the Council House. *Justine.* He moaned and tears streamed down his face.

Brother Raston came to him.

"It should have been me."

"Perhaps."

"I could have been the one to represent the Goddess."

"Yes, but you weren't. There are no easy answers, not for us, not for the gods. Justine knew that."

Sister Hersh visited too. "I am sorry."

"I know."

"I've seen the plans for the monument, it will be beautiful."

"She doesn't need a beautiful monument. She needs to be here talking with me or with Stone playing a game."

"I know, but it is all we have left to offer. All work in the City has stopped except for the work on burying the dead and building the monument. The Chair of the Council is building the casket with her own hands. She was a carpenter before she became Chair."

Patrick just nodded. None of it mattered. It was Ingrid's death again, but worse because he didn't have Justine to live for.

"The Goddess showed up in the Library saying that you sent her there."

"Not just me."

"Who?"

"Her Mother."

"She hasn't acted in the world since it was made."

"She didn't make the world. It was already here. She just picked it from Yggdrasil."

"What...what did she say to you?"

"That she was sorry."

"The Mother apologized to you?"

"I told her in my world, my God did his own dying."

"Brother Raston keeps telling me how different you are. I didn't believe him until now. So, what are we supposed to do with the Goddess?"

"Teach her real Peace."

"You want us to teach the Goddess."

"You'll have plenty of time." Patrick turned back to the window and watched the rain crawl across it. "Will you speak at Justine's service?"

"I serve the Goddess that killed her."

"You're a friend."

"Then I will speak." She left him alone with the rain and his tears.

Two days later Patrick, Davvad, Stone and Barsta carried her through the rain, out to the completed monument. All work stopped in the City and every person who could walk surrounded the site.

"We are a people of peace," Hersh said, "but we forgot too easily that peace must be a choice we make every day. It can't be just a habit or we lose the reason for our peace. Our hospitality needs to be more than custom it needs to be part of us. It must be so ingrained that we can't pass a person worse off than ourselves without sharing what we have. If we are to change, it must be each one of us who changes.

"Justine taught us that. She was a guest, and gave without measure. She showed our children how to play in the midst of calamity. She showed us all how to truly honour each other. She died because we didn't want to. Now she will continue to teach us. When we pass this monument, we must stop and meditate on the gift she gave us. There is a daughter sitting with her father, a son playing games with his friends, while she lies here."

Patrick stepped forward.

"People of Pax," he said. "Justine is with her mother and our God. Our God is also a God of peace, but it's a peace that doesn't come from following rules even if they took three years to write. This peace is knowing that God loves us, no matter where we are or what we have done. Whether we live or whether we die, we belong to God. Whatever Justine did, she did because she trusted God even beyond death. She isn't lost, but found."

The pipers who had come with the Rakkikt army played a plaintive tune for her. The people wept and Justine's service became their memorial for all the lost.

After it was over Patrick went back to their tent, but it was all packed up.

"I will go to relatives while Davvad rebuilds our home." Marisha said. "I will miss her. I will miss you too." She led Boddi away, still attached to her waist by a rope.

Risha and Hishon came and said farewell shyly. They were travelling west with some new friends they had made in the camp. The tent City was disbanding and people returning to rebuild their lives. There was nothing here anymore. Patrick went to find Davvad. He found Stone instead, talking to some of the Rakkikt soldiers.

"Dad's arguing with the Council," Stone said. "I am going with the Rakkikt to teach the peace."

Patrick just nodded and walked to the Council Chambers.

Davvad was there on the steps speaking with the Chair.

"We wish you would reconsider," the Chair of the Council said.

"I have a home to rebuild," Davvad said. "I bid you peace." He took Patrick's elbow and led him away.

"What did they want?" asked Patrick.

"They wanted me to sit in the Empty Seat."

"Someone needs to."

"They can find someone else."

"That's how Justine ended up dead. No one wanted to do what was needed."

Davvad hung his head.

"You are right, friend Patrick. I will tell them I will take the Chair when my home is rebuilt. Marisha may never forgive me."

"She will be proud of you. Lead your people like you lead your family."

Davvad enveloped Patrick in a hug then walked off after the Chair of the Council.

"I'm not sure the Council knows what they're letting themselves in for," Patrick said.

"With luck they won't find out until he is firmly planted in the King's Chair." Hersh joined him on the pavement and watched Davvad talk to the Chair of the Council.

"I wasn't fair with him," Patrick said. "I shouldn't use Justine's name that way."

"What would Justine have said to him?"

"She would have told him to take the seat."

"Well then," Hersh shrugged. "He's doing what she wanted."

With no tent to go to, Patrick went back to the room in the Council House. Davvad was staying down the hall until he was ready to go home to rebuild. Patrick heard him and Stone arguing.

"I thought you went out in the rain to argue," he said to them.

"The Peace must be different now," Davvad said. "It cannot be about avoiding conflict. We have to move past that and learn how to disagree and still keep the peace."

"That's why I need to go," Stone said. "We have to start teaching the Peace to our neighbours or we will be right back where we are now."

"Someone else can go," Davvad said. "You're young yet. I need you with me."

"So which is it? That I'm too young or that you need me safe at home?"

"I am still your father!"

"Patrick," Stone said, "you tell him, if Justine wasn't too young, then neither am I."

"How much do you trust each other?" Patrick said. "If you trust, listen past the words. I won't give you answers."

Patrick went back out to stand by Justine's grave and let the rain pour over him. There had been a gentle, warm rain since he walked up to the City with Justine in his arms. The fields had turned a brilliant green and flowers speckled the expanse. The damage done to the ground had vanished with the rain.

The entire City surrounded him and supported him in his grief. People he had never met hugged him wordlessly. Patrick didn't care. The loss he felt was so overwhelming that nothing anyone did could touch it. Only the faint memory of that love he had felt in the darkness of the tent sustained him. Justine was with that love. He had lost her, but her God had her safe.

"Patrick."

"Stone."

"I came to say goodbye." The young man carried a pack and stood straight.

"I know."

"I loved her." The depth of Stone's pain flashed behind his eyes.

"I know that too."

"I will never love another."

"Justine wouldn't like that. She would want you to be happy. Find someone to love. Have lots of children, teach them the peace. Give it time."

"OK." Stone threw his arms around Patrick. "If I could have died in her place, I would have."

"So would I, son, so would I."

"I'm going north to Rakkikt with the army. The envoys have promised Dad to watch over me. They seemed pleased to have me."

"Good, teach them well, but don't lose yourself."

A little while later Davvad came.

"It is time."

"I know."

"She's not there."

"I know that too."

"I found this in your section of the tent." He handed Patrick a small book. "I think it's for you."

Patrick stepped inside the monument and opened the journal. He saw Justine's handwriting. She had written her name carefully under her mother's name.

Chapter Twenty-five

I'm so scared. Davvad and Marisha have been standing outside all day talking to each other. Boddi is crying and Stone looks like he wants to. These soldiers in white have wrecked everything. I told them you could help. You always help me.

Patrick flipped forward a few pages.

It's better now that we met up with Davvad and Marisha, though now Stone won't hold my hand. I think he's afraid Tammi and Cinda will tease him.

He flipped forward reading a bit here and there.

...Dad's spending all his time at the Library, so Stone and I are just walking all over the Tent City. He sometimes holds my hand. I get all mushy when he does that. I wonder if this is how Dad felt about Mom. We met some people on the West side. They wore leather and stuff. They said they were Westers. They came from the mountains. There weren't a lot of the soldiers in white there, but they were scared anyway. They have relatives in the City. I liked them, but Stone said they talked funny...

...We won! We finally won. It was so awesome. We went all the way into the City and sang the song. Some boys did some neat clapping thing and the guy who was like the Mayor or something came and talked to us. Stone was just as excited as I was. I looked around and everyone had smiles on their faces...

...everything is horrible again. Poor Dad. He was outside the City and met a bunch of the soldiers in white. They told him that their country was taking over the Pax and didn't care about peace, and nobody could go for food anymore. There were heads in the wagon. That's even sadder than it is gross. Stone is

all angry and wanting to raise an army again. No one will let
their kids out of sight so there is no one to play with except Stone
and Boddi, and they're too scared even for Rock, Paper, Knife.
Dad's not coming home tonight so Marisha's going to stay with
me. I almost wish it was Stone, but Dad would kill me...

...Dad's back! but I've never seen him so white. I don't
think I ever want to let him go again....

...I am so mad! And scared too. Dad wants to warn those
awful soldiers that the Goddess will kill them if they don't go
home. I don't think that would be so bad, but then I thought
about Kelly and her missing her dad even though he was mean.
If they're all killed, that is a lot of kids missing their Dads...

...Dad went to talk to the Council. Stone and I had a huge
fight. He was going on and on about building an army. I finally
yelled at him to go look at the heads in the warehouse before he
thought any more about armies and fighting. He went all stiff
and just walked away. I'm sure he hates me now. Marisha's mad
because Stone went off without telling her. Everything's a mess.
I want to go home.

Dad's back from the Council and they wouldn't listen, so
now he's going to go himself. Davvad wanted to, but Dad said
the Goddess meant for him to go. I was so scared, I couldn't even
cry. Then Stone came in and he was crying and talking about
the heads. He just curled up in the corner. I so much wanted
him to come and hold my hand and make me feel better just for
a bit. I went over and held his hand and talked to him and tried
to make him feel better. Dad came and told me he was going,
and he was sorry. I just nodded or something and didn't even

say goodbye. I think he told Davvad and Marisha to take care of me like he didn't think he was coming back...

...Davvad's gone too now, and I think Stone is as scared as I am that his dad won't come back. Marisha saw me writing and getting all blubbery. She suggested that I write a letter to you and maybe it will make me feel better....

Dear Dad, I am so scared, so I thought I would write this down so you could read it when you get back and we could laugh at how silly I'm being. Davvad went off north just after you left. Marisha cried for a long time. It's quiet here without you snoring beside me. I miss you.

Love Justine

Dear Dad, Brother Raston came by this morning. He had a lot of questions about Drasil. He wanted to know if I had met the Goddess. I told him I didn't know any Goddess, but I did know Jesus. He didn't know who Jesus was. I told him all everything I knew about him. I think it upset Brother Raston that our God became so weak. I tried to explain that God's power is love, but don't think I did very well. I'll have to ask the minster when I get home.

It's been cold and windy all day. I hope you're all right. I'm cold so I'm still wearing your sweater. I hope you don't mind. Davvad isn't back and Marisha's worried. I told her it's only been one day, but I'm worried too. Some kids came by today looking for you. The leader said his name is Barsta. He's older than Stone. I think he was one of the boys who stopped us when we arrived. He said he knew you and traded questions for sticks.

You didn't tell me about that. I tried to tell him what it was like back home, but I don't think he understood much.

Dear Dad, It's even colder this morning and the sky is really dark. If we were at home I would think it was going to snow, but they don't know what snow is here. Can you imagine that? They've never seen snow. Brother Raston came back, and Barsta came with him. It's funny, when Barsta is around, Stone holds my hand the whole time. Brother Raston thinks he heard of snow in the mountains.

The food was cold this morning because there was no firewood left, but they wouldn't let Barsta and the others go find more. It's too dangerous. He was all mad, but I told him I would rather eat cold gruel than have his head chopped off. I think Stone and Barsta would be friends if Stone wasn't so worried I'll like Barsta better than him. As if. I haven't told him though. I like holding his hand.

Brother Raston was talking about the Goddess again. He still thinks that she's going to show up and kick butt and send all the soldiers home. I tried to tell him that she sent you to talk to them. He said you don't believe in the Goddess, so how could you let something you didn't believe in tell you what to do.

Then I said that just because you argued about something didn't mean that you didn't believe in it. I told him how you argued with God for ages because of Mom dying. Sister Hersh showed up and dragged Brother Raston away. They were arguing about some book you found for them. Here you are in a completely different universe and you are still doing reports for people. Come on, Dad, it's time to get with it. Just kidding, I'm really proud of how your boss says you're the best report writer in his office. It's like 'Go Dad'. I'm glad you're my Dad. I wish you would come back soon. I miss you.

Love Justine

Dad, it's been days now and you're still gone. I'm starting to get really scared. What if the soldiers just kill you? I like Davvad and Marisha and all, but I want you to be my Dad. Please be careful.

Davvad came home today. Marisha is so happy that she is crying all over the place. Davvad keeps patting her back and going 'There, there, I'm home aren't I?' He met the Rakkikt people not very far north of the City. He thinks they were already on the way, which is pretty much what you said isn't it?

Anyway, he did the whole welcome thing and warned them that bad stuff would happen if they broke the peace. The Rakkikt General made all the soldiers tie their swords into their scabbards. He didn't want any accidents. He seems like a nice enough guy. His armour is all shiny. I could see my face in it. My hair is a mess. I'm going to ask Risha to fix it for me.

The General and the Council have been talking all day about what to do. Davvad got to go 'cause the General wanted him there. He said the Brother who sat on Council was as bad as Raston, thinking that the Goddess was just going to solve the problems. The General said that he hoped she would, but he was going to plan for a battle anyway. Davvad was telling us all about it at supper. The food was warm again because the Rakkikt have these stoves that use other stuff than wood for fuel. They cooked for the whole City. The food was the best in just ages! It was all tomatoey and it reminded me of spaghetti night.

We haven't had spaghetti in way too long. I miss it. I miss you, I miss Mom.

It was funny, Barsta brought some young kids for a visit. They said they were Pauli's kids. We had tea and played Rock, Paper, Knife. Stone tried to teach the oldest boy to juggle and Barsta taught him the fancy clapping he and his friends did for our song. It was strange to be all scared and worried about you and the Pax and everything, then to be playing like there was nothing wrong. I think it was good though.

I had this weird dream last night. This woman came to talk with me. She said she was the Goddess of this land. I asked her if she knew Jesus, but she just gave me a strange look. She said there was a really important job to do, and that I had to do it. I told her you were already doing the job for her and she gave me the look. You know, the one Ms. Hall used to give me before she got nice. She said I had to welcome the Prince of Graffire to the Pax, and I had to do it just right. She said I needed to say the words really clear and give him a cup. I asked what was supposed to be in the cup and she got mad at me. I said I guessed I would do it. After all you can't go around dissing Goddesses and things, but I think it's more than that. I think Jesus would want me to do it.

When I woke up I went to tell the others that the Goddess told me to do this and they were all scared and stuff, but I said, 'She's the Goddess.' So that was that. Risha made my hair look nice and I put on a cleaner dress. Brother Raston found this cup for me. I wanted him to put some stuff in it, but he said it was symbolic. I said I didn't want to give the Prince an empty *cup. What if he wanted to drink out of it? So, he finally said I could put water in it.*

Someone came and said they saw the army coming out of the trees. I've got to go. I'm really scared, but I have to do this, but first I'm going to find Stone and give him a proper kiss and tell him that if he would just wait a little while I would be his girlfriend.

Bye Daddy, I love you.

Justine

Patrick looked up from the page and saw Davvad waiting for him.

"I have to give this to Hersh, for the library."

"It was written for you."

"It's burned into my heart, but I want Hersh to put this in the library. I don't want them to forget that Justine was just a little girl. That she got scared and mad, and was just learning about falling in love."

"I'll wait."

"It's OK, I can catch up to you."

"I'll wait."

"OK."

Patrick left Davvad waiting at the grave and walked through the rain to the City. People turned to him and put their hands over their hearts, some patted him on the back. The children hugged him. It felt like forever before he walked into the shell around the library. He stopped the first Brother he saw.

"I'm looking for Hersh."

"She's in the library, with Her."

Patrick walked to the black doors and knocked on them. The Brother who opened them didn't say anything, but he put his hand over his heart and let him in.

He followed the glow of the Goddess to where she was standing weeping in the circle of the Brothers.

"I think that's enough crying," he said. "You're going to flood the City out."

"The rain isn't mine, Patrick," she said. "The Land is weeping for your daughter." Patrick shrugged.

He handed the book to Hersh. "This is Justine's journal. Please keep it safe. Read it too. Learn from it if you can."

The Goddess looked at him and put her hand over her heart. Patrick looked back at her, then he walked into the circle and hugged her.

"What was that?' she asked.

"Forgiveness," Patrick said. "I need to leave you behind, and I can't if I don't forgive you. Teach her well," he said to the Brothers and Sisters before he left.

He wandered the City until he found himself in a familiar street. then walked along until he saw the leather goods in the window. A knock on the door brought Pauli out. The Wester bowed, then enfolded Patrick in a hug, then bowed again. He brought Patrick through to the back room where Krysa and the children were sitting. The children mobbed him, telling how they had met Justine and how she had welcomed them and treated them so kindly. Krysa poured tea for Patrick and slid the cup to him.

They told him how they had cried at her funeral. The sun shone in the window and Patrick realized that the rain had stopped when he left the Library. It helped him to sit with people who had known Justine. It didn't ease the pain, but it reminded him that the loss had saved two peoples. After a while the children went outside to play.

"I want to tell you a story," Patrick said, and he told them about Hamlan and Darisha. They looked at him a long time with tears in their eyes while they listened to the children play.

"It is a greater gift than we knew that Justine gave us," Krysa finally said. She went into the shop and came back with a small leather bag and a tiny butterfly that could be pinned into a girl's hair.

"My oldest made the butterfly. He was going to give it to Justine, so I give it to you as a comfort. I made this bag. It is a worry bag. You put the things that grieve you or worry you and it is supposed to make your burden lighter." She put the butterfly into the bag and tied it to his belt.

"Your Justine has given us all a new chance at life."

Patrick just hugged her and said his farewells. He went out through the back so that he could thank the oldest boy for the butterfly.

"What's your name?" Patrick asked.

"I changed my name to Justi," the boy said, "if you don't mind."

"Justine would be proud." Patrick turned the butterfly over in his fingers and put it back in the bag. "Will you show me to the gate?" Justi ran in and yelled something to his parents then walked beside Patrick talking the whole way. At the gate, he bowed then ran off.

Patrick smiled and it felt strange.

Chapter Twenty-six

He met Davvad at the grave.

"Let's go."

They walked along the road Patrick had stumbled down, cold and alone in the dark. The army camp was gone, but a big man waited for him in the clearing.

"I guess your masters left you behind."

The man nodded.

"So you can come with us." Patrick said. "What's your name?"

The man shrugged.

"Will you let us name you?"

He nodded

Patrick turned to Davvad, "Davvad, my friend needs a name."

"You can be Paper, since we already have a Stone."

The man nodded at Davvad and smiled. He looked at Patrick and tapped the side of his head.

"Come on then, Paper." Patrick said, "Paper looked after me while I was with the Graffire. He kept me safe."

Davvad stopped and bowed to Paper. "Be welcome in my land, and my home. You will be my brother as long as I have breath."

Paper's eyes widened, then he hugged Davvad and then Patrick.

The birds still sang in the trees as they walked. They didn't need to sleep under the trees. People gave them food at villages that were being cleaned out or rebuilt. Men who used to wear white worked alongside the people of Pax. Patrick would have preferred to sleep under the trees. He was uncomfortable with the reverence that the people gave him.

"I'm no one special," he said to Davvad.

Paper tapped his head and Davvad looked at Patrick.

"I think he is telling me that people are going to thank me anyway. I guess they can't thank Justine, and so I get the thanks instead." Patrick scratched at his chest. All his injuries had vanished while he had spoken with the gods, though he hadn't noticed until after Justine's funeral. For some reason his chest itched. Paper caught his hand gently and looked sympathetically at him.

Patrick borrowed some paper and some charcoal.

"I think it is time that you learned how to read," he said and Paper's eyes widened and he nodded. He had learned the alphabet before the end of the day. By the next day he was writing short words.

They passed many of the soldiers who were now wearing various shades of grey with black arm bands.

"Most of Graffire's army didn't want to go home. They were afraid of the Emperor's reaction," Davvad said.

"As long as they are living in peace." Patrick said.

"As long as they are living in peace." Davvad agreed.

They got to the burned-out village Davvad had called home. Logs were laid out ready for notching. Two men were carrying another one in. When they saw the trio, they put the log down and ran up to them. They threw themselves at Patrick's feet.

"We don't deserve your mercy," the one said.

"We should have done something," the other one said.

Patrick looked at the two men who had guarded him while the Prince's army marched. They hadn't drawn their swords and the Goddess's wrath had missed them.

"Oh, stand up," Patrick said. "If I forgave the Goddess, I'm going to forgive you." They stood uncertainly, then put their hands over their hearts and bowed.

Davvad, Patrick and Paper helped with the rebuilding. The hard work left Patrick too tired to feel sorry for himself. In the evenings he talked with Paper and Davvad. The past slave was mastering writing at an incredible speed.

"Justine would be proud of you," Patrick said to the man. "She loved learning. Use your learning. Don't let doubts hold you back." Paper nodded and tapped the side of his head.

The houses were almost done when Patrick woke one morning and knew what he needed to do.

"I need to borrow an axe," Patrick said and Paper fetched

an axe from the pile of logs. "I'm going to talk to a friend." Davvad and Paper walked with him up the hill to where a tree waited. He hadn't looked properly at Drasil in this world, but the sense of immensity was the same.

Patrick put his hand on the bark.

"You know why I'm here," he said and lifted the axe. Then he heard Drasil the same way Justine must have. Not in words but in vast swirling thoughts. He felt Yggdrasil's grief. It was a grief that extended across universes so vast that it was beyond Patrick's comprehension. How had Justine befriended such a being? He forgave the Goddess who didn't care about Justine; now he needed to forgive her friend who grieved as he did.

He handed the axe to Paper. "I won't be needing this after all." He clasped hands with the man. Then he looked at Davvad. "I am glad we got to be friends. Remember Justine, celebrate, eat spaghetti." The tears started rolling down his face. "I need to go home. She has friends there too."

Davvad clasped Patrick in a bear hug.

"Nothing loved is ever lost," he said.

"I used to say that to Justine," Patrick said.

"She told me."

"It's time for me to go," Patrick hugged the World Tree.

Patrick was swept into the space between the universe and Drasil held him in a hug.

::Forgive me,:: Drasil said into Patrick's soul.::I didn't protect Justine. I promised and I failed.::

"You are not God," Patrick said, "and even you have limits."

"Yes," Drasil said, "for all that I live in the warp and weft of the universe, I am like you, both more and less than what you see. I connect, and because I connect, I love. Justine's heart called out to me and I made her my friend, and the universe was brighter for it."

"She loved you. Now she is gone and the universe is colder for it."

"Nothing loved is ever lost," Drasil said, "Justine told me that."

"She is lost to me," Patrick wailed, "Can't you find her?"

"No, I have lost her too."

"How long must I wait before I see her again?"

Drasil held him while he wept, and water fell on dry worlds and life bloomed. Drasil wept in his own way and stars exploded and scattered themselves as a gift across the lightyears. For a timeless eternity, the friends comforted each other in the spaces between the dimensions.

"I need to go home, Drasil" Patrick said, "If I have a home to return to. It doesn't matter, yet Justine was proud of the work I did, so I will do my work and try to honour hers."

"Go home then, friend. There will be light in your life again."

"No, Drasil. Not in my life. Not ever."

"Not ever is a very long time, Patrick."

They whirled in a last fall toward Patrick's home. For a brief second he felt the touch of something greater than the god who had stood in Patrick's skin and stopped the lightning and grieved for Patrick's child and her own children. It was even more immense than Yggdrasil who was the Tree upon which worlds grew. Yet for all its immensity Patrick felt it knew him and understood his pain. He was engulfed in light that was more than light, a love beyond his comprehension, a promise of comfort.

"Patrick." It was just the merest whisper, but it resounded through his entire being. So familiar he thought he had heard every day of his life. "My child, she was never yours to hold or lose, only to love."

"My Lord," Patrick whispered in reply. "I doubted, and I failed you."

"Love never fails," the whisper came again.

In between the worlds he wept again. He was held and knew he was loved. Loved even more than he loved Justine, and like Justine, sent out into the universe to shine as bright as he knew how. Something whispered in his soul. A WORD filled him beyond comprehension. He glimpsed a PURPOSE.

Love

Patrick found himself hugging the tree in the schoolyard. It was dark and cold. He gave Drasil a final pat, then started the walk home. The huge emotions that filled him while Drasil

220

carried him home wouldn't fit in his body. He felt empty.

He didn't know why he was heading toward a house he was sure would be a burned out wreck. They'd been gone for months; but he had nowhere else to go; so, he walked the familiar sidewalk toward his house. His footsteps became heavier and heavier. For all that she had done in the Pax, the real loss was what Justine could have done in this world. She was so much to so many people. He didn't know how he was going to explain her loss. Yet he knew he wasn't alone. God knew what it was to lose a child.

No matter how slow his steps they eventually brought him home. To his surprise it was still there. There were even lights on inside. He turned up the drive and walked up to the front door. It swung open and Lee stood in the light from the door. For a moment Patrick thought he saw Ingrid standing behind her. She winked and vanished.

"Good grief, you must be frozen!" Lee said, "Come in out of that cold." She pulled him into the house. It smelled of spaghetti sauce. He felt his eyes fill up with tears at the familiar odour. Lee hugged him.

"It's a good thing I came right over when I did, or the sauce would have burned for sure. Justine told me how important spaghetti night is to you."

Patrick opened his mouth to tell her of his loss, his broken heart, but there were no words. Lee had turned away to go back to the kitchen.

"Justine," she called, "your father's home."

The words hit him like a lightning bolt and dropped him to his knees. The shards of his heart exploded into a light that he had never expected. Justine came out of the kitchen and threw herself into his arms. They fell on the floor laughing and crying. Patrick held her tight and felt their tears mingle on their faces. It seemed like forever since they held each other. He sensed God holding them both. Patrick thought that He would be grinning.

"Mom brought me home," Justine whispered. "She said God told her you needed me more than she did. She said to tell you she loved you and it was all right." Patrick didn't try to talk; he just held his daughter and let her warmth melt the ice that had settled in his heart. In the far distance, he felt Yggdrasil rejoice and hold them in his branches.

"Well, that's quite the welcome," Lee said as she came out of the kitchen. "I want to hear this story."

"Stay for supper and we'll tell you all about it," Justine said. She stood up and looked at Lee. "Please?"

"Spaghetti night is for family," Lee said.

"You are part of our family," Patrick said. He reached out an arm to her and she gave him her hand to help him up. "I hope for a very long time." He kissed her.

"Go, Dad!" Justine said, "I'll just go put the noodles on for three." She went into the kitchen and Patrick heard her moving around. He had never known just how much joy his heart could hold.

He held Lee tight and whispered in her ear.

"It doesn't matter who you were, Lee." He kissed her again." I love you now."

"Well, since you put it that way," Lee linked her arm through his, "let's go watch that daughter of yours cook supper."

"Drasil said that the Pax are working things out. They've signed a treaty with Graffire and with Rakkikt. Stone was with the Rakkikt so Davvad got to see him."

"You mean he's still sitting in the King's seat?"

"Yup, but the people need to vote every year to keep him in, because he refuses to be King. He's already campaigning to get someone else elected." Justine laughed, "I wonder what Mr. Mayor would think of that strategy?"

"How is Risha's baby?"

"He's doing really well. I still can't believe they named him Justin."

"I imagine there are more than a few Justins and Justines there."

"Davvad misses you a lot, Dad. He comes to the Tree every chance he gets and tells Drasil all about what's happening. I wish I could go back, but Drasil says I'm dead there and it would be like I was a ghost or something." Justine moved around the table putting out forks for supper. "Kelly is running for class President this year. She wants me to be her vice-president."

"What do you think?"

"It might be fun. Kelly's going to run on an anti-bullying platform. Funny, huh?"

"People change."

"Good thing too. I'd be bored being the same person all the time."

"You just keep getting better."

"Speaking of Kelly, her mom wants me to decorate their new apartment. What do you think?"

"Well, it isn't like it's the first job you've done."

"She wants to pay me. I don't know what to charge. They're my friends."

"You paid Kelly for your dress for Leigh's and my wedding."

"True, she needed the money."

"Don't you?"

"Not really." She sat in the chair and looked at him. For a moment, she looked so much like Ingrid that Patrick's heart skipped a beat, then he smiled.

"I am so proud of you," he said.

"Thanks, Dad, but that doesn't really help."

"Think of what Pastor Daniel said on Sunday. There is a reason we are here. It's our job to live that reason."

"I figured what we did in Pax was a pretty good reason."

"It was, but it isn't over. There is still this world."

She rolled her eyes, "O great," then she laughed.

"At least here, God didn't send someone else to die for him. Our job isn't dying but living for him."

Lee came in the door.

"Oh, it's wet out there," she said. "So, is supper ready?"

"Just have to put the noodles in," Patrick went to the stove. "What did the doctor say?"

"She said that everything is going well and she has no concerns." She pulled something from her purse and put it on the fridge. "Here's the ultrasound. How do you feel about having a boy?"

The Illustrator

Wil Oberdier is a freelance illustrator and fine artist who makes his home in Shelby, Ohio. Experiment is the advice he gives to up and coming students of art and illustration. Wil's unmistakable combination of painting and textures over a loose pencil sketch gives his work mystery and depth beyond the surface of the canvas.

He has won numerous awards of merit both at home and online. More of Wil's work can be seen at wilustration.com.

Acknowledgments

I need to thank all the people who contributed to the Indiegogo campaign to make this book a reality. Without your support this wouldn't exist.

My beta readers helped shape the story into what you just read thanks to all of you and particularly Angela Stevens who went above and beyond beta reading.

My editor Dean C. Moore needs a huge vote of thanks. It is a privilege to work with someone of such skill and dedication.

Other books by Alex

Calliope and the Sea Serpent
Wendigo Whispers
The Devil Reversed
Generation Gap
The Gods Above
Tales of Light and Dark
Like Mushrooms (poetry and photography)
The Heronmaster
Blood and Sparkles, and other stories
Princess of Boring
By the Book
Sarcasm is My Superpower
Playing on Yggdrasil
The Unenchanted Princess

Alex also has stories in:

Words on the Rocks
Beyond the Wail
Collidor Stream Collection 2016